Aɪɴ'ᴛ Nᴏᴛʜɪɴɢ
ʙᴜᴛ ᴛʜᴇ
DEVIL

By Lorelai Watson

AIN'T NOTHING BUT THE DEVIL

Limitless Publishing, LLC
Kailua, HI 96734
www.limitlesspublishing.com

Formatting: Limitless Publishing

ISBN-13: 978-1-64034-540-9
ISBN-10: 1-64034-540-X

DEDICATION

To my parents, who read me countless stories as a child and always encouraged me to chase my dreams. Without you, I never would have fallen in love with words and stories.

To my husband, who's never allowed me to limit my potential.

To my best friend, for reading every draft of this book since it's conception and loving my characters as much as I do.

And finally, to my teachers who told me I would be an author someday. Your encouragement made it happen, and your words were never forgotten.

CHAPTER ONE

The water had grown winter-cold and gray. Droplets of water dripped from an antique brass faucet, marking time like a second hand. It seemed she'd been there for hours, and perhaps she had. She had awoken from her nightmares in a cold sweat, her body pale and shaking, heart pounding with incredible celerity. She had grabbed the knife and their wedding portrait in a frenzy of desperation and filled the tub.

Now the sun was rising, flooding the white-tiled bathroom with blinding orange daylight. Straining to see through the intense glow, she looked into the reflective steel blade between the aged faucet. It balanced over the gray water, biding its time.

Outside, birds were calling through the morning air, heralding yet another day. Jimmy McStott's 1956 Chevy truck sputtered down the road as he made his way to work. The old house groaned when the air conditioning kicked on downstairs. Whispers passed through the walls, spreading the gossip; another tragedy was about to occur. The sounds and

1

sensations battering her mind simply assured a fact she already knew, that life would go on without her.

It's time, she told herself, resolute and, above all, fearless. She shut her red-glazed and swollen eyes to protect them from the brightness of the sun.

She took their wedding picture and forgot to feel the tears streaming down her face. They were the model couple that day, ripped straight from the cover of *The Knot* with bright smiles, bodies fused, their eyes glowing with the evidence of the blind happiness, naivety. But they were clueless about the twists and turns of the road ahead…and the impending impact. Then the crash and burn, crash and burn. Again and again until wedges of steel cooled between them and their injuries tried to heal as time fell away from their weak grasps.

Who knew we'd end up here? she questioned. She couldn't care anymore, no matter how much she wanted to. He was better off without her.

She'd be doing this one last favor for her husband and that would be the end of their road together. Today she was setting them both free from their respective prisons, and they would travel their own singular paths again.

She took the knife by the hilt and twisted the knob until hot water roared once more. It was an ordinary kitchen knife. She had molded her hand to fit the handle many times. Practice made perfect. There were a hundred scars for every time she had told herself that, each one growing deeper.

She sank deep into the tub. Her eyes floated to the coffered ceiling, locked in to the pattern of intersecting lines, and she noticed the way the sunlight arced across them. Her mind wandered to her husband. She envisioned the W, the sounds of heavy Atlanta traffic rising to the heights of his suite. He would already be thinking about the anonymous business of the day ahead, planning his every move so he could execute it to perfection, as he did every day. He was perfect.

She had resented him for being someone like that, for being something she could never completely understand. Every time she looked at her husband, envy ran rampant, causing a knot of tension to take up residence in her heart. While he knew who he was, she was the wallflower lacking the strength to be the main character in her own life.

She heard the scream, saw the blood, and while it hurt like hell for the slightest moment, the pain eventually faded.

The blood looked like scarlet rubies gleaming in the sunlight, dripping from her wrists like a silent stream. The kitchen knife fit back into her skin, widening the stream into a river, deepening it as she pulled it through the mass of flesh and vein.

She marveled at what had happened as though it were magic. Her heart pounded in her chest as she watched the blood surge from her wrists with every beat. The water grew red as the blood billowed and mixed, clouds of scarlet expanding and dissipating into the water one drop at a time.

So pretty, she thought. She withdrew the knife from her wrist to watch the blood fold into the water and flow over the edges of the tub like a scarlet waterfall.

A wave of arctic-cold hit and her vision went

3

hazy. Her body was drifting, slowly…slowly…away. Her senses were beginning to fail when a small black fly landed on the apex of the faucet. Her eyes drew slowly to the creature. It appeared frozen in time, not moving so much as twitching a translucent wing.

The longer it stayed there, unnaturally immobile, the more she began to detect something insidious. She looked into the red-domed eyes of the insect, the scarlet burning into her as it rubbed its forelegs together in anticipation.

Her heartbeat was slowing down…

The blood wasn't erupting from her wrist like it had when she'd first deepened the wound.

Her body was trembling, her fingers and toes growing frigid.

She blinked, trying to get her eyes to refocus. Nothing. Darkness…nothing.

A clouded veil shielded her eyes from the sunlight, but the light grew brighter, sweeping through the room as the sun rose in the distance. Everything in her line of sight was obscure. Her eyes stung with the brightness of a new dawn. Her sight drifted from one place to another, far beyond her control now. The window flooded with the stinging daylight. Her eyes fluttered to the wedding portrait, the pure white-tiled wall where it met the black and white-tiled floor, the fly on the faucet, waiting, watching, anticipating.

The fly buzzed. It flew around the faucet and then landed on the edge of the tub right beside where her head rested in the corner.

I saw a fly buzz when I died, she gasped. *The*

*stillness round my form was like the stillness in the
air between the heaves of the storm.*

The corners grew dark, and she stopped resisting
the force she had invited into her body. She
surrendered over to the darkness, her eyes fixated
on the fly.

CHAPTER TWO

Lee Atwood grimaced at the thought of another day.

Wrong day to feel like this over nothing, he told himself. *Get up, get your shit together.*

He groaned slightly when sunlight pierced into his eyes like pins and reluctantly pushed up off the wild, tangled mass of white silk sheets.

Her arms were wrapping around him before he could even sit up. Lee sighed, but she only held him closer. His lips spread into a crooked smile at the thought of a boa constrictor and some unfortunate jungle animal, though it was less amusing when he realized he was the prey.

"Morning," she murmured, pressing a kiss on his neck.

"Morning." He ran his hands over her arms. Time to play pretend that he wanted to be with her. "Did you sleep well?"

"As always. You're better than sleeping pills."

Lee faked a laugh. "Nice to know you were pleased with last night's performance. I'll be here all week."

"Not tonight, you won't," she whined. Lee couldn't help but admire her as the sunlight washed over her bare body, stolen right from the pages of a magazine, except there was no air-brushing here. Brecklyne Williams was the real deal, with her bright eyes of emerald green and long, wavy auburn hair, but her smile alone could hold him captive. In Brecklyne's eyes, he didn't have a weakness, and he tried his best to make sure it stayed that way.

Lee lowered his body to hers and pressed a full kiss to her lips. He caught the light scent of her perfume and tasted the Irish Cream coffee on her tongue. She had already been up this morning. He pulled his lips away and looked at her enchanting face she had already made up. A little eyeliner, heavy on the mascara. This woman...

"You sound disappointed I won't be around tonight," he noted, lacing his hand through hers.

"I am disappointed," Brecklyne answered. "But today's your big day, and there's the party tonight."

"If you call those lame social conventions parties," Lee groused.

"That's what after-parties are for, and knowing you, you've got one hell of a real party planned already."

"You're getting to know me too well," he replied. "There's a little after-party in the works. Can you make it to that one?"

Brecklyne looked at him blankly, but he knew something was on her mind. As much as she had learned him, he had learned her in return. "What is it?"

"Oh, it's nothing."

"Are you sure?"

"Yeah," Brecklyne said. "Don't worry about it. You've got a big day ahead."

He kissed her one more time for good measure. He had more important things to do than argue with her. "Good. I'm going to take a shower if you don't mind."

"Lee, we've been together over a year now. Do you think I mind?"

"Just because we're sleeping with each other doesn't mean I have to quit being polite," he said, hoping she caught the correction.

He turned the faucet in the large open shower to where the water would be lukewarm. Just as he was about to step in, he heard a soft cry coming from the bedroom. Unwilling to deal with her, Lee jumped in the shower anyway. Maybe if he pretended not to hear her, he could avoid an argument that would be otherwise unavoidable.

He stepped into the shower and went over the day's schedule in his mind, organizing everything into mental checklists. He rethought through every minuscule detail, going through all the mundane motions of preparing to face the thousands of nameless, near-faceless people to whom his day would bring him. When he finished showering, he brushed his braces-straight, whitened teeth and arranged his straight blond hair into a stylish mess.

He knew by the time he was ready, Brecklyne would already be downstairs in one of her filmy negligees that no longer turned him on. But she would look flawless, ready to send him off with a smile painted on her face. He knew why she cried; he knew what she wanted. It was the difference between inviting her to the signing celebration and only inviting her to the after-party, the difference between "being together" and "sleeping together." Brecklyne Williams was in love with him, and they both knew he would never feel the same.

Today was a time for new beginnings, the perfect time to end their madness. If, Lee reasoned in his mind, you could count stifling social conventions as parties and screwing Brecklyne as a legitimate relationship.

He was getting his shit together, getting out of this so-called relationship, and devoting all his energies back where they belonged.

He walked over to a large walk-in closet, most of which was dedicated to Brecklyne's ridiculously large wardrobe. *All courtesy of my Amex,* Lee thought with a shake of his head. He kept a small portion of the closet for his clothes, though he noticed Brecklyne had tried reorganizing his clothing again. After a fruitless search, he yelled at her from inside the closet. "Brecklyne! Where the hell is my suit?"

"Which one, baby?" she yelled back.

Lee rolled his eyes.

It wasn't thirty seconds before Brecklyne was bounding up the stairs and into the closet with Lee.

"The navy Armani with the pinstripes," he said through a tightened jaw, paying her the least amount of attention he could provide. "The new one."

"Oh, you never brought it over," she rattled off

breathlessly. "I put your tux in your garment bag, though. It's in the hall closet downstairs."

"Then where the hell is that suit?"

"Probably at your other house," Brecklyne said, obviously perturbed. She turned around and went back downstairs in a huff.

Lee made a mental note to pack up all the clothes he had stored in Brecklyne's closet next time she was out showing a house or something. He needed a nice, quiet, drama-free breakup.

He settled for a black Burberry, deciding he would have his brother bring his suit down to the office. Lee pulled on a crisp white shirt and walked over to the dresser mirror to make sure everything was in check with his appearance.

When he went to brush back a rogue strand of hair, he noticed something was missing. The absence stuck such a fear in him it was like someone had driven a railroad spike straight into his chest. Frantic, he looked all over the bathroom counters, in the shower and the bed, before spotting it on the floor next to the nightstand. Relieved, Lee slipped his finger back through his wedding band, feeling prepared for the day ahead.

CHAPTER THREE

Adrian's heart pounded in his chest and sweat rolled down his skin. He wasn't certain of the time, but the sun hadn't even made it over the horizon and it was already hotter than hell, a typical Georgia day.

But it was nice to be outside, pounding the track around the old high school football field. He couldn't count the number of times he'd run around this track, trying to outrun all the other guys to impress girls whose names he couldn't remember anymore. Adrian had smoked his first cigarette on top of the press box with the rest of the drumline after band practice, fallen in love for the first time on the forty-yard line, and had his first breakup in the section of the stadium still labeled "Tiger Band" in faded hunter and white paint.

The tiny town of Adairsville wasn't much to talk about unless you were a big history buff, but Adrian Atwood felt a strong connection to the place he'd called home for most of his life. There was practically nothing in the town, save for a few fast-food establishments and small businesses that lasted less than a couple years. There were small subdivisions with vans and SUVs in the driveway, a single grocery store, three schools, about a thousand churches and thousands of acres of farmland.

He paused his thoughts when his cell phone blared in his pocket. Adrian stopped running and took a second to catch his breath.

"Hello?"

"I take it you're running?" his brother's voice emanated from the speaker.

"How did you ever guess?" Adrian asked, trying to slow down his breathing.

"You're not out of breath because you're getting laid," Lee retorted.

"How would you know if I'm getting laid or not?"

"What kind of idiot answers his phone in the middle of sex?"

"Good point."

From the way Lee was suspending his breath over the line, Adrian knew his brother was about to ask him for a favor.

"All right, what is it you need me to do this morning?"

"Jeez, it's just a tiny errand. It's not like I'm gonna ask for a spare kidney or something. You're in Adairsville, right?"

"Yeah, I stayed over at Mom's. You know how she is."

His brother gave an understanding groan. *"It's a minute past ten o'clock. How can you even think of driving to Atlanta this late?"* Lee said, mimicking

12

his mother's high-pitched Southern drawl.

Adrian snickered. "So what is this errand you need done?"

"Run by the house and grab that new Armani I bought last month. And maybe make sure Madeleine's coming tonight."

"Why don't you call her and ask her yourself?" Adrian suggested in annoyance. "It might be a good conversation starter, since you're fighting…again."

"Hell, Adrian, we never stopped fighting. It's been what? A year and a half? I keep expecting to get served with a fat stack of divorce papers any day," his brother muttered.

"Is that what you want?"

Lee scoffed, but then his tone turned somber. *"God, no. But I don't know how to fix it, either."*

"Don't you think you ought to make a special trip up here then? You need to be the one to talk to her, Lee, not me."

"I don't need to argue with her today," Lee countered. *"There are a million things I've got to get accomplished, and further ruining my marriage isn't exactly one of them. Tell her I don't give a damn if she wears t-shirt and sweatpants, I want her to be there tonight."*

"Look, you're being ridiculous. You have nothing important on your plate today. You need to make a trip up, talk this out with your wife, and get your own damned suit already."

"Just get the suit or don't bother showing up on Monday," his brother threatened.

"I wasn't coming in Monday, anyway. I was planning on staying hammered this weekend and having the hangover from hell. Besides, I read the VP job description, and it said nothing about fetching your damn suits."

Adrian conceded, although he didn't know why he catered to Lee so much. "Fine. What time do you need the suit?"

"It doesn't matter. Try to get here by lunch, though; we'll get some junk at The Varsity."

"I just ran four miles. I could use a chili dog to offset the loss of calories."

After hasty goodbyes, Adrian hit the end button and jogged the half-lap down to where he had parked his black Jeep Rubicon. He ran the air conditioning full blast and tried not to think about having to explain to Madeleine that Lee had yet again spent the night in Atlanta, sent him to do his errand running, and that Lee expected her to show up to the ceremony and celebration later. Maddie would be pissed. If his brother didn't get his mind off the company for a while and spend more time with Madeleine, it looked like he would end up losing her. Just like their father had lost their mother.

Adrian pulled out of the parking lot and passed the mayor's house as he made his way up a small hill. The streets of Adairsville were flanked by large, ancient oaks and elms towering over cozy three-bedroom houses and the lofty aging Victorians alike. The paved roads were smooth for the most part, save for the occasional potholes that sometimes made front-page headlines of the *North Bartow News*.

He turned from Franklin Street onto the shaded

14

curved path of Park Street. Trees arched over each side of the road, creating a thick, dark canopy. The house Lee shared (on occasion) with his wife was already in sight. Local historians knew the house as McCollum Manor, and it had been in Madeleine's family since the early 1900s. The house was a two-story white Greek revival with hunter green shutters and doors. Three grand two-story columns flanked the front porch and a balcony overlooking the manicured front lawn.

Adrian pulled into the circular front driveway and parked the Jeep behind Madeleine's BMW sedan. The front porch looked welcoming with rockers on one side, a wicker set on the other, so typical of the Southern home. Adrian walked up to the door and rang the bell. He heard it chime inside the house and propped in the doorframe, waiting for her to answer the door. He ran his fingers through his hair twice in a weak attempt to look somewhat presentable. While he waited, he saw Madeleine's beds of bright purple irises were in full bloom, somehow surviving the blazing Georgia heat and a touch of drought all at the same time. The birds were calling out, hopping across the yard and pecking at the grass. Adrian listened for footsteps on the hardwood floors inside. Nothing. He rang the doorbell again and waited another few minutes. There was a spare key hidden, but the last thing he wanted was to barge in on his sister-in-law.

He decided to call the house. Madeleine would hear the phone even if she was wearing her headphones or was still asleep. He dialed the number.

The phone rang once…twice…again and again until he decided Madeleine would not be answering the door for him.

It occurred to him something wasn't right.

Feeling panicky, Adrian ran his hand over the doorframe, searching by touch for the spare key his brother kept tucked away. When his fingers retrieved the key, he unlocked the door and pushed the front door open.

"Madeleine?" he called out across the foyer.

Silence. In fact, the house was eerily hushed, save for the sound of trickling water.

Dread hit him like a ton of bricks.

"Maddie?"

Nothing.

Something isn't right.

None of it made sense. He bounded up the stairs, skipping steps that creaked beneath his abusive tread. When he reached the top of the stairs, he slowed. His responses did a 180. His stomach turned and a rush of anxiety ran rampant over his entire body. He forced himself to take a step forward off the landing.

Water?

It splashed over his feet, soaking through the mesh surface of his running shoes. There was a thin puddle of water expanding over the dark hardwood floor.

"Maddie?"

It was then his mind fit the pieces of the puzzle together. The ending scene of her last novel.

Don't want to see this. Don't want to see this.

But impulse, or perhaps responsibility, took over

yet again. Against his will, his body moved from the hall to the master bedroom. The trickling grew louder, and cool droplets of water splashed his legs. He touched the cold brass door knob, flung open the door.

Words escaped him, and he stood frozen. He knew he should move, do something, but the blood...There was so much blood he could smell the sickening metallic odor inundating the heavy air. His insides heaved.

"Madeleine!"

He thought he had screamed her name, and perhaps he had. In the next few days, when asked to recall the scene, he never could recall anything with clarity. The only thing he ever remembered with any certainty was that Madeleine's beautiful face, snow white and devoid of life, held the sincerest expression of peace. He knew it was an image he would remember until his dying day.

CHAPTER FOUR

Adrian had tried to distract his mind with a million different things—work, reading the old magazines in the emergency waiting room, listening in on other people's conversations. None of it could take his mind off the images of Madeleine's face, her body covered in blood, the gaping wound in her left wrist, or the scent of her blood constantly lingering in his mind.

Madeleine was always so pretty, even in those awkward high school days when kids picked on her because she was the quiet bookworm of the class. He remembered the oval reading glasses she used to wear, how they always slipped down her nose.

He kept trying to focus on moments when Madeleine was vibrant and happy, when she and Lee were in love, or when she announced she was pregnant.

The pregnancy made him think of all the complications. The moment his brother had walked out of the delivery room door to tell them his son had been stillborn. Never had he seen Lee so

18

helpless.

In less than a second's time, he was back in Cooper's Creek. He was ten, Lee was twelve.

"No way," Adrian had declared. The boys were staring down about a fifteen-foot drop from a waterfall they had discovered while on a hiking trail with their father. It was Lee's idea to sneak away to the magical spot they had discovered on their trek and explore it for themselves.

Adrian had shaken his head. "I am not jumping off that waterfall. Dad's gonna kill us anyway when he finds out we snuck off."

"Don't you ever do anything fun?" Lee had asked with a mocking laugh. But Adrian knew Lee was bluffing; his eyes were filled with terror. Adrian almost wanted to goad him on, but he could only manage a frown.

"If you jump off this rock, you'll break every bone in your body when you hit the water. I know because I watched it on Discovery Channel."

"That's not true. You're a big chicken." Lee took five giant steps backward. He took a steadying breath and broke into a full-speed run. In shock, Adrian had watched his brother fall straight into the water, his body flailing as he sailed through the air. He couldn't even hear the splash over the roar of the waterfall.

"Lee!" he'd screamed through the heavy summer air, watching around the site where his brother had entered the water, marked by white-crested waves that died out as the waterfall pounded into the pond below. Adrian's heart raced;

his brother wasn't resurfacing.

Oh my God, he's dead. Dad will kill me for letting him—

And then Lee emerged from the water, shouting and yelling, his cries echoing through the forest. "Yeah! I did it! Adrian's a big chicken! I did it!"

Looking down at his brother in disbelief, Adrian had decided aloud, "If he can do it…"

He felt like he was ten years old again, in freefall, heading toward a whirlpool of freezing creek water and river rock.

Blood. Red, bloody water. Madeleine. Suicide. Carving out the inside of her wrists.

She looked so peaceful.

He ran straight into the closest bathroom, threw the steel stall door back, and heaved the entire contents of his stomach. Disgusted, he spat up the bile and flushed the mess. He ambled over to the sink and glimpsed himself in the mirror.

You're being weak. Get yourself together.

Adrian forced the cold-water handle on the sink until the water exploded from the faucet. He cupped his hands to catch the water between his palms and splashed water on his face, trying not to think about reaching into cold, bloody water…pulling out her limp body…feeling her slick blood on his own skin…the myriad colored lights of the dance floor reflecting on her skin at prom…his brother's hands moving over her swollen stomach…

They were so happy. How had they ended up like this?

He dried his face, took a big deep breath, and

went back out into the too-loud waiting area, attempting to steel himself against his tumbling thoughts and emotions.

"Adrian!"

He turned to see a welcome sight.

"Em," he breathed, their arms wrapping around one another instinctively. Adrian breathed the scent of her hair and the perfume he'd bought her.

"Your mom called. She said Lee and your dad are stuck in traffic. There was a wreck on 75."

"He'll be hysterical by the time he gets here. He didn't believe me at first, but who would?"

"I'm sorry," Emily murmured. "Are you okay?"

"Not really," Adrian admitted. "But I'm not the one with the greatest needs right now."

Emily's face fell. "I went by your apartment and got you a change of clothes. I wasn't sure if you would need them, but apparently you do," she said, unable to take her eyes off the bloodstains on his shirt.

"Thank you." Adrian noticed his favorite pair of jeans and a Georgia Tech alumni t-shirt had been neatly folded and placed inside the bag Emily handed him. "This is why you're wife material."

"If I'm wife material, you should put a ring on it," Emily replied, holding up a ringless left hand. "Go change before your brother gets here."

CHAPTER FIVE

Disgust. It was the only word Lee could think of to describe his opinion of himself. How could he let her fall into this depression? How dare he be so uninvolved, so uncaring? In his mind he kept seeing Brecklyne, scenes of the two of them making love so many times. Where was Madeleine at those times?

The elevator door opened with a mechanical chime, and Lee's heart raced beyond control. He was going to be sick. He wondered if Adrian and his father could see the fear in his eyes.

I don't want to see her, he thought. *I can't face her, not now.*

"This way," her doctor, a middle-aged man named McGuiness, directed, veering to the left down a darkened, quiet hallway. The past hours had faded one moment into another in an incomprehensible blur. After fighting Atlanta traffic, the hour and a half drive where Lee was left to his own racing thoughts, the doctor's barrage of information he failed at putting into layman's terms, he now stood immobile. He thought he could not have willed his legs to move even if he had wanted to, until he felt his brother's hand on his elbow.

"Lee?" Adrian said, taking a step forward. "Are you ready?"

"I don't want to see her, do I?" Lee whispered.

Adrian exhaled, gathering strength. "Look, it'll be hard, but you're not alone. I'm here, we're all here. And she'll want you in there no matter what you've done," Adrian said, his eyes focused on the door. "Maddie loves you. She always has."

Lee hitched a breath and headed down toward the end of the hallway, through the door.

He stepped into the bright room and felt everything inside him would shatter into a million pieces. His eyes widened when he saw his wife, wires sprouting from sources all over her body. She was as pale as a full winter moon, except for a slight pale pink flush to her lips. Her mouth was slack, forced open with a mouthpiece for the respirator. The machine would emit a prolonged hiss and Madeleine's chest would rise and fall, governed by the machine. Lee ambled to the side of the bed, keeping his eyes locked on Madeleine.

"The respirator isn't permanent," Dr. McGuiness explained. "When she gets some of her strength back, we'll take her off the machines."

His words didn't even register with Lee. He cupped her face in his hand and stroked her smooth skin.

"Hey there, beautiful," Lee said in a sad whisper. He didn't know where to begin. What could he say to her? He looked back to his father and brother, but they were just as clueless.

"I'll leave you alone for a minute," Dr. McGuiness said, "give you some time with your wife. I'll be around if you need me."

Lost in his own thoughts, Lee stared at Madeleine in disbelief. He reached for her hand out of instinct, but when he touched the plastic tubing of the IV, the coarse stitch of the bandage wrapping her skin, his eyes wandered to her wrist.

The bandage was white and pristine, a pretty tattoo attempting to cover up a mistake. She would always bear the scars, but the real damage was on the inside. "I have not been a good husband. I've got to make it up to you somehow."

"Lee, you can't be this hard on yourself," Adrian said gently.

"You have no idea what I have done to her."

A piercing sound, the undeniable scream of a flatline, made his own heart stop for a moment before racing faster than it had all day.

Lee's eyes darted to the heart monitor, and the room opened to utter chaos. Before the three Atwood men could even process what was happening, nurses and Dr. McGuiness flooded over Madeleine, descending on her failing body.

"Lee, get out of the way!" Adrian demanded.

The doctor pressed his hands on Madeleine's chest, beginning CPR. Nurses surrounded the doctor, surrounding Madeleine, performing tasks he couldn't understand.

All Lee could think about was getting to his wife.

He gripped her hand, pleading. "Maddie, I love

you. Don't leave me here, baby!"

A crash cart wheeled through the door. "Get them out of here!"

"Sir, you need to leave so we can help—"

"I am not leaving her again!"

"You can't stay, any of you." A nurse ushered him toward the door, and his brother gripped his arms, pulling him out of the room.

The last thing Lee saw before the door to her room slammed shut and locked was the nurses stripping away her hospital gown, the doctor yelling out a warning to clear, the defibrillator delivering a shock of electricity to her chest and side, making Madeleine's body jolt from the bed, the heart monitor's piercing scream stabbing to the core of his being. Lee panicked at the idea it could be the last time he saw her alive.

CHAPTER SIX

The fluorescent lights and pale walls were giving Lee a headache. All he could think about was getting out of there, of taking his wife back home. They had been able to get her heart beating again, but Madeleine wasn't out of the woods yet.

If she could get better, Lee knew he could fix this. He dreamed of building Maddie a new office, something bright and cheery. She would love him again, be happy again. Then again, what could he do to make it any worse?

Lee's thoughts rocketed around his head violently. The noise in his head became more and more pressing, and he paced the length of the waiting room.

"Lee," his father, Richard, barked. "I know you're worried, son, but you have to calm down. I'm sure the doctors are doing all they can to help Madeleine."

He did not acknowledge his father's words, but he became distinctly aware of his brother's eyes on him as he crossed the room again and again.

Richard plopped down angrily in a rose-colored vinyl chair next to Adrian.

"Maggie Beth, do something with your son," Richard yielded, defeated after trying to convince Lee to stop pacing and cursing at every nurse and doctor in the hospital until he got the information he wanted about Madeleine.

"Lee, baby, you need to eat something," his mother urged, her tone saturated with concern for her eldest son. Lee hated that his mother and father were teaming up again. Divorced for more than twelve years, his parents had put each other down for years, but now they were practically one parental unit again, trying to be the anchor in this storm. "Adrian, why don't you go pick something up for your brother?" his mother suggested.

"I can't even think about eating right now," Lee groused, his stomach turning with nausea. He crossed his arms against his chest and looked around the small area his family had occupied in shifts for the past two days. "Look, I know you're all concerned, and I appreciate it, but I can't even think straight. Nothing's going to be all right until Maddie's back to normal."

His parents exchanged doubtful, worried expressions. Adrian kept his eyes glued on his brother, taking in the details he knew his parents were dismissing. Lee's hands were beginning to shake, a symptom his parents were probably assuming was nothing more than nerves.

"Lee, we might want to go ahead and talk about that," his mother said carefully.

"Jesus Christ," Adrian said under his breath, then

louder, "Now's not the time, Mom."

"I think now's an excellent time," Richard snapped.

"He's not going to want to talk about this right now," Adrian stated firmly.

"What the hell are we talking about exactly?" Lee demanded.

"Madeleine's treatment options," Richard said. "We have been talking with different doctors and—"

"I'm gonna go ahead and state when Dad uses the word 'we,' he is referring to himself and Mom," Adrian interrupted to clarify. "I will have no part in discussing this until Madeleine is able to make her own decisions."

"Adrian, Maddie just tried to commit suicide," his mother implored. "Do you honestly think she's in the right mind to make the best decisions right now?"

"My question is why you've been discussing this without me in the first place," Lee snapped. "Maddie is *my* wife. Her treatment is *my* responsibility. From now on, any discussion of Madeleine's treatment will be discussed with me, got it?"

Richard scoffed. "Son, this is not a damn boardroom you can just waltz in and dominate. This is our family. Now if you want in on a discussion about your wife, sit down and face this like a man."

His mother's mouth fell open and she nudged Richard with her elbow. "For God's sake, Richard. You can't blame him for being out of sorts."

"Exactly. He's not thinking straight, so we have

28

every right to discuss this without him. We're the only ones being reasonable here."

"Here we go," Adrian grumbled. "Typical Atwood behavior. Let's make this all about ourselves." He opened a November 2014 copy of *Field and Stream* and flipped through the pages, trying to ignore the now escalated argument between his parents.

"Lee, baby, we shouldn't have discussed this without you, but—"

"I'll not apologize for it, Maggie Beth. He's just sitting here not saying a damn word, not eating, not taking care of himself. Madeleine's not going to be able to depend on him when she finally gets home," his father argued.

Lee laughed. "What the hell, Dad? You didn't even want me to marry her! Now you pretend to care?"

"May I remind y'all we are in the middle of a hospital waiting room and there are people staring at us like we're a bunch of white trash rednecks?" Adrian pointed out. "Lee, you need to get out of this hospital. You've been here for two days straight."

"I'm not leaving," Lee said with fire burning in his eyes. "Not until Maddie's coming home with me."

"I didn't say leave. Let's step outside for a moment. I could use a cigarette."

"I thought you quit!" Maggie Beth protested.

As if on cue, Lee rolled his eyes and Adrian groaned.

"Yes, let's get the hell out of there," Lee grumbled.

"Those two are driving me crazy. They've done nothing but argue and run each other down for fourteen years, then Maddie gets hurt and now they're best friends, making decisions as parents," Adrian complained as soon as they hit the stifling night air outside the hospital.

"Maddie gets hurt," Lee huffed. "What bullshit, Adrian. She attempted suicide. No point in glossing over the details."

"I figure some kind of hurt had to come first, before she attempted suicide," Adrian responded. "Either way, Maddie got hurt. Literally, figuratively, doesn't matter."

"We should move you to the legal department," Lee responded half-heartedly.

They had walked into a small courtyard between two of the hospital wings where "Floyd Hospital is a smoke-free campus" signs hung on the exterior walls and newly planted saplings extended their willowy branches toward a star-filled sky. Dome lights gave the courtyard an eerie amber glow. In the trees, the ever-present cicadas screamed into the night, broadcasting a message only their fellows would ever understand. Ignoring the signs, Adrian retrieved a cigarette case and lit up.

"Thank you, Jesus," Adrian murmured, exhaling a billowing cloud of smoke. He and Lee plopped down on a wooden bench and stared out into the line of small saplings standing soldier-straight across from them.

"I'd kill for a shot of anything right now."

"Hmmm…maybe you should take the time to detox," Adrian suggested, taking another drag. "I'm surprised no one's noticed how bad you're shaking."

"I swear I'll start taking Antabuse or something if Maddie makes it out of this. Jesus, Adrian, I have got to change. Look at me," Lee said, sticking his shaking hand out. "This is ridiculous."

"Dad was right about one thing, though: you're not taking care of yourself. You've got to stay strong for when Maddie's ready to come home."

"I can't quit until she's okay. I've got to make sure my wife is healthy and happy before I can worry about myself."

Adrian exhaled more smoke, which dissipated into the night air. "I don't like the idea of you taking another drop of alcohol into your body, but you're right about having to focus on Madeleine right now."

"So?"

"I know you don't want to leave in case she wakes up, but I could drive you home and we could stay for a few hours. You can have a drink, take a shower, get some new clothes, hell, take a nap?" Adrian suggested. "You're no good to her in a mess."

Lee knew he was defeated. Adrian always had a way of getting to him in a way his parents had never mastered. "All right, fine. I'll go home long enough to take a shower and pack a few things, and I'll come back later."

"Here," Adrian offered, reaching into his pocket for his keys. "Take my car. Just make sure you give yourself enough time to sober up before you drive it. This one's new."

"I can't thank you enough, Adrian."

"Yeah, yeah," Adrian muttered. "Just go. And don't get a single scratch on my car."

CHAPTER SEVEN

Adrian was worried about Lee. It was now a quarter until one in the afternoon, and Lee had not returned. He struggled to resist the urge to pace the room to get the jittery feeling about his brother out of his system.

Stupid, he raged inwardly. Telling Lee of all people to go home and drink. What was he even thinking? He probably drank himself to death.

Adrian imagined his Jeep Rubicon flipped over in some ditch, his windshield shattered and covered in blood. He called his brother, and the tone droned on over his cell phone while his mind raced.

Lee had been so stalwart about not leaving Madeleine's side, the fact he had not returned was alarming.

Emily had left earlier, leaving Adrian the sole figure standing watch over Madeleine. Though his version of standing watch currently consisted of slumping into the oversized recliner, made to be folded out into a bed for overnight visitors. He had dithered on whether to turn on the television or not, for background noise to drown out the monotonous beeps and hisses of the machines hooked up to Madeleine, but didn't want to risk missing any sound she might make.

Lee would have a fit if he was not here when Madeleine awoke, and it only added another layer to Adrian's worries about his brother. What the hell was keeping him? He'd been gone for hours.

"He probably fell asleep. He's had a rough few nights," Emily had told him before she left.

"I know, but I'm worried, Em," he had replied in a near quaver.

But she knew him and could hear his worries and fears more clearly than any words he could have said. She wrapped her arms around him and laid her head on his shoulder.

"He's fine, Adrian. Maddie will be fine. We'll all have a family picnic in a few weeks, and everything will be okay," she whispered to him, barely audible above the noises of the hospital room. "You can show off that new BMW bike I've seen you eyeing, then Lee will challenge you to a race down Main Street. You on your bike and him in one of those sports car of his. You'll win, naturally."

Adrian buried his face in her hair and laughed quietly. "You always know just what to say, Em. Another reason I love you."

"I love you too, even with your unhealthy love of flashy and way-too-fast vehicles."

Alone in the room again, his worries were building once more. He had not heard from his brother.

The respirator hissed, and Madeleine's chest

inflated with new oxygen. Physically, she would be fine. Emotionally…she could be a total wasteland.

He remembered the day Lee had called him saying he had met the most amazing woman.

Adrian had brushed it off. Lee met the world's most amazing, most gorgeous woman every other week, and he was disinterested in whoever his brother's newest conquest was. That was, until Lee told him his newest girlfriend was an old friend.

He was in disbelief when he found out this most amazing, gorgeous woman was Madeleine McCollum. Was she really interested in a guy like Lee? But then again, it was Lee. Everyone loved him.

As soon as he heard her name, Adrian thought of senior prom with its flashing, gaudy, colored lights. Midnight blue, beaded, satin, strapless dress, her hair swept up, her neck and shoulders exposed. She was breathtaking. It was such a great change from the quiet, bookish Madeleine who had become a close friend over the course of their high school career. He had thought she was cute in a plain way before, but that night she radiated a blinding glow.

"We've only been out the one time. She's in New York right now finishing up her book tour."

"She got published?" Adrian had replied in awe. "That's amazing. She always loved to write."

"Number one bestseller for twenty straight weeks now. Adrian, I'm telling you, this girl is amazing."

A prom-night break up with Leslie Thomas and a lack of date proposals had rendered Adrian and

Madeleine wallflowers. He couldn't believe she even came. He had expected she would declare prom a vapid, bullshit excuse for the preppy kids to make everyone else feel even more like outcasts than they normally did.

She had abandoned her oval glasses for once. Her cornflower blue eyes shined even in all the darkness. He couldn't take his eyes away from her.

Neither said a word but they gravitated toward one other through the dancing crowds. A collision course, for sure. He offered his hand. With some trepidation, she accepted, and their eyes never moved off each other. High school slow-dancing. A coarse waltz of swaying and a couple of turns. No words were spoken. Their eyes stayed locked on one another, but they could feel a tension, like two magnets being held barely out of their attractive reach. The speakers were emanating too much bass, but despite it all, she was the most overwhelming thing in the entire room.

"I heard about Leslie," Madeleine had whispered. "I'm sorry."

"You look amazing," Adrian sputtered.

Even through the dark and the colored lights, he could tell she was blushing.

"Adrian, I get it's a pity dance. You don't have to tell me I look good. You've done your gentlemanly duty."

"One, I would never pity you. I don't have a reason to. So no, this is not a pity dance. Two, I didn't say you look good. I said you look amazing. And I don't give a damn about Leslie Thomas or anyone else in this room right now. I want to enjoy

36

a dance with my best friend."

Madeleine's cheeks had risen with more blush than ever before. Her rare smile made him burst from the inside. He enjoyed making her happy.

"That's better," he breathed, unable to stop grinning.

"What is?"

"You're smiling. I like it much better when you're happy."

She broke their gaze, but she looked elated.

"What are you thinking about?" he asked.

"Nothing," she replied, looking down at her feet.

"Now who's bullshitting who?" he asked with a laugh.

Madeleine stared up to him, getting lost in the gray expanse of his eyes. "I was just wondering…"

"Yeah?"

"Why would anyone ever want to break up with you?"

Her remark had caught Adrian off guard. He wasn't sure how to react. Madeleine had become his best friend in only a year. It was strange how they could understand each other on some deep, subconscious level, but he felt he somehow didn't truly know her. He knew plenty of trivial things about her. Her favorite band was Dave Matthews, her mother was a drunk, her father was dead. They lived in a gorgeous old wreck of a house out on Park Street and his brother had been her first kiss because he thought Adrian must have had a crush on her.

Still, he couldn't explain the force driving him to pull her closer as the twang of a slow country song

37

droned on. Adrian couldn't hear the song, the whispers, only the sound of her breathing as he touched his forehead to hers. He couldn't see the quizzical stares and glares of the clique that had claimed him as their own just because he was the rich kid.

Madeleine was the one he truly fit in with, but the others would never understand. Madeleine had the gift of making something from nothing but a pen and a piece of paper. He knew she was beautiful and imaginative and indescribably different. Madeleine McCollum was an underrated unknown, a bud that would blossom into the most breathtaking flower one of these days.

"Adrian," she murmured.

The sound of her saying his name reverberated through his mind. Her soft, crystalline voice saying his name, calling to him.

"Adrian?"

The second his lips made contact with hers, the entire world as they knew it could have collapsed and Adrian could have cared less.

The faint, raspy whisper called him back to reality and his eyes opened wide.

"Maddie. You're awake."

CHAPTER EIGHT

Her eyes closed and opened. Opened and closed. Bright afternoon sunlight heated the room. Between the layer of stiff hospital sheets and an ugly rose-colored crochet blanket, Madeleine was hot, but articulating her discomfort would be near-impossible in her drugged delirium. She flicked the drip chamber of the IV taped down to her hand. A drop of the clear liquid inside the tube dropped down the spike and Madeleine pictured it exploding and dissipating into her bloodstream, circulating, and filling her body with more of the unfeeling, heavy sensation plaguing her now.

"Madeleine McCollum. And here I thought the next time I saw you, you'd be in a casket."

With great effort, Madeleine lifted her head to see Evelyn Fitch lounged across the room, the smoke from her cigarette snaking up, gray and fading. Evelyn's lips curled into a cunning, frightening grin underneath her innocent Marcel-curled bob. She uncrossed and crossed her infinity-length legs and leaned to the other side of the chair, her beaded, drop-waist dress slinking along her slender body. Evelyn, thankfully enough, only resided in Madeleine's reality, but her constant presence wore her down.

"Cat got your tongue?" Evelyn laughed. "I can't blame you. I'd die of shame if I couldn't even off myself properly."

A hot flush came to Madeleine's face. She had not imagined this stage of outcomes should her suicide attempt fail; embarrassment had never occurred to her. Not only was she going to be forced to face an entire hospital staff who knew what she did, but her family would know what she had been going through, her pain, her fragile mental state.

"W-Where's Adrian?" Madeleine stammered. "He was here earlier."

"Better yet, where's Lee? He's your husband, isn't he?" Evelyn took another drag of her cigarette.

"He'll come. Don't be ridiculous."

"Are you trying to convince me or yourself? You're a lot of things, Madeleine, but stupid's not one of them. Your husband's been gone for months."

She grew quiet, playing with her fingers and pursing her lips. "He'll come. I…we've had our differences, but he wouldn't be that heartless."

"He doesn't love you."

"He might."

"Your marriage is over," Evelyn said, shaking her head. "He'll throw you a pity party, stay for a while out of the little bit of goodness in his heart, and then he'll leave."

40

Two sharp raps on the door resounded, and it clicked open. A petite woman with curled-up red hair wearing a navy pantsuit came in like a tornado. "Missus Atwood? I'm Nancy Tate, and I'll be handling your casework while you're here with us. It's a pleasure to meet you. I am such a big fan of yours. I've read all your books. Love every one of them."

She was speaking so fast Madeleine couldn't even process what she was saying in her high-pitched, Yankee accent. Even Evelyn raised a sharp eyebrow.

"Um, th-thanks," Madeleine stammered. Speaking was difficult on so much pain medicine.

"So anyway, we should get started. You're probably feeling groggy with your morphine drip, but we're just going to go over a couple of things and then I'll leave you to rest, okay?"

Madeleine knew the word she was supposed to respond with, but her lips didn't want to form the sounds. "All right," she slurred. *I sound like Lee,* Madeleine thought as Nancy Tate spouted off too much information to follow.

"First off, I'm not sure if your brother-in-law got to tell you before he left, but you're here with us at Floyd Hospital for the next three days for observation. During this time, your attending physician, Dr. McGuiness, and your psychologist...oh, I see your husband has already found a private psychologist, Dr. Moore. He will check up on you and then he'll want to help you choose a mental health facility or therapy program that will best fit your needs."

41

Evelyn nearly bent double in her chair laughing.

"Wait, mental health facility? Therapy? I—I'm not doing this. Wh-where is my husband?"

"Oh, Madeleine, now you've gone and done it," Evelyn laughed through her tears.

"I'm not sure right now, Mrs. Atwood, but we could wait to discuss this with him if you would prefer," Nancy Tate replied despondently.

"I…would prefer to wait on my husband, yes. This is a little…too much right now…"

"Yes, dealing with these situations often is. I'll let you get back to your rest, and we'll discuss this once you've seen your husband, okay?"

Madeleine looked away from her and stared at the ceiling tiles above her. If she looked hard enough, she could find pictures in the dots in the tiles.

"Mrs. Atwood?"

Oh, look, a dragon. With big wings…

"Yeah…" Madeleine's eyes were trained on the dragon in the tiles. Lee was finally there. "Lee is good at discussing stuff…"

Before Nancy Tate made it out of the room, the door swished open again, followed by footsteps.

Madeleine and Lee both let out a small exhalation of joy and relief.

"Maddie," he breathed as he all but pushed Nancy Tate aside and cupped her face in his hands. He pressed a kiss to her forehead and then his lips lingered on hers, and even through her grogginess, her lips responded to his kiss as a heat spread through her body and her heart beat deep in her chest. She wanted to put her hands on him, throw her arms around him, but she couldn't move her right arm because of the IV. Even her left arm was heavy, and it felt immobile, though she couldn't figure out why.

"You had me so scared," he whispered, locking his eyes on hers. Tears were forming in his eyes, and it broke her heart to see him the least bit sad or upset. Madeleine worked her left arm up but discovered she had no control over her fingers. Though she bade them to move, to wipe the tear falling down her husband's cheek, her fingers remained stiff.

"The tendon in your arm was cut," Lee explained. He took her arm and placed it down on the bed as if she were porcelain. "They did a surgery to fix it, but you won't be able to move your fingers for a while. You'll regain movement. It's just going to take time."

"Wh-what? I can't. I have to write."

"Shhhhh, you will be all right. You can take time off, or I'll type it myself if I have to."

Madeleine was not prepared to deal with this. Not only was she stuck in a more than embarrassing and depressing predicament, but now she wouldn't even be able to write to get her thoughts out about it.

Thoughts swirled until her chest tightened.

"Dr. Moore will want to help you choose a mental health facility or therapy program that will best fit your needs."

Mental health facility, a therapy program….

A stark white room. Institutionally clean and orderly. Spartan like a military barracks. Loose fitting clothing, issued by "them." Group therapy, sob story after sob story, including her own.

Who else will give a damn about my dead babies and an absentee husband? I'll go crazier just having to stay there. Pitch one fit, make a single cut, I'll be in a padded room until I rot.

It would have been so much easier just to die.

"...want to get you home, safe and sound. I promise you I will be there from now on."

"Home?" Madeleine's voice was faint, barely recognizable. Her thoughts slowed, and she could breathe again.

"I'll take you anywhere in the world," Lee pleaded. His hand intertwined with her functional right one. His eyes watered, though he no longer cried.

He sounded so genuine. Real. Vulnerable, even. Lee Atwood was never vulnerable.

"I want to go home," Madeleine whispered. "More than anything. I hate hospitals."

Lee's expression changed. Instead of looking like he was at her mercy, he looked determined, ready to spring into action. "Then let's get you home." It would only be a matter of time before he figured it out.

Lee had already retrieved his phone, no doubt scrolling through his contacts for whoever he knew with a connection to the hospital, when Madeleine reached out and grasped his free hand. He looked down at her, lacing his fingers through hers.

"Thank you," she whispered as another wave of intoxicating morphine took claim of her once again.

Before she fell asleep, she felt his lips on her

cheek and heard him whisper, "I love you so much. I'll do whatever it takes to make you happy again."

Lost in a hazy oblivion that would become a gateway to her dreams, she believed him, and her mind took her away to places filled with golden sunlight.

"Sleep well, princess. There's a world of hurt coming. He's not the prince you've always thought he was," Evelyn whispered.

CHAPTER NINE

"We call these things anchors, Madeleine…"

The voice faded in and out of Madeleine's understanding. She knew she should pay attention, and if she responded well, they would send her home soon enough. Madeleine despised being stuck in bed, the way the nurses' eyes would see her wrists before they would see her, but she supposed she could only blame herself. How long would she be nothing but a pair of scars?

Home, her shelter from the world for so long, called out to her. She longed for the familiar old walls, the bed she occasionally shared with Lee, the backyard where she could sit and write for hours in the stillness while the peaceful call of birds would fill the humid air.

But there also were bad memories of their home. The day her daddy died, the constant drunken state her mother fell into after he died, being penniless after the small amount he'd put away for them was spent. Having to shoulder the cares of the world all alone.

Then she had met the Atwoods. Adrian first, then Lee.

"Madeleine? Maddie? I need you to answer me, please."

Dr. Moore's false familiarity brought her back into focus. Madeleine looked at him, feeling like a child being caught daydreaming in class. She met his eyes, holding an awkward gaze she knew, as a psychiatrist, he would believe she was listening. Madeleine imagined Dr. Moore was smarter than she thought, like he knew she would slip back into her thoughts, eye contact or none. Regardless, the man pressed on, driven by responsibility.

"As I was saying, the people and things keeping you from trying to take your life are called anchors. I know in times like this it's hard to think of them. It may even seem like your anchors wouldn't care or be better off without you. I think you've seen that isn't the case."

Somewhat dumbfounded that he understood so well, Madeleine agreed. "Yeah, that's it. Why keep going when it won't hurt anyone else? No more fighting through every single day of life. Even now, when I know my family cares about me, it feels…logical."

Dr. Moore dropped his voice to a near whisper. "You know you shouldn't be released, right? You're a smart woman. We both know this isn't the best course of action for you."

"I'll be fine. I'm taking my pills like a good girl, going to therapy. My husband will make sure I'm being watched around the clock, I guarantee you."

He gave her a skeptical glance. *For good reason,*

Madeleine made a mental note. Take her meds like a good girl? She'd tried anti-depressants before and didn't like how they'd made her feel. Madeleine knew she'd give it an honest try this time, at least for a couple of weeks, but the second they inhibited her ability to feel, to write, she'd flush the damned things.

Dr. Moore turned a page in his notebook and spoke again. "These anchors, I need you to focus on them. Let's discuss three things you have in your life you can cling to when things get rough. What or who can you rely on in life? What will keep you going between the time you leave this hospital and your first therapy session?"

Madeleine drew a blank. She was beginning to like this guy even if this conversation was being dictated by some legal obligation. She got the impression Dr. Moore didn't want her to go home without knowing for certain she would be safe, no matter how well Lee had padded his pockets to do so.

"I've got to be honest with you," she confessed. "It's only fair I tell you I could list reasons to live all day, but they seem hopeless."

"That's a start, though, and good enough for me."

"It's not like there are things I didn't want to do in life," Madeleine continued. "Like spend more time with my husband and family and keep writing. We always wanted a baby, it just…never worked out."

"Why not?"

Madeleine shrugged, feeling like creeping back

into her shell. How was she supposed to answer this and keep a stiff upper lip? "My body never cooperated with our plans, I guess. We had a son…he was stillborn."

There. She'd explained it. The most painful thing. Now they'd have to talk about him, and she didn't want to talk about Thomas. Her heart had been in enough pain since waking up alive. She didn't know if she could take talking about Thomas.

"I'm sorry," Dr. Moore said kindly. "I can't even imagine how much it must have hurt you to lose him."

Madeleine choked and could only nod, glad he didn't press her for more information she was unwilling to give today.

"Although I still don't want you leaving," Dr. Moore stated, "I think your husband and family will take great care of you, so I need you promise to do something for me, okay?"

"Okay."

"Two things. First, keep a personal journal, if you don't already. Any thoughts that are important to you, or thoughts on repeat all day, write them down."

"I can be a little wordy."

"The wordier the better. I don't expect you to share it with me, just to increase mindfulness. Metacognition, if you will. We can look for patterns together and see how they affect your psyche. Second, I want to talk to you first thing tomorrow. We can call, video chat, whichever you prefer, and we'll keep it short until we can have our first session together next week."

49

Madeleine agreed, somewhat embarrassed, but she tried to accept he was there to help her, and everyone on the entire damned planet already knew there was something wrong with her anyway.

"All right, you're free to go. I've already called in your prescriptions and included instructions for taking them in your discharge paperwork," he rattled before taking a breath and looking her in the eye. "It was a pleasure to meet you, and I'm looking forward to working with you, Madeleine."

She forced a reassuring smile, trying to hold back tears. She was beyond ready to leave.

"I'm sorry to have to put you through this, but this is a contract between you, myself, and the hospital stating you won't try to attempt to suicide again within a certain time frame, which should be written out in the contract. I know it sounds insignificant, but it's one of those things we simply have to do."

A contract? Like a signed piece of paper would stop me if I wanted to try it again, Madeleine thought wryly, though she took the paper and clipboard from Dr. Moore's hands, pretended to read it, and signed it.

"Thank you so much, Madeleine. I'll tell Lee you're ready to leave."

"Thank you, Dr. Moore."

"Please, call me Henry. It makes this whole therapy thing a lot less awkward."

She nodded and smiled, feeling exhausted for what she perceived as no good reason. When he exited the room, Madeleine closed her eyes, unsure of what exactly the future would hold when she and

Lee left the hospital premises.

CHAPTER TEN

The air was laden with the sweet, fragrant scent of ripening peaches. Every breath Madeleine took, she could imagine her mouth filling with the fruit's succulent juice. The setting sun was glowing orange and warm on her skin. The powdery, tilled soil caved beneath her bare feet. Before her, peach trees grew in winding rows as far as the eye could see, with leaves fully unfurled, reaching out toward the sun against a backdrop of a pink and purple sunset. The air was calm, the night cicadas droning their sad melodies into the twilight.

A balmy breeze blew. The trees whispered their secrets down the line, and the peaches bobbed precariously on their stems. The wind toyed with the hem of her eyelet sundress and the soft caress of the summer wind across her exposed shoulders. She closed her eyes and took in the feeling. She was completely at peace and whole. Though directionless, she was purposeful at the same time.

"Madeleine."

She could have sworn she heard her name being

carried on the breeze, though where the voice could have come from, she was not sure. She stopped for a moment and turned in a circle, searching for the source. Nothing made a sound. No breath was drawn, no soil walked upon. Even the cicadas had silenced their droning song.

"Madeleine," it hissed again, this time more audibly.

"Who's there?" she called out. Around her, the breeze had begun to pick up, evolving into a full wind. The sky turned an angry hue of black, starkly different from the soft blue of the waning twilight, and lightning bounded across menacing clouds that had moved in overhead in a matter of seconds. Rain began to fall in explosive droplets, crashing across her arms and legs, stinging her skin. A few paces ahead rose a particularly tall, full peach tree, and Madeleine took shelter beneath its protective limbs. She certainly wasn't afraid of storms. In fact, she loved the way her body tingled with the excitement of danger whenever a bad storm moved through town. She loved the way the air smelled, how the rain sounded as it soaked the needing, dry ground. While the drops of rain found her beneath the branches of tree, for the most part, Madeleine felt safe as she watched the rain come down harder and harder.

"Madeleine."

She looked up into the branches where the sound had come from. Spiraling down the trunk of the tree was a long brown and black snake, the diamond pattern on its back unmistakable. Its forked tongue slithered from its mouth along with another whisper of her name. Her eyes grew wide, and inwardly she was panicking when she saw the nefarious gleam in the elliptical eyes of the diamondback.

"You reek of my domain," it hissed.

She could barely breathe, but she could manage a few words. "Where is your domain?"

The snake's dark amber eyes glistened mischievously. "Just beyond the river Acheron—"

"—return on the whole investment was set at, like, ten-point-eight percent, if I'm remembering correctly. Probably the only wise investment we'd made all—"

"Down, down, down, past the city of Dis—"

"And because I'm not CEO yet, Dad got credit again and—"

"In the Wood of the Suicides, where you belong."

The snake reared back its heavy triangular head, its black tongue whipping through the air. Madeleine was frozen, her heart racing in response to the hiss and the rattle of the diamondback's tail. Lightning stuck, the snake opened its mouth and—

"Do you want peaches on your waffles?"

Madeleine shook her head in slight bewilderment. She had been consumed in thought the entire time Lee was speaking to her. She glanced up from the table to see Lee standing over her, a plate of freshly made waffles in hand. She was sitting at the butcher's table in the middle of their sunny yellow kitchen, morning sunlight beaming through the windows.

"I can get it," she volunteered, but when she grasped the bowl, excruciating pain shot up her wrist. Madeleine hissed in pain, and the bowl slipped through her grasp, the peaches and juice inside splashing across the table. "Damn it." She leaned over the table to clean up the mess with her single functional hand.

"Maddie, don't worry. I'll get it," Lee said, swiping up the bowl.

"It's my mess. I can get it."

"Let me take care of it before you hurt your wrists again," her husband insisted, his eyes locked on hers. Madeleine sat back down while Lee scooped the peaches back into the bowl and wiped down the table.

"So…no sense in pretending this isn't awkward," Madeleine said, her eyes on Lee.

He kept cleaning, his gaze locked on the table. "It's not your fault," Lee denied, his lips forming a hard line at the end of his statement. "You're not the one who moved out."

A hurricane of questions raged in her mind. She said nothing. For now, it was enough he was here.

"I've had plenty of time to think about that over the past few days," Lee insisted, not making eye contact with his wife. "I know it sounds like a load of bullshit, but I don't want to lose you."

He wrapped his hand around hers, his wedding band gleaming in the sunlight. "I promise you, we will fix it. I don't care what it takes." He pressed a kiss to her forehead and backed away, finding and holding her gaze.

Madeleine had to break the stare and think. Lee always knew the right thing to say; it was the follow-through that she'd die waiting for.

Lee seemed to sense her thoughts. His expression tensed, and he went about finishing their breakfast and dishing it out onto plates.

There was a long lull in the conversation. White noise and suffocating tension filled the space around them.

"Lee?"

"Yeah?"

"I'd like that. We need a fresh start," Madeleine affirmed.

"He is a complete stranger," Evelyn chimed in as she strolled into the kitchen. She pressed a kiss to Lee's cheek and punctuated it with a "Morning, darling." He was never the wiser.

Evelyn had propped on the butcher-block island next to where Madeleine sat. She wore a floor-length black lace peignoir and matching chemise. Her dark red hair hung in spiral curls and her make-up was flawless. Madeleine stared down at her attire, a Georgia College and State University t-shirt and a pair of Lee's boxers. Her hair was up in a messy, slept-in bun, and Madeleine was grateful Evelyn was only visible to her.

"Why don't you ask him who he's been fucking the past several months?" Evelyn spat.

"He hasn't slept with anyone else," Madeleine said, carefully taking a sip of her coffee, avoiding Evelyn's eyes.

"You're kidding, right? You know the man's sex drive. If he wasn't fucking you, he was definitely fucking someone else."

"Mom suggested the whole family go out tonight," Lee stated mildly as he over-salted his scrambled eggs. "But we don't have to. I just thought you might want to get out of the house for a bit."

"Yeah, we could do that," Madeleine agreed halfheartedly. The entire family meant Adrian, and therefore Emily, and Madeleine didn't know if she had the strength to do her faking-it routine for an entire night. But there Lee was, giving her an encouraging expression that said he understood she didn't want to, yet he was proud she was doing it anyway. He would not say it out loud, but she knew with a mere glance what was on his mind.

"Wanna take this outside?" he asked, holding two plates of Madeleine's favorite breakfast, waffles with peaches and scrambled eggs with cheese.

Madeleine nodded. *He knows me after all*, she thought with some satisfaction. Evelyn stormed out of the room, muttering something as her heels clicked through the house.

It was a beautiful morning, not too hot yet, with a light breeze blowing. The sun was glowing orange in the sky and shining brilliant—

The bathroom. White tile shining in the light of a rising sun. A tub full of cold, gray water, a fly and the knife—

Shut it out. Don't think about it, Madeleine ordered herself.

Tears.

It was supposed to be over.

"Maddie? Honey, what's wrong?"

"Nothing. Nothing at all, I—"

"You can tell me. I'm here for you."

That's a new concept, Madeleine thought but fought through the thoughts and images spreading like rampant wildfire through her head. She collapsed into one of the metal patio chairs and tried to center her thoughts. Lee set the plates down on the table and knelt at his wife's knees, placing his hands on her thighs.

"This…it happens sometimes," Madeleine explained vaguely. Lee tried to hide the confused expression on his face, which pressed Madeleine to further explain. "I got to thinking about the day I tried it. I had been thinking about it for so long."

Madeleine hated talking about this, especially to Lee. He was never weak; he'd never understand.

"I'm listening. Go on," he urged.

"You wouldn't understand."

"Try me," Lee insisted, pulling the chair close to her.

"I don't even know where to start."

"It is one of your stories. It's your story. If you had to choose a beginning, where would it begin?"

Madeleine pulled her legs up into the chair and hugged them tight to her chest. "Third grade. I was eight, maybe?"

Lee was clearly confused. "What? Eight years old? You've got to be kidding me."

"I told you, you would never understand," Madeleine said defensively.

"No, no, it's not that. I mean, I don't, but I'm willing to try to understand. I'm just surprised an eight year old could even comprehend the concept of death."

"We live in the Bible Belt. Someone's always

trying to help the helpless, like my parents. Once they realize the parents won't bend, they work on the children while their minds are malleable. When you get raised in church, death becomes a common concept. You understand death is merely an extension of life. When things got bad, I felt like, if I could just die, I could go to Heaven where everything is perfect and new."

"But when you say, when things 'got bad,' was there something specific that made this idea of going to Heaven pop into your head?" Lee asked. He was analyzing every word she said.

"I don't know. I don't remember anything specific. But let's face it, Momma and Daddy weren't model parents. I would imagine even after only eight years of being alive, enough had gotten to me to make me want to escape somehow. Trust me, I get it. Most kids imagine running away and joining a circus or going to Neverland or whatever. Heaven sounded pretty good to me, I guess. So one night we were on the back porch, and Momma had bought a cantaloupe for dessert. She asked me to go in a get a knife for her. I pulled one out of the drawer, and this knife was tiny. A thin paring knife with a white plastic handle. I remember thinking I could shove it right into my stomach because no one would ever love me, and I would always be alone. How insane is that?"

Lee shook his head. "Madeleine, I can't believe in seven years of marriage we've never talked about this."

Madeleine gave him a moment to process everything. She had not wanted to tell anyone this, ever, but Lee was especially the last person she wanted to know about her past, how twisted her thoughts had always been. Lee had always been a paradigm of utter perfection in her mind. Sometimes this life still didn't feel real, having the husband a thousand women had wanted, being part of a loving, yet slightly dysfunctional family, getting to write, having her name on more than a few books, having the ability to walk in anywhere and afford anything her heart desired. She didn't feel she deserved any of it because of the darkness creeping around her mind, always threatening to expose itself.

Lee placed his hand on hers and laced their fingers. "I love you so much. We will fix this together. I'm here to support you every step of the way." He leaned over and his lips met hers, sealing his vow.

CHAPTER ELEVEN

The Rice House was a white, two-story antebellum home that had been moved to Barnsley Gardens when it was a family estate, at the turn of the twentieth century. The manicured English gardens surrounding the house gleamed in the aura of summer sun. Normally, the place would have been busier on a Friday evening, as businessmen from Atlanta headed up I-75 for a weekend in Adairsville's tucked away resort.

But tonight, Lee had used his connections, and most likely a small fortune, to buy out the Rice House for their "family get-together." Although she'd been living in the Atwood culture for years, some of the things this family, and their money, had the power to do was staggering for a girl who'd grown up in relative poverty.

The air was sweltering, even as the sun set. Perspiration was forming inside the long sleeves of the midnight-blue dress Madeleine had chosen to wear to cover her bandaged wrists. This dinner would be awkward enough. She wasn't even a full

61

seventy-two hours away from a botched suicide attempt and was supposed to be in a hospital, being watched like a hawk. Having dinner with Adrian Atwood was not on the top of her to-do list.

"Never mind the fact he's seen you naked now," Evelyn had teased as Madeleine was dressing. She had visibly winced at the comment, but Lee was too busy fastening clasps and buttons that put too much strain on her aching wrists. Every time one of his knuckles or fingertips brushed the skin on her back or chest, Madeleine would nearly shudder. The reaction wasn't sexual per se, but the mere sensation of experiencing human touch caused her heart to pound in an aching cadence. It had been months since anyone had touched her.

And now Lee was here, holding her hand as they made their way down the brick path. He rambled on, his words washing over her, his thumb caressing the back of her hand. As nervous as she was about having to face his family, she felt something akin to happiness. Perhaps she'd gotten her old life back.

"Don't sound too eager about it," Evelyn whispered in her ear. "We don't want people thinking you sliced your wrists open for attention, now would we?"

"That's not why I did it," Madeleine hissed.

Lee gently squeezed her hand. "Don't be nervous."

"How'd you know?"

"Because your chest and neck are flushed. That always happens when you're nervous," he responded, placing a kiss on her cheek. "Everyone here loves you. Besides, I'll make it worth your time later."

"Worth my time?"

His eyes glimmered, and he flashed a mischievous, boyish grin that made her blush. The door creaked open, and Adrian stood in the doorway, looking disappointed to see them.

"Nice to see you too," Lee quipped. Madeleine knew her cheeks were already reddening, but it sounded like Adrian was in even more of a bind than she was.

"I need a cigarette." Adrian exhaled and stepped outside, sliding the door closed.

"Mom driving you nuts already?"

"Yes," her brother-in-law groaned. "If she drops one more hint about proposing…"

"Why don't you man up and tell her you're not marrying Emily?" Lee asserted. "Problem solved."

"It's not that simple."

"Why not?"

"Because I'm gonna propose."

Lee's face fell. "Adrian, no."

"You are?" Madeleine asked brightly, her awkwardness beginning to dissipate. She didn't know Emily well, but she was the only woman who'd kept Adrian's attention for more than a few months at a time, and she took care of him.

"See? Maddie's smarter than you, and she approves. You look amazing, by the way," he told her with a sideways grin. The comment burned from her ears to her stomach, but it was better than the awkwardness she had expected from him.

"We'll talk about this later," said Lee. "I'm starving."

He led them through the front door of the house where an over-eager host took over and delivered them to a long table overlooking the grounds.

"Madeleine, that dress is spectacular," Emily said as they approached. "Is it Figue?"

Madeleine smiled back politely, but she hated how she could never tell if Emily was being genuine or if she was so nice all the time. "It is. I've become a big fan," Madeleine lied.

"Have you seen the new fall line yet? It's stunning."

Madeleine worked out a quick lie. "I checked out a few of the pieces, but I haven't bothered to go through at the entire collection yet. But I'm going out first thing and making my poor husband buy it all."

Lee shot her an amused expression, knowing his wife was only doing her best to stay afloat in the conversation.

"I, for one, was looking forward to seeing Nike's new fall line," Adrian intervened, his unique sarcasm shining through.

"Adrian, I swear you would wear nothing but gym shorts and a t-shirt if I'd let you," Emily declared.

"He wouldn't," Maggie Beth interjected. "When the school board banned athletic wear, I thought he was gonna stroke."

"I still think dress codes in public schools are a constitutional violation," Adrian added with a shrug.

"You would, Adrian," Lee laughed.

Everyone at the table was enjoying the

conversation now, Madeleine included, although her stomach was in anxious knots.

This is my family. I don't have to feel this awkward around them. I can relax and have fun tonight, she reminded herself.

"For now," Evelyn chimed. "You are such a hopeless case."

A waiter stepped up to the table and greeted the Atwoods and presented each of them with a wine menu. Madeleine ordered a light Italian Moscato. She rarely drank but figured some wine in her system would help loosen her up.

It didn't take long before the conversation between the Atwood men turned to business. So much had happened during their months of estrangement, Madeleine found it hard to follow. Emily, on the other hand, sounded downright interested and could even throw in a logical two cents now and then. Maggie Beth noticed Madeleine was drowning in the discussion and redirected the conversation.

"Boys, let's drop the business talk and just enjoy our time. It's been too long since we've had our family all together like this, don't you think, Richard?" Maggie Beth asked, working her magic in her own diplomatic way.

He shrugged. "If you say so."

There was a long pause. Eyes darted around or they took sips of their drinks to fill the void. When she caught Richard peering curiously at her sheer sleeves, Madeleine realized she was the elephant in the room. Everyone had the "Event," as she'd come to name it, on their minds but didn't want to bring it up in polite conversation. It was like it never happened, and Madeleine wanted to stand and tell them she was in full agreement. She wanted to forget all about it too, but she couldn't. One minute, she saw it as an opportunity, and the next she'd be cursing the day she met Adrian Atwood for ruining her chance of escaping this life.

"Madeleine, how have you been feeling?" Richard asked. He almost sounded concerned. She and Richard had never shared a warm relationship and likely never would. He was robot-like; Madeleine had figured it was because he had been so opposed to either of his boys having anything to do with her. Her family wasn't suitable, as she'd once overheard in a whispered conversation between him and Lee.

"Much better since being at home," Madeleine said, forcing a pleasant tone.

"Other than being stuck with me," Lee joked.

Adrian grinned. "God help you. I don't recommend living with him."

"He's not so bad," Madeleine teased, genuinely smiling now. Lee and Adrian's sibling camaraderie, and occasional rivalry, had always made being with them enjoyable.

"So you don't think," Richard began hesitantly, "maybe you needed time to convalesce, so to speak? I'm glad you're out and about, I—"

"Dad…" Lee warned.

"What? I'm concerned."

Lee scoffed, and Adrian opened his mouth to speak, but Madeleine placed a steadying hand on Lee's arm. "Lee's been very attentive, and I'm already seeing the best psychologist in Atlanta. I'm much better off at home where I can be comfortable and continue working."

Lee was satisfied with her answer, but Madeleine knew he had no idea how taxing that statement had been to make.

"I read an article about depression the other day from a Methodist minister up in Ellijay. He said depression ain't nothing but the devil," Maggie Beth stated. "He'll lie to you all day about your worth until you believe him."

Madeleine took a sip of her wine. "The devil's a formidable foe."

"He is, but not an impossible one."

Madeleine smiled tersely but didn't agree, and silence set in like a heavy storm cloud. She couldn't help but think if Maggie Beth, or any of the Atwoods, could walk a mile in her shoes maybe they would understand.

Emily was the first to break the silence, asking Lee some banal question to start up a more lighthearted conversation, but Madeleine's attention focused on her in-laws at the end of the table.

Richard appeared lost in thought, staring out the window behind his ex-wife. Maggie Beth was studying his expression, and after about a minute of Richard's mental wandering, Madeleine watched in surprise as Maggie Beth extended her arm across the table and placed her hand over Richard's. He snapped out of his daze, surprised by the hand resting on his own. His eyes flickered up in inquisition to the Atwood matriarch, and she withdrew the gesture, but as her hand lifted,

Richard's fingers wrapped around hers.

Madeleine had to jerk her eyes away from the unexpected exchange taking place and pretend like she had been listening intently to Lee and Emily's conversation the entire time. Madeleine realized Adrian had noticed the small but significant gesture as well. Adrian peered at her, confused and doubting what he had witnessed. A peek back down the table revealed both Richard and Maggie Beth had resumed their normal behavior, though now both of them seemed removed, contemplative. Lee must have said something funny because his deep laugh, highlighted by the musical quality of Emily's, echoed in the otherwise empty room. The sound brought Madeleine and Adrian back from their careful observation.

Madeleine took a sip of her wine, trying to relax and enjoy the rest of the dinner. The remainder of the evening went as any normal, happy family dinner would. They laughed about silly things the boys had done when they were kids, mulled over politics, and dreamed about the future.

"We should do this more often," Maggie Beth remarked. "We should set aside a night every week so we can all catch up in person."

"I think that would be nice, Mom," Adrian responded, placing his arms around her shoulders as the family walked out of Rice House together. Everyone said their goodbyes and went their separate ways. Emily clung to Adrian as they laughed and carried on back to his newest exotic car. Even Richard and Maggie Beth walked side by side, keeping on with their new trend of civil conversation.

She and Lee were alone. Again.

"How about a walk around the ruins?" he suggested. "You've always loved them."

Madeleine was feeling a little tired and didn't want to make the walk in her heels, but she appreciated the fact he knew more than she worried about aching feet. "Never get tired of them."

They started walking toward the ruins of the great Italian-style villa that had been the crowning jewel of the Barnsley estate nearly two centuries earlier. The Civil War and a tornado at the turn of the twentieth century had destroyed its grandeur, and time had taken care of the rest, but Madeleine had found the old house beautiful nonetheless. As they strolled through the English garden to the front landing, Lee's fingers played at the tips of hers until she accepted his hand.

"You look beautiful tonight. I don't think I ever got to tell you." He sounded nervous, keeping his eyes down at his feet as they climbed the wide landing steps to where a grand front door would have once kept the world at bay. "I should have said a lot of things, though. I should have been there for you. Why is it we never realize how much we're hurting other people until the damage is already done?"

Blood rushed to her cheeks as her mouth tensed into a joyous smile. "Sometimes damage can be fixed."

Evelyn laughed from the far side of the verandah, sipping on a glass of wine as the sun began to sink in the distance. "Feeling hopeful now? Where was that hope two days ago?"

"And sometimes it ends up like this." Lee laughed with a nod toward the ruined house.

Madeleine peered up at the towering brick structure and felt its magnetic pull beckoning her inside. "I wonder why they never fixed it," she said, stepping into what she imagined was once a grand foyer, Lee following behind. Madeleine pictured stained glass and black and white marble tile, the hustle and bustle of servants, and laughing children giving the house life again. "How do you let a house this amazing crumble into nothing? It just needed some love."

Lee placed his hands around her waist. Madeleine experienced a shock of alarm at first, not knowing what to expect from him. She turned around into his full embrace, stuck now.

"The walls are here. The foundation's strong. It's beautiful, just in a different way now, and with a little bit of love, it'll be here for years to come."

He held her close to his body and placed a slow, lingering kiss on her forehead. Madeleine breathed in his cologne, the starch ironed into his shirt, and the sweet red wine on his breath. Her heart beating at a slow, steady pace, she placed her hands on the lapels of his suit jacket. She watched the rise and fall of his chest, and with the cicadas droning on into the sunset, her entire body was electrified. It was the most alive she had felt in months.

When their eyes met, so did their lips for the first time in a long, too long, time. Reminded of his kiss, Madeleine collapsed into Lee's arms. His touch was more intoxicating than the wine ever could have been. His hands grasped her hips and their bodies melded together. Every drop of blood within her had turned into hellfire. She clutched the lapels of his suit jacket to stop from peeling it away from his shoulders, unbuttoning his shirt to expose the glorious, soft flesh her fingers were dying to experience again.

"We'll stay here tonight. God knows I don't have the patience to get you home."

CHAPTER TWELVE

"Madeleine McCollum."

Madeleine's breath hitched. *He* was standing in front of her. She was dumbstruck for a moment, then her mind raced with questions. Why would he be here? Surely, he didn't read the book or stand in this line forty-five minutes to get it signed?

Does he remember the day he kissed me? I'll bet he's kissed too many girls to even keep track. Madeleine remembered all too well the sweltering summer day the man standing before her now had given her first kiss. After an entire afternoon of relentless flirting, he had teasingly wrapped her up in his arms, and once their eyes met, the kiss that followed had been so much sweeter than she'd ever imagined a kiss could be.

He was as gorgeous as she remembered. He wore an exquisite jet-black, three-piece suit with a gray shirt and a black patterned tie, his golden hair perfect. Madeleine forced herself to breathe.

I'm an author now, a best-selling one. I can talk to this guy.

"Lee Atwood," she said, trying to keep her cool. "Imagine seeing you here."

She glanced down the line of people waiting to have their copies signed. Conversations with the so-called fans should last thirty seconds or less, and she was certain she had spent that time shocked this golden Apollo had been standing in front of her for the first time in years.

"What can I say? I'm a fan," he said, sliding a copy of her book over so she could sign the title page.

She glanced up at him over her glasses, a skeptical brow raised. He caught her critical gaze and surrendered.

"All right, fine, I haven't read it, but I saw your picture on the display poster and wanted to say hi."

"You waited in line this long to say hi?"

"I had to wait a while, but I may have bought a few people their copies of your book to get ahead."

Incorrigible, these Atwood men, she thought, reminded of Adrian. "Oh. Well, I hope you're getting a good return on your investment."

He gave an amused grin but broke away. She noticed his cheeks were flushed. Satisfied, she leaned back in her chair as his contagious grin spread to her. As much as she was rather enjoying watching this man who had haunted her dreams since he'd first placed that kiss on her lips so long ago, she could tell there were quite a few people in the line getting antsy.

"So how about an autograph?" she said, shaking.

"Would you make it out special? For me?" Lee asked with his damnable, perfect smile and steely blues piercing her through. She remembered the feeling of looking into those same eyes while the hot summer sun bore down oppressively and she melted under his touch. And his kiss...merely remembering it was enough to make her head spin. Her eyes flitted to Lee Atwood's perfect lips, flushed pink, wishing she could remember what he tasted like. Mentally, she stood, grabbed the knot of his tie and, leaning over the table between them, kissed him with an intensity that would make the patient people behind him blush with embarrassment.

She swallowed and shook her head, trying to return from her uncontrollable thoughts back to the real world.

"Um, sure," she finally answered. "What would you like me to write?"

"To my first kiss." Her heart jumped into her throat, but she tried to remain calm as she controlled her shaking hand and wrote as he dictated. "Yes, I would love to have dinner with you tonight."

Madeleine's mouth went slack, in awe of him. She knew she should refuse, but she wanted to accept. She dared to put pen to paper and write. She closed the book, her response forever etched on the inside of his copy. Her cheeks flushed when her hand touched his to exchange the book. He opened it to read her response and laughed, both surprised and amused.

"You'll 'entertain the notion' of going to dinner with me?" he asked with a laugh. "Well played, Miss McCollum."

"I assure you, Mr. Atwood, I don't play. I need

to make sure my schedule can afford an evening out. We're leaving for New York first thing in the morning."

"Oh. Maybe when you get back, if you can't tonight. Anyway, I…great, now I don't even know what I'm saying."

"You? At a loss for words?" Madeleine asked, surprised and somewhat breathless.

"Trust me, it's unusual."

Their eyes locked.

"I would imagine so," said Madeleine. "You've always been so…"

"Verbose?"

Madeleine shrugged. "I would say charming and quick-witted, but—"

"I'll take that compliment any day. Here's my number. Let me know whatever you decide," Lee said, fetching a business card from his wallet.

"A gentleman should be the one to call first," Madeleine said coyly.

He was taken aback. "Oh, really now? By all means, Miss McCollum, I wouldn't want anyone to think you were the one doing all the pursuing here. I'll call you around five maybe?"

She finished writing her number on the back of his business card. "Five sounds perfect, Mr. Atwood. I'm looking forward to it."

"You are something else. Until tonight, Madeleine." He tucked the business card back in his wallet.

"Until then," she uttered, knowing she wanted nothing more than to see him again.

~*~

The last time Madeleine had awoken in her husband's arms, it had felt more like a stranglehold than love. They'd fought the night before. About what, she could not remember, but it was in the weeks leading up to their unofficial separation, so there was no telling what it was over—house remodeling, her typical reclusive behavior at the parties and charity balls he expected her to attend at his side, having another baby, living a normal life again. Things she couldn't interest herself in anymore.

Those should have been the first signs, she'd later figure out while in session with Dr. Moore. She was a quiet, reserved person. Parties and big events weren't her thing. They never had been, and the likelihood she would ever happily attend one was practically nonexistent. Her marriage, though, Lee, that was something she wanted to enjoy. But Madeleine hadn't been able to do her part to fix their marriage, or herself, anymore.

Madeleine nestled into her pillow, not ready to be out of the bed. She turned on her side and grasped the pillow he had slept on. His side of the bed held his warmth; the pillow held his scent. She had done the same the week he had left, clutching his abandoned pillow in her arms, wishing more than anything he was there beside her despite all the pain he had caused.

"He was amazing last night, wasn't he?"

Madeleine shot bolt upright in the bed, covering herself with the sheets as Evelyn flashed a malicious grin up at her, not the least bit concerned for modesty.

"Jesus Christ, Evelyn!" Madeleine hissed. "Have you never heard of boundaries?"

"You're the one who needed me last night. You think you charmed that husband of yours into bed without my influence?" Evelyn scoffed.

"We are married and were long before you came along."

Evelyn smirked. "You got pregnant about the time I came along, though. Coincidence?"

Madeleine considered it for a split second, then shook her head, dismissing Evelyn, as if their thoughts and words were not the same.

She could hear water splashing on tile in the bathroom. Madeleine pushed again at all the dark thoughts in her head, replacing them with the idea to join Lee in the shower.

"You will not keep him interested. Not on your own. He will leave. Again."

Madeleine turned back to Evelyn, who was laying as if she were posing nude for some great work of art. Her perfect body, in stark comparison to Madeleine's own, gleamed in the orange sunrise. "You're wrong. He loves me. We've had a rough patch, but we will fix it. Lee's determined, and there's nothing more powerful than a determined Lee Atwood."

"Unless it has a vagina and an open bottle of whiskey. It doesn't take much."

"Enough! I want you to leave. Get out of my head," Madeleine said with an anger that made her lips tremble. She stood and walked toward the bathroom.

"Are you going to ask him?" Evelyn called as she reached the door. Madeleine gripped the doorjamb in anger, but also to steady her head, which was swooning with the fact she knew Evelyn was right.

"Ask him what?" she quavered.

Evelyn smirked, laughed in condescension, then disappeared from her mind's eye. Madeleine knew exactly what she should have asked him and the answer she should expect. Where had he been all those long months without her?

CHAPTER
THIRTEEN

Madeleine shifted in the oversized and overstuffed white armchair that made her feel tiny. She straightened her posture and crossed her legs to see if it made her feel any more substantial, longing for her antidepressants to kick in. The numbness rendering her near-dead to the world would be better than the nervousness that tensed every muscle in her body. She fished her cell phone from her Louis Vuitton purse to check the time. It was 10:05. Dr. Moore was five minutes late.

Madeleine's eyes searched the room to distract herself from her nervous musings. The room was supposed to be relaxing and peaceful. The walls were meadow green, and the floors were a weathered cedar hardwood. A large corner window provided ample amounts of natural lighting, and the morning sunlight streamed in through the spotted leaves of sweet gum trees and red maples. Two well-chosen but ambiguous paintings covered the walls, the rich, golden colors warming the room.

10:07. In the corner of the room was a desk cluttered in papers and picture frames. It was removed from the area close to her chair, reserved for conversing with patients, analyzing their every thought. Madeleine figured the analysis was the part she feared the most.

What happened if Dr. Moore thought her mental state was beyond therapy and drugs? What happened when he figured out what went on in her head all day, or she didn't live in the same world as everyone else because she talked to her characters? Would he perceive her as merely creative, or was he going to diagnose her with schizophrenia? How long would it take him to lock her up forever in a padded room with a straightjacket? How long would it take Lee to move on with his life? For her literary agent to find a new client?

All the questions circulating in her mind nearly made her sick, but when he popped into his office a full ten minutes late, Madeleine forced it all to come to an abrupt end. Dr. Moore didn't need to know what went on in her mind. It couldn't have been of any real consequence to either of them anyway.

He's here to collect whatever ghastly amount of money Lee is paying him, and I'm here to act sane long enough for him to tell Lee everything's okay with me, Madeleine thought. *It is an act, a dance, I just have to make sure to do the right steps.*

"Hey there, Madeleine. How are you today?"

She plastered on her public face, a small but convincing smile, and shook his outstretched hand. "Pretty good," she responded in a tone much more upbeat than her actual mood. She was irritated he was late, nervous because she could already see through her thin facade, all compiled on top of all the other emotions she had been dealing with over the past few days. She still couldn't get her mind off Lee, the fact she was rather certain he'd had an affair, but she sure as hell wasn't planning on telling this to the good doctor who was sitting across from her.

"How's the recovery going on your wrists? Have you started any physical therapy?"

"Um, yeah. I'm going twice a week. Left wrist hurts, but the right feels better."

"That's good. So, before we begin, let's get a few minor details sorted out. First of all, what goes on in these sessions, or any time we talk, is strictly between you and me. You're the only one in this relationship who can disclose anything to anybody else. Second, I want to know more about you, so we'll get to know each other for now. It could take two sessions, maybe even three or four, but whatever it takes for you to be comfortable telling me what's going on in your world that can better help me treat your depression. And you can call me Henry, if you like."

Madeleine was feeling increasingly apprehensive. Getting to know people was not her strong suit.

"Are you nervous?" he asked.

"Honestly? Yes," Madeleine said. "You have no idea."

"Actually, I do. I won't say I've been through the same situation you're in, but I've faced depression,

I've attempted suicide. I've had to sit across from a psychologist who I didn't know from Adam, who wanted me to tell him thoughts and feelings I had been trying to spare my family and friends from for years."

"Hmmm. Spare. Good word choice," Madeleine contemplated. She took a deep breath and relaxed a bit.

"So you can relate? Having to feel like you're sparing everyone else from what you're having to face every day?"

Somehow, the words and emotions she wanted to keep inside started pouring out. "It feels like a war zone. You have to fight through every single activity. Getting out of bed, talking to people. It's exhausting. Especially when it all seems so pointless. Why would I ever want anyone else to have to understand that? As if some of them even could fathom it at all."

"Some research supports that it takes a certain amount of intelligence for depression to take root. I can't say I completely agree with that theory, but several of the studies have some merit. I can see how you would think certain people could go through life and never further analyze their life or having a purpose, a meaning."

"Must be nice to be them," Madeleine muttered. "To be unable to think like this. I don't want it, but it feels like it's been a part of me for so long."

"How long would that be?" Dr. Moore asked. "When do you think your depression began?"

Madeleine shrugged. She had recently admitted all of this to Lee; how could she tell this man who she had interacted with for only fifteen minutes of her life?

"A couple of years," Madeleine responded, but she regretted the lie. What was the point in lying to this man? Would it ever get any better if she kept internalizing everything? "To be honest, it feels like I've dealt with it off and on my entire life. But the past two years have been the worst."

Curiosity covered the doctor's face. Madeleine bit her lip and braced for his next inevitable question. "How young do you think you were when—"

"Eight," she answered before she could recant her story. "I know that sounds crazy, but it's the first time I thought about...about cutting myself. The first time the idea I could be dead and in a better place must have popped into my head. That idea stuck for a long time, and I would always kind of daydream about it when things went wrong. It was morbid, I know, to fantasize about it so young. Then I'm a teenager, which is hard enough, and to top it all off, literature teachers, by the force of curriculum, introduce me to Shakespeare. *Hamlet*. *They* get it. Hamlet and Ophelia get it. Why face all this? The so-called 'slings and arrows of outrageous fortune.' By God, take control, challenge the world, end the war on your terms. That sounded even better to a teenager who was in control of nothing. Take arms against a sea of troubles, and by opposing them, end them. The end of heartache and pain. It sounded so good after our baby died. I fought for two years, and then two weeks ago, I got up the gumption to follow through. I guess from there, you know the rest of the story."

"Not at all. If you ask me, the good part is just getting started."

Madeleine scoffed. "That's your response? It's not what I expected."

"I'm not here to judge you, Madeleine. I'm too grateful for you being so candid. Your story, while it's your unique journey, is not the first of its kind. I've experienced it myself, and while I never want to face that kind of suffering again, it made me who I am. Like you said, my depression is a part of me. I learned to cherish it in a way. It's the whole reason I wanted to become a psychologist, so I could help people like me."

Madeleine took a moment to process it all, but a wave of comfort washed over her. It helped knowing the doctor understood. Not because he had pored over a bunch of case studies in college, but because he had been faced with every feeling of insignificance, maybe even the same self-doubt and loathing she had.

"Not a single one of my books, short stories, novellas, anything, ever has a clear-cut happy ending."

"How boring would it be if they did?" Dr. Moore replied. "Life doesn't always work that way. But I can promise you, we will work hard to make sure you get as close to your very own happy ending as possible."

Even though she was skeptical, Madeleine thought it was possible a ray of hope had to exist somewhere out there in the universe. If she were lucky, maybe she would at least end up close to it.

~*~

That evening, Adrian joined them for dinner. Adrian's visits throughout the week had once been commonplace, but Lee and Madeleine's estrangement had put a stop to her having much of anything to do with the Atwoods. It was nice to feel a connection to them again, although the conversation went sour halfway into the meal.

"You did what?!"

Adrian shrugged. "She was so…disappointed."

"Who cares, Adrian? Let her be disappointed."

"Christ, Lee, don't act like you don't understand."

"But I don't understand. I don't think she's right for you, and I don't think you need to marry her."

"Stop being such an asshole. I want to marry her. I just don't think now is the time."

"Then obviously you don't need to propose."

Madeleine did not look up from her notebook. Her pen scratched along the parchment paper of her leather-bound writing journal. Ideas were finally striking after a months-long dry spell. She was having to write with her other hand, but the notes were legible enough.

They were all sitting around the dining room table, Lee and Adrian engrossed in their conversation as they ate the steaks Lee had grilled for dinner. Adrian looked over to Madeleine, amused.

"She's off in her own little world, isn't she?" he said.

"Always," Lee responded as he cut a piece of his

steak. "But it's a good sign when she's so immersed in something. Must be another bestseller."

"I don't know so much about this one," Madeleine denied, somewhat absentminded, writing the last sentence before eating her dinner.

"That's what she said about *An Early Grave*," Lee told Adrian. "And how many copies did that sell again?"

Madeleine shrugged. Lee certainly was a lot of things he shouldn't have been, but he was a source of encouragement. She pierced a red-skinned potato with her fork, the skin popping when she bit into the buttery flesh.

"So," she said, flicking her eyes playfully toward Adrian. "You're finally getting married?"

Adrian shook his head but laughed. "Yeah, I guess I am."

"You don't have to propose," Lee argued, exasperated.

"But I told her I would. Maddie, you know what happened, right?" Adrian asked.

Maddie swallowed a cool sip of merlot before responding. "What exactly did you tell her?"

"I asked if she could scrape up enough patience to wait until the end of the year. And I promised her, promised, we would be engaged soon."

"Oh, wow. September is only a few days away. That gives you four months to propose," Madeleine pointed out.

"I don't even know what possessed me to say it. She was so happy. And it's been three years. Isn't it what I should want to do?"

"But do you actually want to marry her?"

Madeleine asked.

"Look, I want to marry her. I just don't feel like it's the right thing to do right now."

Madeleine's heart ached for him. Adrian was a good person, and Madeleine knew he would be an excellent husband and father if he would only give himself the chance.

"In other words, he doesn't want to marry her. At least not now. I don't think she's right for you anyway. Good for you, sure, but not the one." Lee's tone was filled with victory, as if he had already brought them around to his point of view.

Madeleine rolled her eyes. "Ugh, I loathe that expression."

"You're the one for me." Lee grinned. Madeleine wanted to lash out at him, demand to know why if she was the one he would ever leave her, but she kept her thoughts hidden inside. She was angry with him but couldn't truly feel the heart-pounding, fearsome rage she knew should have been consuming her. Instead, overwhelming numbness of calm kept washing over her.

Side effects, she thought glumly and before long probably would be feeling the similar numbing effects of the antidepressants. She had felt that way the first time she'd been prescribed them and held faint hope she'd feel any differently this time around.

"You need to be honest with her," Madeleine told Adrian. "If you think something is wrong, tell her. If she truly loves you, she'll be understanding."

"Hurt, but understanding," her husband added.

Once everyone had finished their dinner,

Madeleine stood to take their plates, but when she reached for Adrian's, Lee swept in.

"You'll hurt your wrists," he protested, taking them from her hands. "I wish you would let me get someone in here to cook and clean."

"I like to cook, and I don't mind cleaning up my own house," Madeleine said defensively.

Adrian toyed with his phone, pretending not to hear or care about the short exchange.

"I'm supposed to be the one taking care of you right now, and I think I can handle a few dishes," Lee countered. He took the small stack of dishes and walked off into the kitchen.

Madeleine exhaled deeply and sank back into her chair when she heard the water in the sink turn on.

"He can probably count on one hand how many times he's washed dishes, right?" Adrian mentioned with a grin. "He could put them in the dishwasher and they still wouldn't come out clean."

"I'll bet you're right." Madeleine watched Lee fill the sink with water and soap.

"Just let him do his thing and take care of you for a while. I know you want to handle things yourself, but take a break. It won't hurt him to do a few things around here."

"I'm not helpless."

"I know you're not."

"And he's…he's so—"

"Frustrating?" Adrian cut in. "I know he is. Where do you think I got it?"

"You're both pretty frustrating sometimes. At least I've only got to put up with Lee, right?"

"Hmmm, I'm over here quite a bit. I'd say you

got stuck with both of us. No wonder Mom loves you so much. You've saved her a load of trouble."

She couldn't help the laugh that escaped. She also could not remember the last time she had laughed. Out of the corner of her eye, Madeleine saw Lee was looking back curiously through the doorway, and she could have sworn a satisfied smile played at his lips. Madeleine wasn't sure what to think about this. For a man so bent on making her happy, he definitely knew how to make her miserable too.

Adrian's phone buzzed on the table, heralding a call from Emily. Madeleine gave him an encouraging nod; he exhaled and answered his phone.

"Hey, Em."

Picking up her notebook and pen, Madeleine went into the kitchen to give Adrian some privacy. She wanted nothing more than to wrap her arms around Lee's waist and rest her head on his shoulder. She wanted the numbness to go away, the memory of all their pain erased, to stop hating herself for being so weak when all she wanted was her old life back. But she set down her notebook and settled in the corner of the counter instead, watching Lee dunk the last dish into the warm, soapy water.

"Emily called?" Lee asked.

"Yeah."

Lee finished wiping down the dish and placed it in the dishwasher. Even through the numbness, Madeleine wanted to embrace him, relish the time he was here. Eventually, Lee wouldn't be spending so much time at home. Whether he left again, or just got back into the routine of a sixty- to seventy-hour work week and business trips, he would not be here like this for long.

She longed to go to him. They had said they would fix this, they had made love the night before, so why was she so nervous to initiate any kind of affection?

Evelyn scoffed as she prepared a cup of coffee. "He doesn't care about you."

"Yes, he does."

"You're falling for that? 'Oh, Madeleine, I can't live without you,'" she mimicked. "But I'm gonna leave for six months and fuck God knows who while you sit here and rot. Face it, he won. And it was so easy."

Wounded, Madeleine couldn't even look at Evelyn. "I love him despite everything. I knew he couldn't have been faithful. I'm not stupid. But it doesn't change the fact I've only wanted for him to come home, to come back to me."

Evelyn shook her head. "Weak."

Madeleine ran her fingers through her hair, confusion wracking her brain. In an attempt to distract herself, she grabbed a box of her Earl Gray tea and a kettle. She laid them out on the counter and began to rifle through the cabinet for her favorite teacup. Lee noticed the kettle and filled it with water for her, then set it on the stove and turned on the eye. Madeleine put too much sugar in the bottom of the teacup and placed it on the counter next to the stove. For a moment, their eyes met in an awkward exchange, and Madeleine longed to be close to him.

Oh, what the hell, she figured, wrapping her arms around him and resting her head on his chest.

He embraced her in reciprocation. "I love you so much," he whispered.

"I love you too."

They stood there in each other's embrace in the middle of the kitchen until Adrian came wandering in on his cell.

"I'll see you Monday. I'll be back tomorrow night. Yeah, I'm crashing at Lee and Maddie's."

"I love how he just invites himself," Lee responded sarcastically.

Madeleine broke their embrace when the teakettle began to whistle. She and Lee both went to get it, but with Adrian's words in the back of her mind, she let Lee pour the water for her and even let him serve the tea to her at the butcher table. He placed a kiss on her forehead before stepping out of the room to make a few business calls.

For the moment, a warmth crept through the emotional numbness. She sipped her tea and flipped her notebook open to the last page she was on before having to stop to eat, feeling a satisfaction as her pen glided over the paper once more. Things were going to work out with Lee, she was writing again…she could not think of many more things she could possibly want.

She felt a presence behind her, and Adrian broke the silence. "From what little I've read, this new book sounds interesting."

Madeleine's heart skipped a beat and she went to shut her notebook, but her fingers caught the tip of her teacup, spilling the hot tea all over the paper. "No!"

"Maddie, I'm sorry. I'll grab some paper towels."

The warmth that had begun creeping up on her was now gone, and the numbness iced over her emotions once again, although Madeleine wanted to be extremely angry with Adrian for both reading over her shoulder and ruining her notes.

Adrian made his way back to Madeleine with a wad of paper towels. She snatched them from his hands and began to blot the paper.

"We could take a hair dryer to them," he suggested.

"Why would you even be reading over my shoulder anyway? I don't even let Lee read anything."

"Lee doesn't even get to read it? You're married."

"No one reads anything less than a final draft. It—it's just a…a thing I have."

"I hate to tell you, but I've been reading over your shoulder since junior year of high school."

"Adrian Atwood!"

"What? I've always liked your work. I quite literally have got to be your first fan, and I'm your brother-in-law, and I still don't have a single autographed copy of your books," Adrian replied matter-of-factly. "I like your books, rough draft or published-perfect. Are you honestly afraid I'm going to criticize it or something?"

Madeleine kept blotting the papers one at a time. A calm wave of understanding washed over her, the warmth of a genuine compliment. "I didn't know you read them."

"I love your books."

There was an elongated, nervous pause between them.

"I'll go get a hair dryer. I would hate to have ruined the next great Madeleine McCollum novel."

Madeleine reminded herself to relax. She could fix this. "You know the best thing do for wet paper?" Adrian shrugged.

She began taking the pages with her notes out, carefully tearing the perforated edges along the top of the paper. Fifteen double-sided pages in all. "Heat makes the ink run," Madeleine explained. "You stick the pages between wax paper and put it in the freezer."

Adrian went to a cabinet and pulled out a box of wax paper and handed it to Madeleine. "You would expect an engineer to think of something like that."

"Considering you know how to construct robots and space shuttles and whatever else it is you guys work on over there at Atwood Technologies," Madeleine joked.

"We don't make the shuttles, only the avionics systems," he said shyly, placing one of the pages between the wax paper.

"Oh, so the important part of the space shuttle?" she asked facetiously.

"Yes, the important part. So now you stick these in the freezer?"

"For a few minutes." Madeleine stacked his sheets on hers. "Then they have to air dry. As long as I can see what I've written to guide me through a rough draft, I should be all right."

"I'm sorry I read over your shoulder. I didn't know you were so sensitive about your work being read."

"It's fine." A smile crept over her face. "Besides, you kind of gave me an ego boost there."

"If I were you, I'd never need an ego boost," Adrian said flatly.

She cast her eyes to her bare feet. "I could use them all the time. Just to feel what I imagine must be…normal."

Madeleine did not see his cheerful expression fade or the hurt he felt for her so plainly written across his face.

"Maddie…" He faltered, unsure what to say.

"I think I'm going to head up to bed," she said.

"Yeah, I'm sure you're tired. Sorry, again. I promise I'll try to be stealthier about reading over your shoulder in the future."

"Or you could stop altogether."

"Or you could do your brother-in-law a favor and start emailing a chapter here and there. I should get first fan privileges."

Madeleine shook her head dismissively but couldn't help but wear an eye-crinkling smile. "Goodnight, Adrian."

"'Night."

CHAPTER FOURTEEN

Another week passed, and the board began asking questions about when Lee would come back. Madeleine insisted she would be fine, that he didn't have to stay and protect her. Begrudgingly, Lee told his father he would come back to work, and within a month, he and Madeleine had settled into a comfortable routine that greatly resembled their life before they'd lost baby Thomas. Lee was happiest he'd been in two years, and Adrian was the first to notice.

"You look better, healthier. I knew that if you would just go back home—"

"Yeah, yeah," he muttered. "You were right. Happy?"

"I am, actually. Now if I can only get you to stop drinking so much."

"Jesus Christ, Adrian." He laughed. "One thing at a time."

Incessant phone calls from Brecklyne convinced

him of a need for closure. She had to know he was done. On one early October morning, Lee was staring at his watch in apprehension. She was late. He took another sip of his bitter black coffee, his nerves frazzling.

He was sitting in the Marietta Diner amid the masses of people cramming in for breakfast while the black-clad waitresses hustled from table to table with long-abused carafes of coffee, expertly filling the anonymous white mugs used a thousand times before. He kept checking his watch as the creeping sensation of dread had his stomach knotting. Had it not been for that looming sense of foreboding, Lee would have had a hard time believing he was in the diner at all, as if it were all some out-of-body experience. The clanging of plates and spoons and knives and forks, the loud, rhythmic dialogue between the cooks and waitresses, the conversations of fellow diners, all of it was so easily shut away from his mind. He was not thinking about anything in general, but he kept casting his eyes from table to table, people watching as he drank his coffee and obsessively glanced at the dial on his watch, seeing the seconds of his life fleeting away into the impossible chasm of time.

She was twenty minutes late. He should take it as a sign, a second chance, and leave. Forget going to work today. Go home to Madeleine. They were planning on attending Atlanta's biggest even of the season, the Swan House Ball, later that evening, anyway. They could spend the day together with nothing more to do than prepare for the always-grand event.

Yet his body was rigid, unwilling to move. Hadn't he agreed to meet her? Hadn't he missed Brecklyne to some extent? He had fully expected this was something he could handle, but it was proving to be just another stupid decision that could cost him everything he genuinely held close to his heart, and those things numbered a precious few. This time, he wasn't even sure he couldn't lose his brother over this. Lee thought of how Adrian had begged him to stop seeing Brecklyne in the first place, how he exasperatingly explained every terrible, though likely, outcome. Adrian had been right in the end. Yet Madeleine was there by his side. They had been given a second chance, and Lee knew he didn't deserve it.

"Are you waiting on the rest of your party, sir?" the waitress asked as she refilled the unremarkable white mug. He nodded silently and took a sip of coffee so hot he likened it to hellfire. The waitress had caught him off guard, lost in his own thoughts about Madeleine, how pretty she was curled up next to him asleep this morning, how very guilty he felt about leaving her, the premeditated actions on his mind gnawing at his spirit. He had taken one more long gaze before closing their bedroom door and wished a million times over he was a stronger man or that he'd never decided to steal her away from his brother when they were young. Adrian would have been a good husband; he never would have been unfaithful. And simply because good things should happen to good people, he imagined they'd have a houseful of beautiful children and all the happiness in the world.

He hated himself for robbing her of that. For taking a complex girl who craved nothing but a simple life and small pleasures and making her live in a world he knew she could never survive in. It was like taking a lamb from its flock and expecting it to live among a pack of wolves for the rest of its life. Madeleine had done nothing in her life to deserve that, nothing but fall in love with the wrong man. What could he do about it now? Set her free, hurt her even more than he already had?

"I can't believe you showed," came a voice that, although soft, overshadowed the entirety of the diner chaos. From the moment he had laid eyes on Brecklyne, all he could think about was how very badly he wanted to claim her as his own, and she had been like malleable clay in his hands from their first conversation. All the charm and wit and money and allure had been enough to bewitch her into his complete submission.

"I don't know why we're here," he admitted softly as she sat down across from him. The waitress strolled up to take their orders. Brecklyne ordered a coffee with her low-fat, low-calorie, gluten-free (what Lee classified as "hippie") breakfast; he ordered his usual, bacon, eggs, and hash browns, though he didn't feel like eating anything at all.

Brecklyne waited patiently for the waitress to leave before continuing their conversation. "I thought we were happy together."

Lee shook his head. "I don't even know anymore, Brecklyne. I can't say I don't miss you, but I do know that this isn't how I want to live the rest of my life."

"No one is forcing you to live it this way either."

"I didn't come here to argue with you about it," he snapped. "I've already made up my mind."

"But you miss me, and you agreed to meet me here in the first place."

Lee swallowed, taking her humbling blow. "I love my wife, and I want our lives to get back to normal."

Brecklyne threw him a steely glare and crossed her arms. He awaited her response, almost like a child waiting for a punishment. Why did he ever allow her to have so much power over him? This had to stop. Then he noticed a glistening teardrop welling in her eye.

"Do you really love her that much?" she cried. The first tear fell, but Brecklyne swiped it away like it was acid. She always hated it when he saw her cry, but today she was too distraught to care.

Lee stared at her blankly, unsure of what to say, so he decided to simply be truthful for once. "Yes, I love her that much. That's what I'm trying to tell you."

"But your actions always say otherwise," she choked. "If you love her so much, why would you leave her to be with me?"

"Hell, Brecklyne, who do you think I am? I am not the knight in shining armor figure you've got painted in your mind. I'm the the antagonist in this story. There is no hero."

"That much is obvious," she fired back through a stronger flow of tears.

Lee flicked his eyes over the other tables to make

sure Brecklyne wasn't attracting any attention. The idea of being seen with her now scared him in a way it never had before. "Why would you want me anyway? I'm telling you, you're going to be better off. You're going to find someone who loves you and can treat you right. Then you'll see that all of this was a huge waste of your life."

Brecklyne stared at him contemplatively for a moment. "All I ever wanted, from the first time I met you, was for you to be a part of my life. For the past two years, you have been all I could ever think about, then Madeleine decides she's better off dead and you decide she's all *you've* ever wanted."

"It was a huge wake-up call, yes."

"No, it was the universe telling you that you couldn't have everything your way for once in your life and you didn't like—"

"Bacon, eggs, and hash browns?"

They both looked up, feeling caught red-handed in the middle of a crime as their waitress slid Lee's plate in front of him. "Brecklyne, we can't keep doing this. I'm sorry. I didn't want to hurt you, but I've got a wife who I've hurt enough already, and I can't bear to hurt again."

He took out more than enough cash to pay for their meals and tossed it on the table. "I've got to get to work. I'm sorry, but I can't do this anymore.

Lee had made it a few steps away when she spoke up. "What are you going to do if she finds out?"

He turned to stare her down, eyes glaring as the world tinged red. "You wouldn't dare."

"The truth always has a way of coming out, Lee.

I'd never have to say a word."

Lee clenched his jaw, nervousness and anger swelling into a great lump in his chest. Before he could say anything he might regret later, he turned on his heel and left.

~*~

Later that night, Lee was unable to concentrate on nothing more than a glass of Gentleman Jack. He was clenching his hands in his pockets, standing in the hotel elevator, impatiently watching the lighted floor display, waiting for the floor to the suite he'd reserved for them that weekend. He had half a mind to see if Maddie wanted to stay in. She hated these things anyway. He could drink, she could write; they'd be one happy little family.

When he unlocked the door to the suite, he could practically feel a crystal highball on his lips and a smooth whiskey burning down his throat, and he was thinking of excuses he could give to Madeleine for wanting to hole up in the hotel suite when he had insisted they attend the Swan Ball. But then he opened the hotel door and saw his wife and everything faded away.

Madeleine was finishing getting ready, fastening a gold waterfall earring in the bedroom mirror. She was wearing a one-shoulder, floor-length emerald gown that hugged at the hips and breasts, accentuating the hourglass figure she rarely showed off. Her hair was up in some complicated style he was sure had taken hours and a thousand pins to accomplish. There was no way she wouldn't the

101

belle of the whole damned ball, though she would be the last person to think it.

"You, Mr. Atwood, are very late," she said, keeping her eyes on the mirror while she fiddled with a stray strand of her up-do.

He wrapped his arms around her, holding her tight against his body. Madeleine relaxed his arms and rested her cheek against his shoulder.

"Rough day?" she asked softly, and he could tell from her tone that she was genuinely worried.

"Terrible," Lee choked, praying Madeleine didn't say anything about it. Everything came rushing back—Brecklyne, the fact that the mere sight of her filled him with a guilt so heavy he could hardly breathe, and worst of all, the feeling of impending doom that he was about to lose the only woman he had ever loved.

"Lee? What's going on?" she asked.

Lee tightened his hold on her, and Madeleine acquiesced to his needs as she always did. He searched for an excuse, something to tell her instead of the truth. "It's a lot of stress with the company, that's all. I can handle it, get it all figured out. I have to, right?"

"You're not the CEO yet. You can let your father handle something every once in a while."

"I'd rather die than ask him for help," Lee grumbled. He stepped back to admire her once again. "Enough about all that. I don't want to talk about it for the next two days, besides...damn, you're gorgeous."

"Really?" she asked with a blush. "I wasn't sure about this dress."

"It would look better on the floor."

"You're such an ass," Madeleine said with a coy grin. "We're going to be late. You need to get ready."

"Let's just stay in," he suggested, unsure if he was serious. "You don't want to go."

Madeleine eyed him curiously. "It must have been a really terrible day. We always go to the infernal Swan Ball. If you don't want to go, we certainly don't have to, but Doctor Moore says I should get outside my comfort zone every now and then and try to be more social."

"If you insist, I suppose we'll go," Lee replied.

"Oh, I sure as hell don't want to go. I just know that you normally like to. Besides, I look too good to stay in." She playfully struck a pose.

Lee laughed at her and placed a kiss on her cheek. "Fine, we'll go. But if it's not fun this year, we're leaving and going to the Varsity to heckle Tech fans."

"Ugh, it's never fun, only bearable. Get dressed or we might miss something exciting."

Snickering, Lee started preparing for the night ahead.

Madeleine sat down at an ornate desk at the opposite end of the bedroom, scribbling a few sentences here and there on the hotel stationary while she waited for him.

"Jesus," he uttered minutes later. "Guess what I forgot to pack?"

"Your cufflinks?" Madeleine asked absently.

"How'd you guess?"

"You always forget them," Madeleine said.

"Lucky for you I spotted them on the dresser right before I left. They're in that small bag in the bathroom."

"Another reason why I love you so much," he remarked, stepping into the marble bathroom. He spotted the bag sitting on the wide vanity and rifled through it for the black velvet box that would contain the cufflinks Madeleine had purchased as part of a Christmas gift when they first started dating. They had always been his favorite simply because they were from her.

Lee fished out the box, but as he did, the bag toppled over, spilling its contents. An amber prescription bottle skidded across the marble surface, littering it with tiny, circular pills that fell with a clatter, and he groaned. Automatically recognizing the pills as Madeleine's antidepressants, he cursed and hurriedly began scooping the pills back into the bottle, counting to make sure he had gotten them all.

He counted fourteen pills, then decided to check the original quantity against the date. "Damn it," he cursed when he realized. "Madeleine!"

He read the label once more, to check before confronting his wife. *Refill after: 8/13 Qty: 30*

Fourteen pills left. An entire damned month.

"What's the matter? Aren't your cufflinks in the—"

Madeleine had stopped in the doorway, her eyes locked on the bottle clenched in his hand.

"I don't even know what to say to you right now," Lee seethed. "I can't think of a single reason why you wouldn't be taking these."

She took a shuddering breath. "You don't know what it's like being on antidepressants, and especially not for me."

"Then tell me, Maddie, because I can't figure out why you're doing this to yourself, and to me, all over again."

"What does any of this have to do with you? Lee, you truly possess a remarkable ability to make everything about you."

Struck silent, Lee was overcome with a feeling of wretchedness. Anger swelled in his veins, quickening his pulse, but at the same time, he was weighed down with utter despondency. Frozen in place, he could not think of anything to say or do.

His lips formed a hard line, but the strike of pain in his heart must have radiated through his eyes as he kept them glued to her. "I worry about you taking your pills because I don't want to lose you. Is having a desire to keep my wife alive and safe that self-centered?"

Lee grabbed the box of cufflinks off the counter. Slowly and deliberately, he finished dressing while Madeleine sank down on a very uncomfortable armchair in the bedroom, her mind rushing with thoughts of what injustices she and her husband had inflicted on one another. She flicked her eyes at Lee, who was slipping on his tuxedo jacket.

"Let's go," he said coldly, stepping out of the bedroom door. "We're already late."

CHAPTER FIFTEEN

The car ride reminded Madeleine of the ride home from the hospital, the tense silence suffocating any attempt to make peace with her husband. She hated the anti-depressants. They weren't supposed to make her feel numb, but it was just her luck she was one of those rare cases.

They glanced at each other, searching for what to say, how to feel, but there was a black void where understanding should have been. The journey was much too short for Madeleine, who had been pondering all day how she would carry on throughout the ball, playing out the possible conversations in her mind, rehearsing different scenarios in her mind over and over. She knew how to describe the new book when the inevitable question arose, what to say and not to say when people asked about Atwood Technologies business.

She was still drawing a blank for "How are you?" which would be code for "Have you thought any more about slitting your wrists lately?" Respond with "Fantastic!" and they'd all be smirking and wondering what drugs she was hyped up on. Respond with "Fine. How are you?" and they'd think she was barely holding on, ready to heave herself off the top of a tall roof.

Butterflies swarmed in her stomach as the familiar stretch of road beckoned them ahead.

The Swan House was as beautiful as ever, glowing warm in the autumn night.

"Ready?" Lee said when they pulled up to the front and waited for the valet.

"As ready as I'll ever be," she breathed. A liveried valet opened the door, and Lee passed off the keys. Lee offered the crook of his elbow and Madeleine laced her arm though, though grudgingly, knowing the night would be filled with nothing but put-on affection and forced smiles. They were the newest faces of the Atwood clan, old Atlanta society, a staple at these events. Everything was just dandy—happy marriage, fulfilling lives, and an ever-flowing fountain of money. What could be wrong with people like them?

Prepare the face to meet the faces you will meet, Madeleine quoted as they stepped through the doors into the foyer, and she tightened her grip around Lee's forearm. They may have been angry with each other, but he was her greatest hope for survival. His eyes cut toward her in a near-glare, but he must have noticed her nervous expression. Lee wrapped his hand tight around hers.

The black and white patterned marble floors glistened in the light, and the foyer alone looked like a palace. Madeleine's eyes widened in a certain delight every time she walked into the Swan House, although it served to intimidate as much as inspire wonder.

"Mr. and Mrs. Atwood," a man with a very complicated-looking camera greeted them. "Mind if we get a picture for *Social Season*?"

They posed for the obligatory photo while Madeleine wondered if their painted smiles would be obvious in print. As soon as the flashbulbs stopped, they sauntered toward the bar.

"You two couldn't show up somewhere on time if your lives depended on it," Adrian called out with his typical flippant air from a corner close to the bar.

"Haven't you ever heard of being fashionably late?" Lee countered. "Then again, you and fashionable don't belong in the same sentence."

The group gave a light laugh at the brothers' exchange. While Lee and Adrian were bantering, Madeleine looked from face to face of each of the people in the group. She remembered seeing all them before but was having a hard time matching them with a name, occupation, reputation, anything.

This caused her stomach to knot.

Everyone always knew her and Lee, sometimes better than they should, and it bothered her. Had they always been such good gossip fodder? Did any of them know or suspect Lee had been having an affair? Was it with one of these women?

That thought alone was terrifying.

"Wonder who he prefers in bed?" Evelyn mused.

Madeleine's heart raced, keeping time with the

paranoid thoughts wracking her mind. "I do everything he wants, right? I've tried everything he ever wanted to do to me."

"But was she better than you?"

"More than likely," Madeleine admitted. "Are you helping me out or making me feel even worse tonight? I could use a hand here, and since you're my creation anyway…"

"That's what you think, and you're mistaken," Evelyn said. "We're too different for me to be your so-called creation. You can't make this up."

"I've got thousands of readers who would beg to differ."

"Then handle it on your own, miss socialite," Evelyn said with a scoff. "You don't need my help if you created me, right?"

Evelyn slinked off through the party and circulated with the guests as if they were all good friends she had known a million years.

Useless characters, Madeleine thought, annoyed.

"Madeleine, you're gorgeous as always," Emily said, snapping her back to reality.

Emily was the one who was always gorgeous. Adrian couldn't keep his eyes or his hands off her, and that was saying something for mister self-control. She regretted Lee didn't share the same disposition.

"Look at you. You're the one who's always the trendsetter around here. Always a year ahead of us," Madeleine said in genuine compliment. Emily *always* outshone all of them.

The woman next to Emily agreed. "I know, right? I always feel out of style around her. It must

109

be the eye for art." It was a reference to Emily's job as a curator at the High Museum, where she was always receiving some accolade for whatever it was curators did; Madeleine wasn't sure.

Lee had acquired two drinks from the bar, a flute of champagne and a highball of whisky. He knew she didn't like to drink very much, but holding a glass made her feel less awkward. For this small but meaningful gesture, her eyes met his in silent gratitude. She caught his saddened gaze as she took the glass, and it was her turn to feel confused as she took the glass of champagne.

When do we get it all figured out? When does it become like it was before?

Madeleine lamented the possibility it never would. Hadn't it all been too good to be true anyway? It couldn't have lasted a lifetime.

She stayed afloat in small talk among the ever-changing flow of people, using Lee as a crutch. Madeleine couldn't help but wonder if she and her husband looked as fake as they felt.

Lee, predictably enough, kept going back to the bar for drinks. After the third or fourth time, he settled with a bottle and chatted with some hotshot executive from Boeing she'd met before and didn't like. This left her to fend for herself, and the panic set in.

"Maddie Atwood, I haven't seen you in forever," came a chipper voice like nails on a chalkboard. Maisy Stewart was coming in for a greeting hug as if they were old friends. Nothing could be further from the truth. Maisy had not liked Madeleine from the day she'd met her, and all because of Lee. She'd been one of his many conquests before he'd met Madeleine, and she hadn't made the cut when it came down to actual relationships. Maisy had publicly stated on more than one occasion, always behind Madeleine's back, how she never understood what made Lee pick her over everybody else. Honestly, Madeleine couldn't quite figure it out either.

"Hello, Maisy," Madeleine replied as enthusiastically as she could in her most polite happy-voice. "You look stunning as always."

"I love this dress," Maisy gushed, eyeing the tight little number making Madeleine even more self-conscious.

"I was just admiring yours," Madeleine lied.

Maisy's face fell, and she lowered her head toward Maddie. "I've been meaning to call you. How have you been?"

Taken off-guard, Madeleine had to think fast, to straighten her thoughts from the tangle they had become, but her mind was already filling with blood-red social panic. She figured Maisy would have had an extra pep in her step if her suicide attempt had been successful.

"It's all right. If you don't want to say anything, I understand."

"I-I'm better. Thank you," Madeleine stammered, plastering a reassuring smile to her face. Her heart was beating too quickly, and heat rose through her chest to her cheeks.

"You're so brave," Maisy continued. "Coming out here so soon after…everyone thinks you're so strong. Especially considering the situation."

111

"Yes, well, I'm getting to where I need to be," Madeleine said, searching desperately for an exit. Her stomach seized up.

"Men can be so thoughtless. They don't know how their actions affect us."

Madeleine's heart raced even more, feeling like the beats of a hummingbird's wings in her chest. "Maisy, I'm not sure we're talking about the same—"

"Madeleine, there you are," Emily chimed. "I've been looking everywhere for you. I've got a favor to ask. Hi there, Maisy," she added as a dull afterthought. Maisy gave a resentful smirk.

The panic rising in her chest quelled as Emily approached and took her by the arm. "Our head curator found out you're Adrian's sister-in-law and is dying to meet you. He's a big fan of your work, and it would be an amazing opportunity for me to kiss up," she said. "Do you think you can spare a minute to come say hello? It would make his night."

Madeleine nodded with trepidation, feeling very much indebted to Emily. "Sure," she agreed, trying to recover her happy facade. Although she had wanted to see where her conversation with Maisy was heading, she couldn't have been more grateful for an out. "Nice seeing you again, Maisy."

"Oh, Maddie, one last thing before you go," she said, digging through her clutch. She retrieved a business card and handed it to Madeleine. "This is Dr. Houghton's number. He does all my nips and tucks. I was thinking when you're up to it, you should talk to him about your wrists."

Madeleine's heart skipped a beat. "My wrists?"

"Yes," Maisy affirmed, condescension thinly veiled. "Do you really want to wear a failed suicide attempt like a badge of honor?"

"Maisy, that's enough," Emily warned.

"I'm only trying to be helpful, Emily. You can put your claws back up."

"Keep talking and you're gonna need more than a little nip-tuck to fix that face," Emily said through clenched jaws.

Madeleine felt every eye in the room was on them. The last thing she wanted to do was cry, but it was coming like a dammed-up river released. With no options left, she stood tall and lifted her chin, tears already blurring her eyes. She could feel their stares, amusement for the evening, as her heels clicked in time across the marble tile as quickly as she could without breaking out into a full-on dash through Swan House.

CHAPTER SIXTEEN

As she escaped out onto the back terrace, past the anonymous party-goers, down the steps and tiered fountains out to the gardens, that burning, kick-in-the-gut sensation of shame burst inside her. Everyone knew. There went Madeleine McCollum Atwood, the outsider, married to Lee Atwood, one of their own. Writer. Shy. How typical. Depressed, obviously. Weren't all writers? Botched suicide attempt survivor.

They would all know too their marriage was equally as botched, held together with some half-assed placed bandage over a gaping wound. They could all see how fake it was, and they'd wonder why Lee, the golden boy, had ever married her. They'd understand why he had slept with someone else.

Madeleine made it to a great length of the folly, an arc of columns where vines hung over the foundational wall in wispy trails which bordered the property. It was darker here, and no one wandered out this far away from all the excitement. She slumped against the wall, giving little care to snagging her expensive dress. God knew she could only wear it this once anyway without someone questioning how long it would be before Atwood Technologies would downsize. Since the Atwoods couldn't afford another two-grand dress for the latest charity ball, disaster was surely imminent. Lee certainly couldn't let anyone think less of his precious company.

Out there, alone in the darkness, Madeleine sobbed, allowing the dammed river to rage. Everything had culminated into one moment. Lee, the shame of the entire world knowing how much she struggled just to get out of the bed in the mornings, feeling like an utter failure no much how she accomplished. There had to be an end to it somewhere, some solution so she could be happy again, but for the life of her, all Madeleine could think of was how she had wanted to put an end to everything once and for all. The world didn't want her; she didn't want the world or a single thing it offered anymore.

"Maddie?"

Relief flooded her. The rustling she had heard was only Adrian and not some anonymous society ass. She swiped and dabbed at her makeup, but knew it was pointless. Adrian already knew when she was upset, and he always found her at her worst moments.

"I'm over here," she surrendered in a half-squelched sob. There was more rustling, and he

115

emerged from the hedgerows, making his way into the folly.

His face dropped when he saw her. "Maddie, come on, you can't let these people get to you."

"I don't care about fitting in with people like that," she denied through her tears. "The only reason I'd ever care to fit in with them is…never mind. It doesn't even matter anymore."

"You just want to make Lee happy." Madeleine was surprised he understood. He sat next to her, and she noticed the bottle of amaretto in his hand. "I thought you could use a drink so I grabbed your favorite. Wasn't thoughtful enough to steal glasses, though. Mind drinking it straight out of the bottle?"

"No," she said with a shuddering cry. Then she remembered. "It's almost like senior prom all over again."

"Prom sucked. You broke my heart." Adrian laughed, settling down next to her against the wall. He twisted the top from the bottle and took a sip before passing it to her. She blanched from the taste. Adrian snickered, but Madeleine threw the bottle back and took another burning swig.

"You were drunk when you asked me out," she sniffed.

"Half-drunk. Super close to being in my right mind," he corrected. "You, however—"

"It was the first time I had ever even touched alcohol," Madeleine defended with a hint of a grin. "And I didn't break your heart."

"You certainly did. I had a crush on you, but you never noticed."

"Okay, 'half-drunk' and your girlfriend had

dumped you. I figured it was alcohol and heartbreak talking. 'Worked up the nerve.' You, the most pursued boy in school, and me. Like that would have worked."

"It could have." Adrian took another swig of amaretto. "And you made out with me, but you wouldn't date me. How very unladylike."

"Ugh, do you have any idea how awkward that was when Lee and I dated? I've never had the heart to tell him."

"It was a little awkward." He passed her the bottle. "You and Lee, though…Meeting you was the best thing that ever happened to him. I could get over it when I saw how happy he was. But hell, I still wouldn't tell him about it to this day."

"He wouldn't get that defensive over me." Madeleine laughed, taking another sip.

"Yes he would," Adrian insisted. "If he'd been a few more shots along in there, Lee would've kicked Brent McCanless' ass."

"Why?"

Adrian laughed. "He kept making comments about the way you look in that dress, your backside in particular."

"You must be joking."

"No, ma'am. Mr. McCanless is an admirer. He'll be lucky if Lee hasn't ousted him from his seat on the board by Monday morning."

"Oh God." Madeleine grinned, feeling better than she had in days. "It's always nice to know when a man finds you attractive."

"Let me assure you, he's not the only one. It's one reason Maisy's acting like such a bitch."

"Acting? You mean it's all pretend?"

"Let me rephrase that. It's why she's not on her best possible behavior. She's jealous and letting her true colors show. Here you are, after going through one of the worst events in your life, and you look amazing. Not a single person in there can disagree. You even pretended to be happy until Maisy got to you."

Madeleine shook her head. "You noticed that?"

"That you're unhappy? I'll admit, you're good at hiding it. If I didn't know you any better, I'd be convinced you had the perfect life. But you do this thing with your hands when you're nervous, like they're always twisting at whatever's close by. And every time you say something, you sit there and study the faces of everyone around you to make sure you didn't say the wrong thing. You were scared to death in there."

Madeleine shrugged. "That doesn't mean I'm unhappy. Maybe I hate parties."

"Which you do," Adrian responded. "But then there's the moments in between the conversations and it's just you, standing in the middle of this crowded room, not putting on a performance. You're so lost, and you only want to find your way back home."

Madeleine stared at him, astonished he had noticed so much. It was a wonder there were people in the world like Adrian who could see so much while others, like Lee, couldn't see past their own noses.

He cleared his throat, dragging her from her musings. "You should come dance with me. We haven't danced in forever."

Madeleine blushed. "Then you know all too well I'm no good."

"You love it anyway. Besides, we look so damn good no one will ever notice. Maybe Lee will catch Brent checking you out and beat the hell out of him. It might be the one chance we have of livening up this party."

They stood and made their way back to the house. Madeleine hesitated for a moment before stepping inside, but Adrian encouraged her onward.

"There's no one in here any better than you. They may think they are, but they're not. You're kinder, smarter, more accomplished. Not to mention you're prettier and, what pisses them off the most, wealthier."

"You'll make a good husband...whenever you get married."

"I hope so," Adrian said, visibly uncomfortable.

"You will be. No doubt about it."

He shrugged.

"I'm not the only one with a confidence problem."

Adrian offered the crook of his arm. "At least neither of us is alone."

She laced her arm through his, and every head turned as they walked through the door together.

"Chin up. They're no better than you. They're no better than anyone. Oh, and don't forget to smile."

"Now we'll pretend we're gossiping and making an amusing remark about the subject of our conversation. Look over there at Maisy's most current married lover, Dane Ashby. I'm going to whisper, aaannnddd now we share a conspiratorial laugh."

Madeleine laughed in earnest as he continued his narration. "Nice job, we've got everyone's eyes. Now we'll make our way to the dance floor, share one dance, and then we'll get Lee back to the hotel before he embarrasses the hell out of all of us."

Madeleine spotted her husband at the bar, talking in animated gestures very uncharacteristic of Lee. She could tell by the way his bow tie hung slack and the way he was struggling to hold his posture he had drank more than he could handle.

"Are you sure we shouldn't get him now? He's obviously wasted."

"Oh, no. If we go now, we won't look nonchalant enough about it, and then people will talk about how they think Lee Atwood has a drinking problem."

"He does," Madeleine added drily.

"You're not happy enough, Mrs. Atwood. Enjoy a dance for once and we'll take care of him later. You've got to show all of Atlanta society how strong you are."

The jazz band was only a few measures into "Moonlight Serenade" when they stepped out onto the parquet dance floor. Adrian wrapped his arm around her, clasped her hand, and they joined the other couples on the floor.

She noticed eyes were on them at every corner, making her thankful Adrian was a good dancer. She and Lee had avoided dancing like the plague. Neither of them was good at it. Following Adrian's steps were easy enough, and he could compensate for her when she missed a step. About halfway through the song, she got into a good rhythm and the steps came with minimal concentration.

"See? You're not so bad," he said.

"No, I'm pretty bad. I've just got a good lead to follow. Thank you, by the way."

"For?"

"Everything. Coming to get me. Sharing the first conversation I've had in weeks that didn't involve the status of my mental health. For picking a girlfriend who doesn't mind standing up for me."

"Sometimes you need a good cry," Adrian said dismissively. "Doesn't mean you'll throw yourself off the roof."

"It's nice to know someone gets it. I'm not some ticking time-bomb, ready to commit suicide at the slightest infraction. It took a lot more than a night like this one to...motivate me, I suppose you could say."

"I'm glad you're getting better. Going to therapy, giving medication a shot."

"I-I quit taking my antidepressants," she stammered. "I didn't like the way they made me feel. It wasn't me anymore."

Adrian swallowed, mulling over what she had admitted.

"I don't want to be happy if it's not real," Madeleine went on. "It's not right when things happen that should make me sad or angry and I can't feel them."

"Did your doctor say you could quit taking them?"

Madeleine hesitated. She didn't understand why

she was compelled to tell him this in the first place when she had wanted to keep it all from Lee.

"You can't just quit taking them, Maddie. It might not have been the right medication for you, or the dosage might have been too much. I understand why you quit taking them. I get it. I wouldn't want to be happy just because I was on medication either. Just tell Lee you will talk to your doctor at the next visit. He may be able to help."

"What if he's not?"

"Hell, Maddie, I don't know. You can always try heroin like everyone else. You're about the only one here trying to medicate correctly."

"You're hilarious."

"Talk to him about it. Promise me."

"I'll tell you what, Adrian, if it'll make you happy."

"You being happy would make me happy," Adrian said.

Madeleine felt a tugging sensation in her chest and wasn't sure how to respond to him. Again, he had saved her. She was embarrassed, realizing what a burden she must be to him, to Lee. But the difference between Lee and Adrian was Lee preferred to pretend everything was fine, and Adrian dutifully strapped on his armor and rode into battle every time.

"You're making a habit of coming to my rescue."

"I don't mean to. It's just that…you were my best friend in high school, believe it or not. I was more myself around you than anyone else. You mean so much to my family and to me. You always have. I don't want anything to happen to you."

Madeleine flushed. She could have hugged him right there in the middle of the dance floor, but she didn't want to call any more attention to herself.

"What's wrong?" Adrian asked, concerned.

"What?"

"You're tearing up."

"Oh, I'm sorry," Madeleine apologized. "I didn't even realize. It's just…it's been a long time since anyone's said anything like that to me. Lee did, but…"

"I should have already told you. No one ever does, though. We don't tell people how much we think of them until it's too late. All those sentiments, the things you want to say, get piled up across the years to make a pretty eulogy. But what good are words when they're not delivered in the right way or time?"

"Useless." She filed away his words for use in her writing later.

The song ended with applause for the band, and Madeleine and Adrian walked off the dance floor to where Emily was standing with Lee at the bar.

Lee grinned drunkenly at Madeleine.

"You look soooo pretty out there dancing," he slurred. "You should do it more often. I think it makes you happy."

"She might, if she had a partner with any rhythm," Adrian joked. "How much have you had?"

"Lost count. Johnny here gave up and left the bottle." Lee pointed toward the bartender and poured another shot.

Adrian grabbed the shot glass and knocked it

back before Lee even realized Emily had taken the bottle and returned it to the bartender with a stern expression on her face.

"Let's get out of here. This party's boring," Lee declared at an embarrassing volume. He slipped his arm around Madeleine's waist and with surprising litheness stood and led the group out the doors of Swan House, giving hearty goodbyes to anyone he even remotely knew on the way out.

"How is he even walking in a straight line?" Emily asked Adrian in a disapproving whisper.

"Lots of practice, and I am damned good at it," Lee fired back.

Madeleine tried not to laugh since she could see Emily was embarrassed, especially since she'd come to her rescue against Maisy. Adrian sniggered but was silenced by a menacing glare from Emily.

"Sure you're good to drive, Mads?" Adrian asked when Madeleine closed the door behind Lee and walked around to the driver's side.

"I am. Thank you…for everything." She got into the car. "You're always having to save me these days."

"I don't save you. You've been saving yourself. I only help. You could have left, but you went back in and faced them all. I'm proud of you."

Before she even knew what was happening, he wrapped his arms around her in a surprise hug. Madeleine was in a haze. She felt awkward, embarrassed, but he was so warm in the biting October air. And he didn't smell like alcohol; his words were his own. For a moment, she simply appreciated being shown a bit of affection not sparked by an insatiable sex drive or Jack Daniels, but actual emotion. She flushed when she caught sight of Emily staring at them. She pulled away from him, her heart pounding.

"Emily is waiting on you, I'm sure. Tell her I'm sorry about Lee," Madeleine said.

"She'll be fine. Call me if you need anything like getting this asshole out of the car."

Madeleine laughed, half out of relief. The dreadful Swan Ball was over.

CHAPTER SEVENTEEN

The end of October had heralded Richard's sixtieth birthday, and the announcement he would, again, step down and retire as CEO of Atwood Technologies. It also meant Lee would finally become the CEO he'd wanted to be since he was a young child, and Adrian would begrudgingly step up to become vice president. Naturally, the Atwoods threw a party.

Atwood culture had always fascinated Madeleine. Parties for every little accomplishment in life were so very foreign to her, yet she knew from movies and books this was what normal people did, no matter if they were rich or poor. She could not help but wonder if she'd come from a more similar, or more normal, background, maybe she could understand the people who had become her family.

She also didn't understand why Maggie Beth would want a single iota to do with this party in the first place, but from the moment Lee had mentioned throwing his father a joint birthday-and-retirement celebration, she had immediately taken over the planning. When Adrian pressed her for a reason, her argument was any party thrown by Lee would feature more alcohol than a prohibition party and a few bags of convenience store potato chips. Adrian let it go, but neither he nor Madeleine quite believed there was nothing more to Maggie Beth's new interest in her ex-husband.

"I cannot believe your parents are getting along this well," Madeleine told Adrian as they sat together at the bar.

Adrian spied his parents across the crowd. "Ashton Kutcher is going to pop out any minute and tell us we've been punked. After fourteen years of not-so-subtle insults and never speaking, here they are acting like they never got a divorce at all."

"Maybe some people are better off divorced," Madeleine said, spotting Lee within the sea of people circulating on Richard's lawn. As her husband schmoozed with the corporate elite of Atlanta, Madeleine wondered if they too would be better off apart. Better people, nicer to each other, less of each other's drama. Things had been better ever since their bout of reconciliation after the Swan Ball, but so much of their relationship seemed forced, disingenuous. Madeleine had decided to stay the course; it would get better with time.

When she glanced back over to Adrian, he looked concerned. He started to say something, but Emily popped up to the bar, all utter feminine cuteness. Madeleine downed her drink, questioning why she was so annoyed by this. Adrian being smitten over Emily had been the status quo for years, and she'd always been happy for him.

Had she taken her pills? She had, after breakfast, right? Right before working on that new chapter. She had followed Adrian's advice and spoken to Dr. Moore about the dosage of her medication. It took a leap of faith, but she was taking them every day without fail. Thus far, she felt better, but Madeleine knew all too well it would be weeks before her antidepressants would take full effect again.

"Mads, where's Lee?" Adrian asked, breaking her trance. She had not even noticed Maggie Beth had wandered up the bar to join them.

Madeleine searched for Lee where she had spotted him earlier, but he had disappeared. "He was with Dennis earlier, but now I can't see where he is. You can't keep up with Lee at a party."

"I wanted him to say something to the guests tonight before we bring out the cake, especially since this was all this doing," Maggie Beth said.

Adrian snorted and shook around the leftover ice and liquor in his glass before taking one last drink. "Yeah, okay. It was all Lee."

"You helped too, I know," Maggie Beth said in a false, apologetic coo.

"Not really. Throwing him a party was my idea, and Lee made it a joint retirement party. Other than that, we did nothing. You took over and did everything else. Lee and I would have come up with something way classier and cost-effective."

Maggie Beth raised a skeptical brow. "Like what?"

"Like a trip to the Clermont Lounge."

Madeleine nearly spit out her drink laughing, but his mother groaned and Emily rolled her eyes.

"Someone appreciates my jokes!"

"Classiest place in town," Madeleine quipped.

"And some of the dancers are Dad's age. Maybe he could find a date."

Madeleine laughed again but noticed something had struck a chord with Maggie Beth, whose cheeks flushed. "I don't know how I raised such an awful child. Find your brother."

She walked off from the bar to rejoin Richard in the crowd, and Madeleine peered over at Adrian, who narrowed his brow in confusion. "You'd think she'd be used to my stupid humor by now."

Madeleine smirked. "I don't think that's the issue."

"She's fine." Emily waved it off. She pulled Adrian close by the lapels on his sports jacket. "Go find Lee and let's see if we can't duck out of here early."

"Yes, ma'am." Adrian struck off through the crowd to find Lee.

Madeleine yet again had to check the feeling of annoyance at the happy couple and ordered another drink. Maybe if she were drunk, Lee would take full advantage of the situation. There was no maybe about it. He undoubtedly would.

As much as she despised the thought of giving in to her husband, Madeleine needed to be touched, held, kissed…to feel he desired her in some way, no matter how small. He'd been distant ever since the Swan Ball and was drinking even more than usual, but Madeleine supposed she could understand.

With Adrian and Maggie Beth's departure, however, Madeleine was all alone at the bar with Emily. While Emily had been a bit of a fixture in their family for three years now, and Madeleine admired her kindness, they never had quite developed a close relationship. Yet there was one particular thing that had been on Madeleine's mind she wanted to tell Emily, and she supposed now was as good a time as any to tell her.

"I never thanked you, Emily, for the other night at the Swan Ball," Madeleine said.

"You don't have to thank me. It was the right thing to do."

"Not many people would actually do it. You don't know what it means to me."

Emily took a gulp of her wine. "I've never told you this, but you aren't the person I thought you would be. I was nervous as hell to meet you when Adrian wanted to introduce me to his family."

"Oh Lord, why?" Madeleine laughed. "You're never nervous."

"It's true. Whether it was because you snagged Lee or because you're an Atlanta celebrity, I know dozens of people who want to be you."

"I can't for the life of me imagine anybody wanting to be me. Judging from Maisy, I was thinking my life was nothing but a second round of high school. Nothing but boy drama, cliques, bullies, and embarrassment."

Emily studied Madeleine for a while, which made her increasingly uncomfortable. "When I first moved to Atlanta, I used to pick up those *Social*

130

Season magazines, and in every single issue, there you were. I always used to see you in your ball gowns and at all your book signings, and then you would be in a picture with Lee, and he looked at you like you hung the moon. I wanted all that. Everyone does."

Madeleine didn't know quite what to say. She wasn't sure if she was more flattered or embarrassed.

"You know what would piss off every single one of those empty-headed bitches, Maddie?"

"Wish I did. I'd do it in a second out of spite."

"Be happy." Emily laughed, as if it were as obvious as the nose on her face. "Keep kicking ass in the literary world. Stay with Lee and make it work. Have another baby, or hell, get a dog. Do whatever will make you happy, and I promise you, they'll all die of jealousy."

Madeleine smiled, for Emily's sake. It was a nice thought. And it would be so much easier than being miserable. She supposed to Emily, to anyone on the outside, the solution was so easy, to simply reach out and claim her happiness.

However, they didn't see how that felt on the inside, how the glossy pages of a magazine could never tell the entire story. Just because it looked good didn't mean it was good. The prettiest things in nature were often poisonous, and it was no different in human life.

Madeleine was caught between living in a dream world of manufactured happiness and being true to herself. Could this marriage be worth saving? Was this life Lee providing the cure for a past anyone would be grateful to leave behind? What if this new book didn't do well? She didn't know if she could handle an impending divorce and the downward spiral of her career.

"Now that you know the truth, Emily," she asked, "would you still want to be me?"

Emily shook her head. "Not for every red cent the Atwoods have. No offense. You've been through hell. I know it's hard. Adrian worries about you."

"He does?" Madeleine asked, genuinely surprised.

"Oh God, yes. I think he feels responsible for Lee. Like he ought to be, I don't know, his brother's keeper, I guess?"

Madeleine didn't know why it hadn't occurred to her sooner, but it made so much sense. Adrian's unwavering loyalty to his family, his friends…it was why he was always there, coming to the rescue. "You got yourself a good one there. He'll make a good husband."

Emily raised her brows. "If he ever proposes."

"He's afraid," Madeleine explained. "Of what, I'm not sure. I know he's told Lee more than once he's worried."

"I wish he'd stop. Between you and me, I love that man, but I don't want to wait forever."

"Madeleine? Emily? Did anyone find Lee yet?" Maggie Beth huffed, pushing her way back to the bar.

"We'll find him, Maggie Beth," Madeleine assured her, hoping if she got Emily alone again, she could convince her to be more patient with

Adrian. He'd done so much for her, the least she could do was try and return the favor.

CHAPTER EIGHTEEN

Lee had known they would be searching for him soon. He sat at his father's desk, cradling a bottle of Jack and staring up at the ceiling when Adrian walked in.

"How much have you had?"

Lee poured his fifth glass of whiskey for the night. "This is my second, thank you very much."

"Bullshit." Adrian saw through his almost-slurred words even easier than Lee thought. "You said you would quit when Maddie got better. She's better. Now what's the excuse?"

Lee sneered. "Adrian, I work a sixty-hour week, every week of the year. Between trying to be a decent husband and keeping our company running, when do you think I've got time to focus on myself?"

"You've got to. This is going to end up killing you."

"Great." Lee downed his "second" whiskey. "I

can rest when I'm dead."

Adrian wrinkled his face in disgust, and Lee thought, perhaps, disappointment. "Jesus Christ, Lee. If you don't care enough about yourself, don't you care about everyone else in your life?"

Lee peered suspiciously at Adrian. "You and Maddie have the same, exact problem."

"Which is?"

"You care too much about what everyone else thinks about you," Lee sneered. "Like Maddie at the Swan House. As if Maisy Stewart—*Maisy fucking Stewart*—has anything on her. Madeleine's worth a thousand women like Maisy."

"And you could have been the one to tell her that if you weren't three sheets to the wind, embarrassing yourself at the bar," Adrian retorted.

"And you, you're the worst. You're about to marry a woman you have no business marrying just because she expects a proposal." Lee laughed. "You're going to ruin your life because you can't stand disappointing people."

"You're drunk."

"Isn't there an expression about drunks telling the truth? Are you uncomfortable with the truth?"

"It's not the truth," Adrian groused.

"You don't sound convinced." Lee smirked. "I'll tell you what. You look me in the eyes and tell me you're absolutely in love with Emily and I'll leave you alone about it. I'll never bring it up again. But I've known you since birth and I know about everything there is to know about you, so don't think you can lie to me."

Adrian glared at his brother, his jaw clenched.

Lee could see his brother's balled fist in the pocket of his jacket, possibly keeping himself from punching him. Lee stared on at him, his steely, expectant expression attempting to burn a hole through his brother's face. "You're not saying anything."

"I don't have to justify myself or explain anything to you."

"You don't love her. Just admit it."

Adrian took a deep breath, trying his best to calm down. He swiped the bottle of Jack and his brother's glass and poured a drink. He took a long swig and smacked the glass down on the desk. "Well…don't we all deserve a shot at a marriage as miserable as yours?"

Sarcasm was always Adrian's best defense.

Just then they both heard footfalls and Madeleine's voice calling, "Emily, wait—"

Adrian stood and ran out to the hall. Lee followed behind, moving slower to keep his balance.

"How much did she hear?"

Madeleine looked at Adrian with pity. "More than enough."

Dejected, Adrian dashed off down the hall after her. "Emily!"

Even as drunk as he was, Lee's stomach was already sinking in guilt. He sat there, frozen, in the doorway of his father's office, waiting on the fallout as his brother ran down the hallway, leaving him alone with Madeleine.

"Lee, what the hell have you done now?" she demanded, pushing past him and closing the door behind her.

Lee automatically went on the defensive, even if he knew he was partially at fault. "Me? What did I do? How is this my fault?"

"You've been against him marrying her since the second he said he would propose. He loves her."

Lee laughed. "No, Madeleine, he doesn't. I think I know him better than you."

"He does!" Madeleine insisted. "And just because our marriage has gone straight to hell doesn't mean you have to spoil Adrian's chances too!"

Lee didn't know if it was as apparent, but it felt like she'd knocked the wind out of him. He was miserable without her. Even in this state where things were so treacherously hanging in limbo, he was happier than he'd ever been with Brecklyne. But he didn't want to be hurt. He couldn't let her think he was wounded, much less that the wound she'd inflicted was gaping.

Lee flipped through his father's ancient Rolodex. "If you're so miserable, here's my father's divorce lawyer," he spat, ripping out the yellowed business card and holding it out toward her.

"Lee, that's not what I meant. I shouldn't have said it," Madeleine protested.

"I hear he's excellent. He'll get you every dime of alimony you deserve for being so damned miserable," Lee slurred, taking a drink straight from the bottle as he walked out of the library.

The sound of her crying ripped the gaping wound even wider, but he'd won.

A victory under his belt, he celebrated by

numbing himself to every bit of pain it caused.

CHAPTER NINETEEN

Adrian hadn't been able to catch up with Emily. She'd made it out of his father's winding house, and he'd lost her in the crowd before he could ever catch up. He'd called her non-stop, trying to get her to answer, and even jumped in his car and made his way to her house before he decided she didn't want to speak to him and giving her space for a while was the best.

He sent her a text apologizing, telling her he loved her, he was just being vindictive in the moment and trying his best to hurt Lee, all while wondering what would possess him not to insist to his brother he loved Emily. Lee would believe him if he said it. It was the truth.

Yet Adrian couldn't get the question out of his head. *Isn't it true?*

When he came to a red light, he decided it was smarter to go home and call it a night. He didn't want to be within a hundred-mile radius of Lee right now. And he wanted a cigarette. A quick stop into a rather shady-looking convenience store solved his problem. He got a few odd stares stepping out of his McLaren, but he didn't even bother to lock it as he went in and half-pleaded for a box of Camel menthols.

"You know that stuff has glass in it, right?" the clerk grumbled as she slapped a pack on the scratched surface of the counter.

"Fiberglass, actually, but that's a myth. There's no fiberglass in cigarettes," Adrian corrected her.

"No shit?" she asked, her interest piqued.

"No shit."

"Hmmmm…$5.35."

"Jesus. These things just keep getting pricier."

She eyed him up and down skeptically. "You got the money."

He shrugged and swiped his debit card.

"Psssh. You're blessed, boy. You don't even know."

Adrian pressed his lips together and had to admit he was humbled. He thanked her as he took his cigarettes, but he knew he owed her much more. Her words brought him a sort of clarity. Although it was the last thing he wanted to do, he went back to his father's party. He could tell his parents goodbye and check on Madeleine before he left. God knew Madeleine had more deal with than she deserved.

When he got to the dying party and found Madeleine and his father, he wished he'd just stayed away. Or, better yet, went to Emily's and begged forgiveness.

"Did you talk to Emily?" Madeleine asked as

soon as he found her sitting alone in a folding chair dragged away from the main gathering.

It was clear she'd been crying. Her eyeliner was smudged and her eyes were weary. But he wasn't going to mention it unless she did.

"No, I didn't, but she needs time to be alone anyway. I can't blame her for not wanting to talk to me."

"Adrian, I'm so sorry. Do you want me to talk to her?"

He did not want to put even more on Madeleine than she was already handling. And it was his mess; he wouldn't ask anyone else to clean it up. "We'll work it out. I'm not worried about that. It's only a matter of time and me jumping through a few hoops to fix things."

It was clear Madeleine did not understand, but she carried on. "Either way, you shouldn't have to. Look, I've got a favor to ask, but I think we'll need help."

"What's wrong?"

"It's Lee. Follow me," she requested wearily. He followed, but only out of respect for her, not his brother. He couldn't care less what Lee needed.

When they got to the living room, they met his father smoldering in anger with his arms crossed. "What the hell is this?" Richard asked them, motioning toward the sofa.

Lee was passed out on the couch, the now-empty bottle of Gentleman Jack clutched in his hand.

"I was going to put him in the car, but he won't wake up and I can't carry him myself," Madeleine explained. "I'm sorry. I know this is embarrassing."

"How often does this happen?" Richard questioned.

Adrian saw Maddie's nervous glance, but Richard cursed under his breath in disgust. Adrian started to speak, but Richard cut him off. "Adrian, don't even bother standing up for him."

"He said he was getting help. He had a plan in place."

"He *said*. He *had*. He's passed the hell out on my couch. Good intentions without following through mean nothing."

Adrian shoved his hands in his pockets, and Madeleine muffled a sniffle, possibly in an attempt to stop from tearing up. He knew his father could see straight through the facade. Richard walked over to the sofa where his oldest son lay with his empty bottle of whiskey in a slack hold around the bottleneck.

"Madeleine, you two will stay here for tonight. I'll let my housekeeper know. She'll make sure you have everything you need."

"Richard, no, we couldn't bother anyone with—"

"You're staying. Even if we got him in the car, what would you do with him when you got home, Madeleine? It's not your responsibility to put up with this behavior. Adrian, help me get him down the hall before your mother sees him."

They had barely heaved him up and gotten him into the hallway when Maggie Beth rounded the corner. Madeleine assumed the party was over and the last guests had gone home for the night.

"Oh my God! Is he drunk?!" Maggie Beth exclaimed, rushing toward them.

Richard and Adrian rolled their eyes and kept lugging Lee down the hall.

"Calm down, Maggie Beth," Richard huffed, obviously struggling with the dead weight his son had become.

When they neared the guest bedroom, Madeleine was wringing her hands in anxiety. Adrian could practically see her thoughts in her eyes. She must have been worried about Lee, the family, blaming herself for everything. Adrian could practically hear her in his mind, almost as clearly as if she had said it aloud. Perhaps he knew her too well.

They lugged Lee onto the bed and took a step back. Maggie Beth sat down next to him and tried to get him to come to.

"Lee, baby, wake up," she said, patting his cheek. Lee gave an annoyed grunt and turned over. His mother's eyes filled with tears. "What if he vomits in the middle of the night? What if he suffocates on it? Do you think it could be alcohol poisoning?"

"Mom," Adrian said, putting his arm around her, trying to comfort her. "He's fine."

"He is not fine, Adrian!" Maggie Beth erupted. "This is not okay!"

Adrian was clearly at a loss.

Richard threw his hands up. "Don't look at me. Your mother's right. This is ridiculous. I knew he was a drinker. I knew he drank more than he should. But this? I had no idea. And apparently it's a pretty normal occurrence."

"It wasn't, though," Madeleine explained shakily, on the verge of tears. "Not until…until…"

"Until they lost Thomas," Adrian said. "That's when it started."

The room filled with overwhelming quiet until Maggie Beth let out a sob, breaking the silence. Richard went to put his hands on her shoulders, to provide the mother of his children with some semblance of comfort. Madeleine spun and walked out of the room, and Adrian knew he had to follow her.

In the hallway, she instantly broke down. "I can't do this!" she sobbed. "I can't take care of him. I can't make this marriage work."

Adrian stood dumbfounded for the longest time. He didn't know what to say. Madeleine was right. He didn't want her to be. He wanted, above all, for her to be happy, for his brother to be the man he knew he was on the inside. He didn't have an answer for her. All he knew to do was wrap her up in his arms and let her cry.

"We're gonna fix this. I promise. I don't know how, but we'll get him better and get you both back on track."

Madeleine stayed locked into his arms. "And if it doesn't work?" she wept. "What then?"

"We'll keep trying, Maddie. I promise."

CHAPTER TWENTY

It was impulse that drove him to his mother's house. Or maybe he had decided it was time to make a move toward the future.

He couldn't be sure which, but it felt like the right time. She had forgiven him for his verbal missteps at his father's party, accepting he had said the entirely wrong thing for the entirely wrong reasons. It was not out of character for him, anyway.

"I wasn't expecting you, Adrian," his mother said as he came bounding up her front porch steps. "I'm about to head out to meet someone."

"It won't take long, I promise. You remember how you always told me I could have Gram's ring?"

Maggie Beth cupped both hands over her mouth and gasped in happiness. "Adrian," she squealed, standing on her tiptoes to hug her son. "I could not be any more excited for you. Let's run in and get it."

Adrian followed his mother to her bedroom where she took out a small fireproof safe that stayed hidden beneath a loose floorboard in her closet. For all the Atwoods were worth, their most prized family heirlooms were trusted to a woman who wasn't born an Atwood and distrusted banks.

Maggie Beth unlocked the safe and handed her son a sterling silver box with an engraved initial "A" on the top. Although it needed a bit of polish, Adrian decided it would have to do. His mother handed it to him, clasping his hand and the ring box before relinquishing it.

"Every new Atwood bride since 1920 has worn this ring at some point. It means a lot to this family, and I want you to be certain Emily is the one you want to be wearing this ring. Marriages are no picnic. They require a lot of work and patience."

"And faithfulness," Adrian added, thinking of his brother.

"Especially that," Maggie Beth agreed. "And if it helps, I think Emily is perfect for you. I know you're worried about being a good husband and—"

"How? I haven't said anything about it."

"Moms know." Maggie Beth let go of the box, leaving it in her son's hand. "And moms also know when their sons are being too hard on themselves. You'll be an amazing husband, Adrian."

Relieved, he hugged his mother. "Thanks, I needed to hear that."

Maggie Beth pulled back and dabbed at her eyes. "Now, when are you going to ask her?"

"I was thinking I'd do it tonight."

Maggie Beth frowned. "Tonight? Just like that? You're not planning anything special?"

Adrian bit his lower lip. In his frenzy of impulse,

he had not considered what a huge moment a proposal was going to be for both of them. He opened the box to see the ring one last time before he—hopefully—put it on Emily's finger. "Think she'll like it?" he asked nervously.

"Baby, it's a two carat, antique ring with a good story. Any woman would flip her lid."

Adrian told his mother goodbye and drove straight to Atlanta, the pit in his stomach growing deeper and deeper the closer he got. By the time he pulled into the parking lot of the High Museum, his heart was about to pound out of his chest.

"Hey, Rose. Emily's giving tours today, right?" he asked nervously when he got to the admissions desk in the lobby.

"Hello, Mr. Atwood. Emily's last tour left about fifteen minutes ago. You might be able to catch up with them in photography. I'm sure you know the way."

"Photography," Adrian repeated, nearly out of breath. It was serendipitously perfect. Photography was where they had first met.

He took off toward the photography wing, and once he had spotted Emily's tour, he ducked into the back of the group.

"Now, this work is my personal favorite in our photography exhibit, *Eleanor, Chicago* by Henry Callahan. Eleanor appears in countless numbers of her husband's photographs. It is difficult for one to imagine what Callahan's career would have been like without her."

Adrian's palms were sweating as Emily further explained her favorite photograph. He grasped at the ring box in his pocket. Never would he have imagined just three years ago he had been standing in a tour group not any different from the one he was in now, finishing off an assignment for a fluff class for his master's degree. The photograph she was talking about was the very one that had sparked their first conversation.

It was now or never. He cleared his throat.

"Moving to the next photograph in our collection—"

"The first time I saw this photograph, I told you she wasn't anywhere near as pretty as you," he said over the hushed murmurs of the group. "And I haven't changed my mind."

Emily's eyes lit up. It was comforting, until Adrian realized he was about to propose to her in front of twenty complete strangers, and their eyes were all now glued to him. He made his way through the group.

"And then, thinking I was doing an excellent job of hitting on you, I asked you out on a date, but you turned me down."

"You were so cocky," Emily said, her choked indicating she suspected he was up to something.

"Somehow, I wore you down. We went out on our first date, and I've never wanted to be apart from you since."

The women in the crowd collectively crooned.

Adrian knelt on one knee, too focused on Emily to care people in the group were taking pictures and videos on their cell phones.

"This was my gram's ring, but it's been in the family almost a hundred years now," he explained, taking the ring out of his pocket. "The first time my grandfather proposed to her, she turned him down. She didn't think he was ready for marriage. Grandpa always said she was right. Whether he was sixty or seventy when he told the story, he always said he still wasn't ready for marriage."

Behind him, people laughed lightly, and Adrian become anxious again.

"The point is, no matter how much older or wiser my grandfather got, being married always presented a challenge. But there was always an upside to the story. Grandpa always said as long as you had a good woman by your side, patient enough to put up with an Atwood man, you could get through anything.

"Emily, you're the one I want to be with for the rest of my life, for better or worse. You're the only woman I've ever dreamed of starting my own family with. So…" he opened the lid from the ring box, "…would you do me the honor of becoming Mrs. Emily Atwood?"

Tears in her eyes, Emily could only nod to accept his proposal. She threw her arms around Adrian when he stood, and he held her tight.

"Was it that bad of a proposal?" he joked, his heart fluttering in his chest.

"It was perfect," Emily said through her tears.

"Good, because it was completely unplanned."

"Liar," she accused. "That was too well timed."

"No, it was just meant to be."

149

CHAPTER
TWENTY-ONE

Madeleine was sitting at the coffee shop in the same building as Atwood Technologies, waiting for Lee to meet up with her for lunch. He was already thirty minutes late, as Madeleine suspected he would be, but she didn't mind. Truth be told, she wasn't looking forward to lunch with her husband. They were going to "talk things over" since they had been skirting around their issues since the Swan Ball. She was sure he and Adrian had worked together to concoct some strategy to get him to stop drinking, and she could only hope it would work.

She'd act pleased, she'd accept his apology. But nothing would solve the problem. He'd be an alcoholic, and she'd fall for his bullshit every time. Though it was getting old, this fetid, rotting love was holding on strong. Sometimes she wished she could give it up.

The café was in the middle of the concourse. It was an excellent place to people watch and an even

150

better place to write, even if the coffee she always felt obliged to order was terrible. Her coffee sat untouched, probably lukewarm and even more disgusting than it already was when she ordered it.

"Madeleine Atwood."

Madeleine glanced up to see a tall, slender woman towering over her table. She had glistening auburn hair and stunning green eyes, although they were puffy and sunken into dark circles. Madeleine knew all too well—this woman was another troubled soul trying to disguise her inward burdens and failing.

Madeleine gave an obligatory smile. "Hello."

"Mind if I take this seat?"

"Um, no, go ahead," Madeleine replied, trying not to allow her anxiety to take hold. She didn't have the faintest clue who this woman was.

The woman sat as she took an initial sip of her coffee. Madeleine was searching her mind for this woman's face or searching for something about her that could identify who she was. She did not like that this woman knew who she was and referred to her as Atwood instead of McCollum. Simple logic told her she was someone Lee had introduced to her when he was trying to help her make friends in the Buckhead circles, or she could be a reader who had done a good bit of research to find out about her personal life.

"Ugh…they always burn the beans here," the mysterious woman groused. "I don't even know why I bother."

"Oh, yeah. I only order it so I'm not just taking up their table out here."

"Why don't you just go to Lee's office?"

Atwood Technologies employee, Madeleine conjectured. *Did I meet her at one of the company parties? Working for my husband would explain the bags under her eyes.*

"I think I make Janice nervous, to be honest," Madeleine confessed. "She thinks she has to jump through hoops to keep me entertained while I'm there. I don't want to bother her."

The woman stared at her peculiarly. "Strange thing for the wife of the CEO to say. You're kind of the queen of the castle, don't you think?"

"Atwood Technologies is Lee's domain, not mine. I hardly have the right to show up and interrupt people's work days."

"Haven't you figured this out yet?" Evelyn whispered in her ear. "Don't you know who she is?"

Madeleine ignored Evelyn's commentary, focusing entirely on attempting to remember who this woman could possibly be. "What department do you work in?" she asked.

The woman's face cracked into a devious smirk. "You don't have a clue who I am, do you?"

"I'm sorry, I'm terrible with faces," Madeleine apologized.

"You've never seen me. Probably never even heard of me."

Confusion and fear were quickly setting in. "Then who are you?"

"Brecklyne Williams. I'm a real estate broker. I worked with Lee when he wanted to buy this property down on Lake Lanier."

"Okay, but—"

"You were expecting a baby boy," she continued, "and Lee thought it would be the perfect weekend getaway without going too far from home. It was supposed to be a gift for the 'mother of his children and love of his life.' Those were his exact words. He can be romantic when he wants to, can't he?"

Something inside Madeleine broke. She stared, shocked and disgusted at the smirking woman across from her, the hate swelling inside her so much she could feel it surging through her veins with every beat of her heart. It was almost enough to make her miss the numbness the higher dosage of anti-depressants had once forced upon her.

So this was her. The mysterious enemy without a face.

"It wasn't long after, a few months maybe, he started calling, ready to sell the house. He just didn't think he could bring himself to come to a place he'd planned on spending time with his son. It took a while for the house to sell, so we were in contact a lot. When it sold, I thought he was going to break down right there in my office. It was heartbreaking for me too. I hugged him, and one thing led to another and—"

"Are you kidding me?" Madeleine blurted. "You have some gall."

Brecklyne shrugged. "Given Lee's personality, would you expect him to pick a woman with none?"

Madeleine sat back in her chair, taking in Brecklyne Williams. Her interior was molten, but she was bound and determined to remain frozen on the outside. She had wondered now for months

153

what this woman was like, what it was that made her so much better. Brecklyne was certainly beautiful, much more than her plain-Jane self. Back when she first dated Lee, this was exactly the kind of woman she would have pictured him being with.

Madeleine sneered, channeling her anger into a shield. And then she laughed.

Brecklyne was confused, though quickly regained her composure "God, you must be as crazy as he said you were."

"Oh, I hope I'm living up to your expectations, because you certainly aren't living up to mine," Madeleine lied. "Where did Lee meet you? Moreland Avenue?"

"Aren't you clever?" Brecklyne smirked. "No wonder he's so bored with you."

"It doesn't take much to keep Lee interested. Any set of open legs will do," Madeleine said, pointedly eyeing the woman she had been trying to imagine for months now.

"He was set on divorcing you before you went all psycho and slit your wrists, right? How's that healing, by the way?"

Her comment hit a chink in Maddie's armor of rage. It wasn't true. It couldn't be. Why else would he have been so insistent they stay together? If he wanted a divorce, he would have given her one by now.

Madeleine's cheeks grew red hot. Her frozen exterior was melting, not a minute into this confrontation. Inside she was crashing and burning, struggling to keep the tears at bay, even though she had rationalized Brecklyne was lying. She quickly realized the only thing keeping her from completely losing her grip on herself was the feeling of her fingernails digging into the flesh of her palm.

"Leave me for you," Maddie jeered, lifting her chin to look down her nose at the woman across the table. "You poor thing. Did you actually believe him? Do you really think you're special?"

Brecklyne leaned over the table and peered at her. "Lee does. He loves *me*. He wants to be with me. And you can believe the second he thinks you're mentally stable enough, he's going to come right back where he truly belongs."

"What the hell are you doing here?"

Madeleine felt she was drowning. She could faintly hear her husband's gravelly voice, see his face contorted in anger.

Brecklyne smirked. "I told you the truth would come out."

"You bitch. You did this just to hurt us. My wife, my family was off limits. That was our *one* damned rule."

"I know you love me. We would be so much happier together."

"Damn it, Brecklyne, we will never be together!"

As if she were in the grips of a titan, the steel grasp squeezing out every bit of air she would fruitlessly try to inhale. Her heart was racing, her palms sweating, her head swooning. Black and white dots danced across the concourse before they all converged to a gray, consuming haze.

She grasped her husband's forearm. "Lee—"

His face, fading from anger to alarm as he spoke her name, was the last thing she remembered before falling to the floor.

CHAPTER
TWENTY-TWO

"Sounds like a panic attack," Dr. Moore said placidly. "Has it ever happened before?"

"No," Madeleine answered. "And it would happen then. In front of *her*."

"It's understandable, Maddie. It was a highly stressful situation. Most people experience a panic attack at least once."

Madeleine tried to judge Henry's expression. Over the past few months, they had developed a somewhat trusting relationship, but Madeleine found she tired of him after a while. She could never tell if he was genuinely worried about her or if he was just that good of a psychologist. His tones were often too lacking in real feeling.

"It's not something I'll have to take more pills for?"

"Not unless it happens more often. Here, sit. You shouldn't be pacing around after a fainting spell. Rest."

157

Madeleine flopped against the thin emergency room bed. She crossed her legs to keep them still, but she found she could not. She was too anxious. Too angry. More than anything, she wanted to run and never come back, never see Lee for the rest of her life.

"Tell me what you're thinking."

"Do we have to do a session now?" Madeleine groaned, crossing her arms across her chest like a sullen teenager.

"This isn't a session. As a human being, I need to know what you're thinking and how you're feeling."

"Why?"

"Because I'm concerned."

"About me trying to kill myself again?"

The room fell silent. Henry cleared his throat before he answered. "Yes."

"No, Henry, I wouldn't dare think about that again," she muttered.

"The cynicism is what scares me."

Madeleine shrugged. She longed for a cigarette. Not for the sake of nicotine, but just for the sense of having a vice that could relieve some of this tension. Adrian would have one if he were here. She wondered if he'd come if she called.

"Maddie?"

"I'm not the same person I was," she asserted. "You don't have to worry about me. I just want to go home."

Henry knew she was shutting down, and he didn't dare follow. Noticing his defeated expression, Madeleine felt somewhat guilty.

"You can go home as soon as the nurse comes in with your discharge papers. Want me to send Lee in?"

Pinpricks of anger twinged throughout her body. "No. I'll drive home myself."

"You probably shouldn't drive. Just in case."

"Then I'll call a taxi."

"Adrian's here," he suggested.

"He is?"

"Of course."

Madeleine peered at him with a furrowed brow. "What does that mean?"

Henry shrugged. "You guys are close, right? That's what I've gathered from your sessions."

"It's a more recent development. I guess it's just surprising someone cares."

"Your family loves you very much, Madeleine. You've got a good support system. You just don't realize it."

Madeleine nodded, but only to acknowledge she heard him speaking. She knew Adrian, Richard, and Maggie Beth cared about her, and deep down, she knew Lee loved her. What Brecklyne had told her had all been lies. But now she was the one confused about their marriage. Was Lee worth this much heartbreak?

Henry put on his coat and fished his keys out of his pocket.

"Do you think you could do me a favor?" Madeleine asked, somewhat timidly.

"Sure."

"Ask Adrian if he'll drive me home? I don't want to see Lee. Not for a while. I need some time

159

to think. That's not an unreasonable request, is it?"

"No, it isn't. I'll call you in the morning, if that's all right. You can come in for your session tomorrow, or you can cancel it. We'll discuss it then, okay?"

"Okay. Thank you. It means a lot."

Henry left the room. As soon as the door clicked closed, fear spread through Madeleine like wildfire. She knew she could not trust herself alone, knew how easy it was to give in to those dark thoughts troubling her mind in the middle of the night.

"If you're this worried about spending a single night all by yourself, how are you ever going to leave him?" Evelyn questioned, sitting on the wide windowsill. "I don't even know why you're worried about it. He's usually never home any—"

"Mads?"

There was something about Adrian's presence that made her break, comfortable enough to fall apart. He didn't say a word, as if he somehow knew words weren't what she needed, but wrapped his arms around her and held her close. Typically, it would have been awkward, but that day, it wasn't. A simple hug was exactly what she needed.

The rest of the afternoon went in a blur. She spoke with Lee, only enough to tell him she didn't want him to come home that night. She needed time to think. Surprisingly, he didn't fight it, and she was thankful he let her have her way for once. The car ride home with Adrian was silent, both too caught up in their own thoughts. She could tell Adrian was angry. He scared her as she noticed the McLaren's speedometer kept climbing higher and higher, his way of subduing his mood. Perhaps for her sake, but Madeleine couldn't be too sure about that.

"Thanks for driving me," she said when they pulled up into the driveway of her home. How much longer was it going to be *their* home? "I promise, one day I'll slay my own dragons. I'm sick of being the damsel in distress all the time."

Adrian shifted into park. "Um, let's hope your dragons do an awful lot of shrinking. I don't know any damsels, or knights, for that matter, who could fight all this alone."

"Don't have much of a choice anymore. It's either fight it or run away."

"I knew about it," he spluttered, looking down at his steering wheel, his fingers fiddling nervously. "I'm…I'm so sorry. I should have told you."

"Adrian, it wasn't your place to tell me," Madeleine said in the most comforting tone she could muster. She placed her hand on his shoulder.

Adrian's face was crestfallen. "Wouldn't it have been easier coming from anyone other than her?"

"Lee should have told me. If it was up to Lee, I wouldn't know a single bit of the truth."

"I don't know what he's thinking," Adrian grumbled.

"I don't even think I know who he is anymore."

"He's your husband. And he loves you. He made a stupid mistake, and he's already paying for it."

"He was sleeping with her when I tried to kill myself. That's the only reason he ended it. Guilt."

"Maybe so, but you are the one he loves. Lee loves no one easily. It was always different with you. For what it's worth, I think it is."

"Adrian, I don't know if I can be with him. God knows I love him, but enough is enough," Madeleine said matter-of-factly.

The air grew thicker in the tense silence that fell between them.

Adrian swallowed, his hands gripping at the steering wheel. "I'd miss you. Not that something so small would make a difference. But I wouldn't blame you if you left him."

Madeleine's vision blurred. "That's not at all small to me. You don't understand how much it means to hear someone say they would miss me."

Adrian rested his hand on her forearm. "Maddie, I've got to admit I don't feel comfortable leaving you here all by yourself."

"I'll be fine," she tried to assure him, although she wasn't so sure it was the truth.

CHAPTER TWENTY-THREE

Lee had never understood. He had never fathomed wanting to die. Only selfish people would ever take their own life. While he didn't want to think of Madeleine that way, his mind was set.

She was crazy; she was selfish.

Although he loved her, he couldn't understand her like he thought he eventually would in those days before he fell so in love with her that understanding her didn't matter so much.

Yet lying there in his father's guest bedroom, staring at the shadows on the ceiling, he felt the sting of her absence like never before.

Lee finally understood.

Guilt weighed so heavy all he could think about was how everyone would be better off if he was dead.

CHAPTER
TWENTY-FOUR

Madeleine had spent the night writing nonstop. She had given up trying to sleep at midnight, then trudged downstairs to brew a kettle of Earl Gray and sit until the ideas quit coming. Her thoughts were a blurry mess of scene after scene, repeating endlessly, until she had captured everything completely. She wasn't sure how long it had been, but she had watched the dawn break and stream through her windows.

"Sleep well, Mads?" Evelyn chimed.

"Don't call me Mads."

"Why not? Adrian does it."

"Precisely."

"Oh, you and Mr. Handsome have exclusive nicknames now?"

"Quit calling him that."

"Why? It's fitting. And don't deny it," Evelyn said, flopping into the chair across from Madeleine's desk. "That Adrian Atwood is keen, to

164

put it lightly."

Madeleine kept typing.

"Oh, come on now. Don't pretend you haven't noticed how fetching he is."

Madeleine stared flatly at Evelyn. "What is it you're getting at?"

Evelyn leaned in. "Adrian has the most beautiful set of mysterious gray eyes I've ever seen on a man. He's tall, well built, and he's got a smile that could make a nun sweat. Do I even have to mention his ass?"

"No, you do not have to mention his ass," Madeleine grumbled, turning her attention back to the screen. "What's a better word for 'prudish?'"

"Try 'Madeleine Atwood.'"

"I hardly think I'm being prudish because I choose not to check out my brother-in-law's backside."

"He's about to not be your brother-in-law anymore, isn't he?"

Madeleine ceased typing and looked over her glasses at Evelyn, her mouth slightly ajar. "I-I don't know. I haven't made up my mind about…that yet."

"*That?* You're not even going to refer to the problem as 'Lee' anymore?"

Madeleine sighed deeply. "Yes. Lee is the problem. Happy?"

"You know what you need to do," Evelyn said, thumbing through an issue of *Elle*. "You'd just have to get up the courage to do it again."

The words stung, but for just a split second, Madeleine thought that maybe—

"No. That…that's ridiculous."

"*Is* it so ridiculous?"

Madeleine stood, narrowed her eyes at Evelyn, and then whipped into the living room, straight to the antique cabinet kept for the collection of bottles her husband deigned to share with any guests.

"Going to numb the pain instead?"

"The pain, the tiniest idea of committing suicide…you. Whatever it takes to escape for just a bit."

The cabinet was fully stocked. She vaguely remembered a promise or two he was going to stop drinking so much, but that promise had long stood broken. For once, glad he'd never followed through, she grabbed the bottle and took a long, burning swig of whiskey. It made her feel her lungs were on fire, but Madeleine kept drinking until her chest grew accustomed to the feel and her nerves uncrossed and held their fire. She settled onto the sofa and took long sips while contemplating life. The sun was high and bright, shining through the windows, when the front door eased open and Lee walked into the foyer.

"You look like hell," Madeleine said when she saw him, tipping back the bottle again. He had dark circles under his eyes and yesterday's clothes were wrinkled to ruin.

Lee sat on the edge of the sofa. "Didn't get a wink of sleep."

Madeleine huffed. "Tell me about it. I think I wrote half a novel last night."

"I'm sorry," Lee said, his eyes welling. "I am so sorry."

"Jesus, Lee. You'll be just fine without me.

166

You've made it the past several months just fine."

"No I haven't," Lee sputtered. "I've been keeping myself numb to everything. I love you."

Madeleine sneered. "Bullshit." She took another drink from the bottle.

Her body wracked with a terrible sob. Lee moved as close to her as he could, leaned in, and tried to put his hand on her shoulder, but Madeleine balled up her fist and pushed him away. Lee wrested the bottle from her hand. "I think you've had enough for now." His voice was gentle, even after her burst of almost-violence.

"Don't you dare lecture me about having too much to drink!" She shot her hand out to grab the bottle back from him, but he moved it away from her. "You've gotten all the anesthetic you've ever needed. When you've even had the slightest inkling your life isn't going the way you want, you just numb everything!"

"Maddie, take it from me, it's not going to fix it. Come here."

Lee tried to wrap her in his arms, but Madeleine forced him away. "Get away from me."

"Maddie…"

"Don't Maddie me," she slurred, sinking down on the floor. "Do you have any idea what this is like? You don't have a damned clue."

"No. You're right, I don't. But I—"

"I mean she—this *slut* who *knew* you were married—decides she wants you, and you—you fall for her! My entire life, what fragile existence it was, is completely ruined because of her!"

"Maddie, no," he said, sinking down next to her.

167

"Nothing has to change."

She snorted a laugh. "You're hilarious."

"No one ever said this has to be the end for us. Fuck Brecklyne, she—"

"Check, already done," Madeleine spat.

"Do you still love me?"

"I wish I didn't."

Lee clenched his jaw, the muscle visibly tightening under the pressure. "The words won't be of much value to you, but I love you. I want you. I have fucked up beyond what you should ever have to forgive. But I promise you—"

Madeleine interrupted him with a laugh, but he grasped her hand and finished before she could speak. "I promise you, I'll be everything you need. We've been through hell. I just want us to find our way back to where we were. We used to be so happy together."

She couldn't deny Lee was right. They had been happy together, and he was all she had ever wanted. "How do you get back to Heaven when you're in Hell?"

"I don't have the answer to that, Maddie. I wish I did."

She took another swig of whiskey and offered him the bottle. He took it and drank without comment.

For a few silent minutes, that was all they did. Drink, hunkered down on their living room floor, both equally scared of the uncertainty of their future together.

"Why don't you get out of this house, Madeleine? I don't know why we even moved here in the first place. There are too many bad memories here."

"And go where?"

"You don't realize your net worth contains a couple of commas, do you? You can go anywhere in the world. It'll help you clear your head."

Maddie choked back a laugh. "The world is a big place, Lee. I might never come back."

"Then you won't have to worry about me anymore," he said. "Hell, use the beach house if you don't want any distractions. God knows there's nothing to do on Tybee this time of the year."

The image of a beach floated through her mind, and she could almost feel the sand beneath her feet and the sea breeze ruffling her hair. The more she thought about it, the better it sounded. Distraction-free and hundreds of miles away from Lee.

"I can call right now and have it ready for you by this evening. Just say the word."

"Okay," Madeleine agreed, not completely sold on staying in anything owned by the Atwoods, but Lee was right. She needed to get out of this house, away from its ghosts, away from the present haunting her just as much as the past.

CHAPTER TWENTY-FIVE

Madeleine left her suitcase and bags on the entryway floor and walked through the doors of the beach house on Chatham Avenue. It was a gorgeous house, quiet and peaceful, and not half as pretentious as the other Atwood houses. But it was devoid of life. Madeleine was not sure if she liked the overwhelming sound of her own breath. It was too much like the days after Lee had left.

Except she was the one who left this time. And even though he deserved it, there would have been no peace living with him while she worked out what it was she wanted to do, what she needed to do. She also didn't know if she was ready to stand against the overwhelming loneliness.

Evelyn's eyes wandered at their new surroundings, despondent and searching. "We could have gone anywhere. Anywhere, Madeleine! Paris, London, Rome! Bloody hell."

"It'll be relaxing. I can get a lot of work done,

and—"

"And think about Lee while pretending to not think about Lee."

"Precisely."

She didn't even bother unpacking. Instead, she reached for her laptop bag, carried it to the living room, plugged in her headphones, and got to work. Madeleine touched the keys, the insertion point on the blank page waiting expectantly. There were so many emotions inside, trying to surface through the chemical fog of the anti-depressants. She wanted to cry, scream, rage, but she just couldn't feel the need anymore.

Put it into words, she told herself.

She pressed the first key, typed a first line, and let it flow. Every suppressed emotion wound together to form words and sentences and paragraphs.

Life.

Something from nothing.

Madeleine didn't even realize the time until her phone vibrated on the table and forced her back into the real world. Lee was calling. She sent the call straight to voicemail. Refocusing, she typed a few more lines until the phone vibrated yet again, her husband's name and picture heralding another call.

"Pocketful of nopes," she muttered, declining the call again.

"Persistent, isn't he?" Evelyn chimed. "You might as well pick up. You're dying to talk to him."

"Obviously not," Madeleine hissed through a clenched jaw. She resigned to sending him a text later, to at least let him know she'd made it down to

171

Tybee alive.

About the time she got back into the flow of writing, the phone rang again.

Out of sheer frustration, she picked it up. "Yes, I'm here. Alive and without incident. And on a scale of one to ten, my likelihood of committing suicide is a solid two. Yes, I've taken my meds and—"

"Bad day?"

Madeleine laughed. "Oh, thank God, Adrian. I thought you were Lee again."

"Aww, that's not very nice."

"I know he's your brother, but can you blame me for not wanting to talk to him?"

"Honestly? No."

"Are you calling to keep tabs on me?"

"Yep. Boss's orders."

"You're kidding."

"Nope. Lee says he knows you don't want to talk to him, so he's asked me to check up on you now and then."

"Wow, Adrian. That makes me not want to speak to you," Madeleine replied, only half joking. "Does he want you to spy and see if I'm planning on taking him for all he's worth?"

"No. He just wants to make sure you're okay, and you've got everything you need. Honest to God. He's a downright mess. I think he'd give every dime he has to get you back."

A pause in conversation gave her time she needed to process. What was she supposed to say to him? Her husband's brother? If she wasn't talking to Lee, why the hell would she talk to Adrian?

"Really, how are you? I could guess, but the question is more to show concern."

"So are you actually asking or not?" Madeleine laughed. For all his charm, Adrian could be as awkward as she was.

"I'm asking only if you want to be asked. If you don't want to be asked, I'm just calling to let you know I care."

"Hmm, are you sure you went to Tech and not law school?"

"I live in the corporate world now, sweet pea. Doublespeak is my second language."

"It's Lee's native tongue," Madeleine groused.

"Burn. So, how are you? Yes, I'm asking."

Madeleine swallowed anxiously. Now that the initial shock and anger had worn off, she was sad.

"I'm fine," she said. "I've been here a couple of hours, and I've done nothing but tune out the world and write. All things considered, I'm doing better than I would have six months ago."

"July twelfth. It feels like it happened yesterday."

July twelfth was a date she knew all too well. It should have been carved on her tombstone by now. If she'd died, she wouldn't have had to endure another round of pain. Lee could replace her with a better, shinier woman that matched him better. Adrian could be making the Atwoods another million or being the man of Emily's dreams instead of checking on his depressive, anxiety-ridden sister-in-law.

Her thoughts were racing, over-thinking a thousand different theories of how the world would be a little less complicated if she was dead.

"I can't forget it," he continued. *"I think it was the worst day of my life."*

"W-What?" Madeleine stammered.

Adrian cleaned his throat. *"I've never wanted to die. I have no idea what that's like. So I get it must sound childish to you because your lowest point was infinitely lower than mine. But I've never watched anyone die, and there you were, dying right in front of me. Minutes away from being gone forever. I didn't have a clue how to stop the bleeding. Got enough wits to call 911, and I just sat there, clenching both your wrists in a towel as tight as I could until the ambulance got there. I hadn't prayed in years, but I started back July twelfth."*

Her throat clenched and her eyes stung with tears. She knew, when Adrian had said he cared, it was real—no intentions to decipher, no put-on caring out of obligation. She instinctively knew she could trust him as she always had, and something about the ability to trust made the world feel slightly less lonely.

CHAPTER
TWENTY-SIX

"What are your goals for the future, Madeleine?"

She sat there for a moment, staring blankly at the digital rendering of her therapist on her laptop screen. She almost wanted to laugh at such a silly question. The corners of her mouth tugged in a grin.

"You look like you have something on your mind," Dr. Moore prodded. "We're open here. You can say whatever is on your mind."

"Okay." She shrugged with a shake of her head. "I think I'm still in survival mode. My goal is to get through the day without some major breakdown."

"That's good. It's important to focus on a day at a time when you're dealing with depression. What are you doing to get through the day?"

Again, Madeleine had to scoff. "Right now I'm writing. Sometimes I think it's the one thing keeping me together. There's a story to be told."

She was already tiring with this conversation. Didn't doctors, people who studied psychology, understand goal-setting was beyond her capabilities right now?

"Do you just realize that's a long-term goal? To finish a book?" Henry's expression was almost smug.

Madeleine furrowed her brow. "It only takes me a matter of months, so it's not too long of a goal. The new book's halfway written."

"Really? We talked about you starting it just a few sessions ago."

"I know. Ever since…Lee and I separated," she said, choosing her words tactfully, "I've had nothing but time to myself. And I'd rather write than cry, so why not?"

"Sometimes you need a good cry. It's okay to cry if you need to."

"Yes, but crying doesn't fix the problem. It's an emotional release. If I can get the same effect doing something I love and make a few bucks doing it, why not?"

Henry grinned. "You've got me there. So answer this then: after this book, what do you do?"

"It depends on the sales, but it's not unlikely I'll go on tour for book signings and readings, maybe the occasional lecture if I can manage it. The anxiety meds will help with those, I hope. It'll be interesting to see. I loathe tours. It's something I'd like to enjoy. I've just never been able to. Every time I've been on a tour, I've missed Lee." Madeleine thought for a moment. "I guess maybe this time I won't be missing him so much."

That idea hurt. She missed him, even in that moment. She could see it concerned Henry, but he gave her time to process.

"It's also okay to miss him."

Madeleine squeezed her eyes tight to blink out the tears before they could fall. In all her months of therapy, she'd never managed not to cry, and she didn't want to waste any more tears on Lee Atwood.

Which didn't mean she wouldn't, but she certainly didn't want to.

"I don't want to talk about him today."

"We don't have to talk about him. Let's move on. What do you want to talk about?"

Madeleine tried to shake the thought of Lee. "I've made some progress, I think," she began, but her voice was overlapping some random memory of Lee like two songs playing over one another. "I've been socializing more."

"That's wonderful. Are you making some strong connections?"

"Kind of, but it's hard to say not knowing what the future holds. I'm going out with Julia tonight. She's an old college classmate. We haven't spoken in years, but we randomly bumped into each other in a bookstore in Savannah last week."

"That's great! Connecting with others can help in many ways."

"I talk to Adrian every day, which is good. We were good friends before college, but I can't imagine if Lee and I get a divorce, he'd keep speaking to me."

"Why do you think that?"

"He's a great guy, but he loves his brother. We may be friends, but blood runs thicker than water for Adrian."

"Just take it one day at a time. Appreciate the relationship and support as long as you can."

"I'm trying to. It's just hard when it won't be there one day."

"Do you necessarily know that?"

"No, but—"

"Can you trust Adrian?"

"I want to."

"Is he a trustworthy person?"

"Extremely," Madeleine answered in all certainty.

"So do you think he deserves a chance?"

"I...I don't know. It's hard to let go and trust, even when I have no actual reason to doubt his motives."

Dr. Moore's expression told her he understood. "Don't let fear get the better of you. Even though it's hard, let go and trust."

The night had started out awkward and uncomfortable for Madeleine. Even though Julia and her husband Will had been more than friendly, she was unsure of what to say and do, what details to share and which to keep to herself. She didn't think she could bear to admit to this perfect couple her marriage was hanging in the balance, so she wove some more fiction into her life, telling them she always went somewhere in isolation to write her newest book. Lee and their marriage were just fabulous, and life as a famous author and richer-than-God executive couldn't be better.

178

As the night wore on, they ended up at the Bohemian Hotel on River Street, drinking cocktails at the rooftop bar that towered over Savannah. The glittering black Savannah River snaked through the landscape, ferrying boats back to the Atlantic on yet another journey. Julia and Will were seated at the bar, downing one drink after another. Madeleine had a decent buzz going, but the alcohol made her feel disconnected from her friends and the crowd. She ended up excusing herself, claiming she needed air, and went over to the outer wall of the roof overlooking River Street.

A behemoth of a barge sounded its blaring horn as it approached the bridge. Madeleine settled into the cushions of a black rattan sofa with her watered-down cocktail and let loneliness sink in. She didn't think Dr. Moore would appreciate her shutting herself off when she was supposed to be socializing, but this was simply who she was.

Or was it?

It wasn't that she didn't want friends, but making them was exhausting, no matter how much she liked them. Madeleine took her phone out of her purse just to have something to distract her mind and noticed she had a missed call from Adrian. It was late, but calling him back was tempting.

She could always blame it on the fact she was tipsy. Before she knew it, he was answering.

"Hello?"

Adrian sounded tired. "Hey. Just saw I missed your call. I was out with some friends."

He took a moment to respond. *"Seriously?"*

Madeleine laughed. "Don't sound so surprised."

"No, no, I'm not surprised. I just didn't know you had friends down there."

"Not really. They're more like acquaintances. Good people."

"You've been drinking."

"You can tell?"

"Yeah, you sound too relaxed."

"Adrian Flynn! What's wrong with me being relaxed now and then?"

He laughed. *"Nothing. I'm worried you're out drinking with acquaintances in a city 250 miles away, but other than that, I'm glad you're having out having fun."*

"I am having fun."

"So why are you calling me? Can't be too fun if I'm able to interrupt."

"I think you're plenty of fun. Hey, you remember in high school when you did that thing to Coach Adams' computer where you flipped the screen upside down?"

"Control-alt-down arrow! Got him every time."

"He turned the whole damned screen upside down," Madeleine laughed. "That was hilarious."

"I do it to Dad sometimes, but then I get in trouble with Lee."

"Ugh, Lee. Let's not." She realized then just how drunk she was.

"Hmm, that's not a good sign. I guess you've talked then?"

"No. I don't want to talk to him. No offense. I just…I'm enjoying the time away. And it still hurts."

Adrian was silent for a few fleeting seconds.

Madeleine leaned her head back and stared up at the starry sky.

"Yeah, Maddie, of course it hurts. I can't even imagine. It's got to feel like having the rug pulled out from under your feet."

"Except the rug was covering a black hole. And I just keep falling through."

"It will get better. I'm here to help in any way I can."

Madeleine thought back to her conversation with Henry. He'd asked her to trust, but she wasn't sure if she could. "Adrian?"

"Yes, ma'am?"

She nearly snorted. "Bless your little Southern heart. Aren't you just the cutest?"

Even tipsy, it one made her blush as soon as it came out of her mouth, but Adrian just laughed. *"My mama trained me well."*

"Are you gonna talk to me if Lee and I get a divorce?"

"Yes," he replied without even the slightest hesitation.

"Wow. I'm impressed."

"Why in the world would you be impressed?"

"Because! Why would you want to talk to your brother's ex-wife?"

"Because my brother's ex-wife was my friend first. He just came along and swept you off your feet. Why should I lose my friend because he's an idiot?"

"Blood's thicker than water," she quoted Adrian's own words.

Adrian exhaled over the line. *"Not in this case."*

CHAPTER TWENTY-SEVEN

Madeleine awoke on Christmas Eve to a knock on the door. A delivery man had her sign for a van-full of gifts. Save for a few from Richard, Maggie Beth, and Adrian, they were all from Lee. Some were what Lee considered small—designer handbags, perfumes, well-chosen clothes, and jewelry that fit her simple style, but exuded wealth regardless. To top it all off was a black velvet box containing a silver key and a keychain with a QR code.

"Oh, dear Jesus," Madeleine mused. "What could this be?"

"Definitely real estate." Evelyn nodded, impressed.

"You think so?"

"He's bought you some enormous mansion to impress you. Don't let it impress you now," Evelyn said with a grin.

"That would be Lee's style. Only one way to

find out." Madeleine scanned the QR code with her phone. Once it loaded, there it was. The most ridiculously expensive but wonderful gift he could have gotten her. It was a warm, sun-filled house in a tiny town in Northern England. From the small garden out back, you could see the remains of an ancient castle, and the sea glistened not far in the distance.

As she scrolled through the pictures, she couldn't help but fall in love with the house. There was a cozy sunroom with a gorgeous desk overlooking foggy moor and castle, a perfect place to write.

She was torn. How could she accept it? Buying her a house was a grand gesture meant to reel her back in, and knowing this was simply a tactic cheapened the entire gift.

Madeleine threw the idea around in her head for a moment and then called him. *"Well, if this isn't the best Christmas present I've ever gotten,"* Lee greeted, sounding excited to hear from her.

"Lee—"

"It's the house, isn't it? I knew you would say it was too much."

"Yes, it's too much!" she exclaimed, then guilt settled in and made her soften her tone. "I mean, it's perfect, but—"

"But you don't know if you want to come home and you don't feel you should accept it. Or is it the fact you think I'm trying to bribe you?"

"Both," she sputtered, irritated he knew exactly what she was thinking. "Are you?"

"Trying to bribe you? Only if it worked."

"Lee—"

"This is the way I see it. If we get a divorce, which we won't, I can rest easier knowing you've got either a place to make a fresh start or a strong investment property you can rely on if you needed the money. Either way, that house would be your new favorite place to write."

Madeleine had to admit, he knew her well.

"I'm just trying to take care of you and show you I love you in about the only way I can right now. You deserve it, no matter what."

Once their call was over, Madeleine felt terrible. For days, she debated whether she was being too hard on him or if he deserved it. Evelyn insisted she was much too hard on her loving, apologetic husband. Madeleine thought he was lucky he wasn't rotting in a shallow grave where no one would ever find him. She knew for a fact she loved him, and she always would.

However, that didn't mean she wanted to be his wife. What kind of marriage would they have? Would she constantly fear that every business trip was some hook-up? Would she become one of those paranoid women constantly checking up on their husbands? She shuddered at the thought.

Time slipped by, and the gray winter days bled into one another. By the time a new year rolled around, Madeleine settled into a comfortable routine. Every morning, she'd have breakfast at the cafe a mile down the beach where she'd read the paper and drink her coffee. Then it was back home to write until Adrian called on his lunch break. At first, their conversations had been minimal, keeping up with their respective worlds, and Adrian's semi-subtle hints that Lee was more than remorseful. By January, a call a day had evolved into two—one at lunch, and another later in the evening, when they'd both quit working for the day.

"I think your parents are *together*," she announced one night.

For a moment, there was nothing but a few crackles of dead air over the line. Madeleine waited expectantly, staring at the bedroom ceiling, unable to stop smiling. Although she wasn't quite sure why, the sound of Adrian's voice, particularly lately, brought her a sense of contentment she thought she had lost years ago.

"Say that again?" Adrian laughed after a long moment of silence. *"I'm not sure I heard you right."*

"They had lunch together a few days ago. Your mother called and told me all about it," Madeleine reported. "And she sounded so happy. Cupcake-phase, gushing Richard this and Richard that."

"You are so full of it."

"I swear! Call her up."

"I would, but it's nearly one a.m."

Madeleine peered at her wristwatch. "Oh my gosh. I'm sorry to keep you up this late."

"I just now realized it," Adrian responded with a lilt. *"And I'm close with the boss, so if I'm late to work—"*

"You'll still get fussed out."

"Yeah, pretty much."

"Goodnight, Adrian."

"Night, Mads."

She hung up the phone and snuggled into her

185

pillow, a creeping feeling of satisfaction spreading like a match-light in the darkness.

CHAPTER
TWENTY-EIGHT

With a smile of satisfaction, Madeleine finished the chapter and emailed it off to her editor, who had been waiting days for more chapters. She was excited someone else was having as much fun reading it as she was writing it. Who had known three months of practical isolation would help fuel her creative spark and make her feel something similar to happy? Checking the clock, she felt even more fulfilled. It was 1:00, and Adrian would call any minute.

"I don't know why you get so excited about him calling," Evelyn complained from across the living room. She was sitting on an armchair, Madeleine's paperback copy of *Anna Karenina* open in her hands. "You're like a dog waiting on its master. How ridiculous and demeaning, Madeleine."

"You're upset because I have someone to talk to other than you?" Madeleine countered, shutting down her laptop.

"Hardly," Evelyn harrumphed. "He's only talking to you so he can run off and tell Lee every word you tell him. He never called you before. Those phone calls are for nothing but gleaning information."

The satisfaction was sucked right out of her body. She had not thought for a moment Adrian would be capable of something so underhanded. Would he do that to her?

"We've spoken nearly every day. We were on the phone until nearly one a.m. last night," Madeleine argued. "He wouldn't do such just to tell Lee everything."

Evelyn shrugged, not even bothering to look up from the book. "The longer you talk, the more information he gets. Maybe Lee thinks Adrian can get some sort of evidence to use against you if you divorce him. He married you without a prenuptial agreement, remember? Lee wouldn't want you getting one grubby finger on his money unless he was getting something back out of it."

"Lee's called a thousand times. He's concerned about me, our marriage. The Atwoods have more money than God. I guarantee you, Lee isn't worried about a little bit of alimony. Not that I would ever want it."

Evelyn stared at Madeleine, her green eyes wide. She gave a short, snorting laugh. "Go over there to that mirror and take a good long look at yourself. Go on now."

Curious, Madeleine did as she said. The mirror hung over the mantle in the living room, reflecting the ocean view from the window across the room.

She walked up close to inspect her appearance, and Evelyn followed closely, placing her hands on her shoulders and her face next to Madeleine's.

Side by side with Evelyn's doubtless beauty, the comparison was stark.

"Tsk, tsk, Maddie. See those bags under your eyes? For someone who's supposed to be relaxing, getting away from the world, you've not been sleeping very well. And are those crow's feet forming? You're only thirty-two! Better be thinking about a nip-tuck there to keep that husband of yours interested. Who am I kidding? Crow's feet are the least of your worries. It's that plain-Jane face that's the problem. Even with make-up, you've only ever been…eh, acceptable, I suppose would be the word. Ah, Jesus. No wonder Lee cheated on you. As always, he's simply too damned good for you."

Madeleine's heartbeat rose in her chest, her throat already closing. "He doesn't care. He loves me."

"Does he? I'm thinking there's never been a single person in this world who actually cares about you."

Just then, Madeleine's phone rang from the desk where she had left it. Feeling short of breath and wanting nothing more than to answer it, she knew it must have been Lee or Adrian, or Maggie Beth, anyone who actually cared. She would prove Evelyn wrong. There were people who cared, weren't there?

Evelyn's grip on her shoulders tightened, pushing her toward the mirror. "You're not good enough for him. Not good enough for any of them.

And don't think I don't see the thoughts running through your head, no matter how brief they may be. That handsome brother-in-law of yours…part of you has always wanted him, admit it."

Madeleine grimaced, disgusted with Evelyn, with herself. "Yeah, when I was a kid, but I fell in love with Lee."

Evelyn threw back her head and laughed. "Oh, Maddie, please. It never stopped. Never. He was the only one who ever took pity on you, and you loved him for it. And Lee, he was just too damned cocky to think a girl could want his younger brother more than him, so he kissed you, just to hurt his own brother."

Evelyn's voice had become strangely seductive, her hands running across Madeleine's shoulders and down her sides and hips. "Like a common whore, you fell for the first man who showed you the least bit of physical affection."

"Take your hands off me," Madeleine ordered, grasping Evelyn's hands and forcing them off her.

Evelyn snickered. "Uncomfortable with your own body, Madeleine? I wonder if Adrian could make himself as comfortable with your body as his brother is?"

"Stop it!"

"You're not as pretty as Emily, though. I doubt he'd risk losing his sweet princess for a piece of ass he never got as a teenager. Maybe you can spin the conquest angle. How many men get to fuck their brother's wife?"

"I said stop!" Madeleine hit the mantle with her hand.

"You know you want him. It must be so exhausting living in such constant denial."

"Get out of my head! Getoutofmyhead! Getoutofmyhead! Getoutofmyhead!"

A dark veil shattered and fell in a million pieces to the ground. Her eyes stung with bright, white light washing the house in its impossible illumination. Madeleine's heart was racing, quick, shortened breaths rushing in and out of her lungs, powered by the overwhelming sense of fear and loneliness coursing rampant in her veins. Her phone buzzed again on the desk, and she jolted to pick it up.

"Adrian?" she said in a tone she hoped didn't sound as desperate as it was.

"I am exhausted," Adrian said, his tone bright and comforting. *"This cute blonde kept me up all night, and I had to beg for a lunch break from the boss from hell."*

Madeleine closed her eyes tight, squeezing out the tears.

"Maddie? What's wrong?"

She cursed her inability to hide from him or his uncanny ability to know when she needed someone to assure her everything would be okay.

"I am just so glad you called," she said tearfully. "I think being here alone is getting to me."

"Then come home. Not necessarily home with Lee—that's your decision. But…"

"But what?"

"Just be closer. That way, if something happened to you or you're lonely, I—we—could be close by."

191

She put her hand over her chest, and she could no longer feel her heart's threats to pound out of it. Something felt different, comfortable, secure, and Madeleine wanted to commit the feeling to memory by savoring every second of that fleeting moment.

"I'll drive down there right now if I have to," he offered when she did not respond.

"I know you would. But you don't have to. You do enough for me already."

"Emily and I could come down for the weekend if you wanted. I have some things to do at work Friday morning, but I could leave that afternoon. We'd be there in time to go to Screaming Mimi's for dinner."

"Eh, I like Vinnie Van Go-go's better."

"Vinnie Van's it is," he said. *"Lee will be jealous."*

Madeleine swallowed at the mention of her husband. "Speaking of Lee, how is he?"

"Hmm, do you want the truth or a pathetic lie?"

She was hoping Lee would be getting over things. That maybe he would change or at least show her that he would be fine all alone, and if she wanted to, she could move on.

"He's no better?"

"He's not taking this well. Your leaving him is a reality check he desperately needed, but he's drinking. Like a lot. People at work are noticing."

Madeleine groaned. "He can't, not when he's just started as CEO. He's wanted this since he was four years old."

"I know. But it's not your job to fix him, either, Maddie. You've got your own issues to sort out

192

right now. Lee's got to make a conscious decision to be who he needs to be."

"That's a lot for someone who doesn't even want to get out of bed in the mornings," she answered.

She didn't know if Lee was struggling like she was, but she could identify. People did not know how strong depression was, how it had the power to turn your own mind against you, no matter how hard you fought.

"Look, if you want to, call him. Maybe it would make him feel better if you just checked in and let him know you're alive," Adrian suggested. *"You do what you're comfortable with."*

Madeleine didn't even want to think about speaking to him, completely unsure of what she would even say to the man she loved so much but resented so much.

"Do you love my brother?"

Madeleine was sure of the honest answer in her heart. "Yes, I love him, but—"

"Then that's enough, Madeleine. Call him. What do the two of you have to lose?"

All things considered, Madeleine knew Adrian was right. She and Lee were nothing but a stack of divorce papers away from being out of each other's lives forever. What could a simple phone call hurt?

CHAPTER
TWENTY-NINE

The entire point of leaving Lee had been to figure out what she wanted. After spending three months away from him, she couldn't decide if their marriage, if the path their lives had taken, was a beautiful wreck or a continuous maze down a path of certain destruction. She hadn't been able to bring herself to call Lee. Whether it was pride or fear that kept her from calling, she didn't know, yet every time she picked up the phone to call him, her follow-through waned.

The red dawn cast an eerie glow over the gray ghost town that was Tybee Island. Winds whipped down the deserted beach, bowling over the tufts of drying seaweed abandoned by the receding tides. Typically bustling shore-side shops and restaurants faced the bleak horizon, awaiting the bright, hazy days of another summer.

Red sky at morning, sailors take warning, Madeleine remembered.

She faithfully popped her pills, one for depression and one for anxiety, and swallowed them down with a sip of water. She then brushed her teeth and prepared for the day, doing it all in a lazy haze of routine. She wrote, unsure of what she was even writing, but there were words and plot on a page, and she figured it would have to be good enough for now.

Madeleine had gotten into the habit of taking long strolls on the beach at dusk, when it seemed like she was the only person left in the world. There was a certain peace in it but an overwhelming loneliness. She kept imagining the ocean swallowing her up, her body sinking to the depths. Within months, she would be of no consequence to anyone for the rest of eternity. She couldn't get the idea out of her mind every time her toes strayed into the water's reach.

Madeleine kept this to herself, carefully shrouding her thoughts and faking her way through her therapy sessions.

When her mind wasn't focused on a death at sea, it was free to bounce back and forth between Lee and, occasionally, Adrian.

This particularly dour morning, she paid no mind to the headline on the paper as she slid quarters into the newsstand out of habit. Bitter hate was rising like bile in her stomach, burning her inside. The logical side of her, trained by Dr. Moore to notice when her thoughts turned to the negative, failed to cajole her raging spirit.

She ordered a pecan pancake, but it grew cold while the blank page of her notebook stared at her, taunting her for her lack of action.

"Damn it all. There's nothing left when even the words have left me."

"Wonder what Lee's up to?" Evelyn said, staring out the window to the ocean waves as she sipped on her coffee.

"Screw Lee," Madeleine grumbled, keeping her eyes on the page.

Evelyn raised an eyebrow. "That's certainly an idea. It might help to relieve some tension in your shoulders…among other places. You could use a good lay."

"A good lay, as you so eloquently put it, is the last thing I need."

"Lee could certainly get the job done right. It was the one thing you could never fault the man for."

That much was true, although Madeleine hated to admit it, but their relationship was doomed. She couldn't go back, even if she knew for certain she wanted to. There was no doubt she loved him, but there simply was no way she could trust the man ever again.

Fighting a serious urge to sink down on the tiled floor and weep, Madeleine haphazardly threw a twenty down on the table and grabbed her notebook and pen, practically running out of the restaurant. The tears came hard and fast the second she made it out the door and rushed toward the gray expanse of the shoreline that would take her back to the beach house.

CHAPTER THIRTY

The smell of her Burberry perfume stirred his senses, her skin beneath his hands soft and smooth. Her body rocked against his, making his blood sear through his veins. Fire engulfed him, fogging his mind even better than the finest whiskey. He pressed his lips to her neck, feeling her fire pulsing just beneath the thin layer of her flesh.

"Lee…"

He wasn't even sure how it had come to this. She had come strolling back up the gray strip of beach, notebook and pen in hand, staring out dismally to the sea. In that moment, he had hoped she was thinking of him, missing him to even a fraction of the intensity he had missed her.

Yet Madeleine hadn't exactly been happy to see him.

"What are you doing here?" she had asked, steel-toned and stalwart when she spotted him.

Although it had cut him straight to the core, he knew he deserved it.

"Maddie, come on," he pleaded. "We need to

talk, face to face."

"Today isn't a good day for me, Lee." Madeleine breezed by him to get to the house.

"Looks like a perfect day to me, Madeleine," he protested, following close behind. "We're here, same time, same place, and we've had three months to think about what we want. There's no time like the present."

She glared at him, her mouth forming a hard line as she stared him down. "I am so tired of being your weak, compliant little wife," she groused, the pain rising from her core and out her mouth without even a thought. It was pure, pent-up emotion that spewed from inside that had been squelched and hidden for months. "I don't want you here. I don't want you in my life at all."

She took five silent steps and had her hand on the front door handle when he spoke again.

"You said you loved me. Just a few weeks ago. Have you really changed your mind that quickly?"

He hissed in pleasure as she ground her hips slow and hard against his, over and over, then faster until it sent his head spiraling. There was nothing in the world other than her, and she was everything he could ever want or need.

"I'm not going to be able to stop."

"I'm still your wife," she whispered. "You don't have to stop."

"Thought you didn't love me—ah, *fuck*—"

Hadn't she said that? Lee wondered bitterly. She'd said she didn't love him and they were through.

"I meant it," she seethed. He could tell she was

on the brink. "I-don't-love-you…"

"Liar." He gripped her hips roughly and brought her crashing down on him over and over, arching up to meet her every time. Her fingers grasped at his shoulders, her entire body tensing at once. He lost any modicum of control he might have been grasping to when Madeleine cried out, and it wasn't long before they were laying side by side, trying to catch their breath, their bodies humming a song only they knew.

Lee lovingly wrapped his arms around her, wanting to draw her close after her long absence. He relished the feeling of her skin, the mystery of how soft her body could be against his, the barely there smell of her body wash and perfume lingering. She was his home, and he wondered if it were possible she had ever thought the same of him.

Madeleine turned into him. "We shouldn't have done this."

Lee cradled her head in his hand and kissed her. "I'm still your husband. We can have sex whenever the hell we feel like it," he said between kisses that became more and more passionate.

Madeleine broke away. "I'm supposed to be clearing my head, figuring things out. How am I supposed to do that when you'll drive six hours just to fuck me?"

"I didn't drive six hours just to fuck you. I fully intend on taking you home with me."

"Are you even sure you want me because you love me and not just because you feel guilty?"

She sat up and turned away, rummaging for her clothes scattered in a trail across the floor.

He sat up. "Madeleine, I've sat here for weeks doing little more than trying to drink this all away. This hurts like hell. Please, just come back. I'll be everything you need me to be."

She stared at him like he'd grown a second head. "How exactly do you picture our lives working out from now on? How am I supposed to trust you?"

"I know it will take time, but I promise I will prove it to you."

"Time? More like the rest of our lives. I knew when you left and you didn't come back for months. I knew it. But I didn't want to listen to myself, didn't want it to be true. Then that…that *woman* sat across from me and told me how you had planned on divorcing me for her."

He shook his head in denial. "I never said that. I never indicated to her in any way I wanted to leave you."

Madeleine scoffed. "Lee, seriously? *Wanted* to leave? You already had left me! You were with her all that time! So maybe the words never came out of your mouth, but your actions said every word you wouldn't be man enough to say."

Lee was silent, mentally cursing. This was not the way he had wanted this to go, sex included. He stood and began searching for his clothes. "Did you mean it?" he asked.

"What?"

"When you said you didn't love me?"

"I don't know," she stated flatly. "I'm just…confused."

Lee took a sharp breath. He had to think of something to say that would convince her. "I lost my wedding band the morning you tried to kill yourself, Madeleine. I found it minutes later, but it sent me in a panic. I looked everywhere for it. I can remember how suffocating it felt, just missing a symbol that's so easily replaced. But I'm not going to find another Madeleine anywhere else."

She stood dazed for a moment, perhaps unsure what to say. Lee imagined for the tiniest moment that he was unearthing the love he'd buried deep below his sins. He stepped toward her and took her hand in his. Madeleine flinched at his touch and crossed her arms tight across her chest.

"Lee, I love you. There's not a doubt in my mind about that. But the simple truth is that I don't trust you, and I'm tired of being weak. I'm tired of *always* having to be saved by someone else. I can't get any peace about going back home with you."

Lee stood there a moment, a bit bowled over by what she had said. While he couldn't deny she had every reason to feel that way, he was becoming bitter. Madeleine was simply stringing him along at this point. She knew when she left that she was never coming back. "So we're just going to give up on our marriage, out of nothing but pride, because you don't want to look weak?"

She stared him down, her eyes narrowing in an angry, steely gaze. "I've done everything I possibly can. I may not have a ton of self-respect, but I've got just enough to say enough is enough."

"I've apologized over and over, Madeleine," Lee fumed. "I am doing everything I can to make this work, and nothing I do is good enough."

Madeleine   scoffed   in   open-mouthed

201

astonishment. "Nothing you do is good enough? What have you done? Came home? Been an actual husband?"

"Yes! It should show you that I am serious about fixing this!" he said, putting his hands on her shoulders as if the meager show of affection would appeal to her sensibilities. "I just want my wife and my old life back. I know I messed up, but I would do anything to get it back."

This time, Madeleine let the tears fall. Lee could tell they were not born out of sadness, but sheer exhaustion with the entire situation. "I know you would, Lee. I know," she sobbed. "It's all too little too late for me. I needed you. For six months I was completely alone, just dying for the occasions you would come home. Oh, you'd be drunk and a complete pain in the ass, but you'd be with me and that was all that mattered."

She paused for a moment to push away the tears rolling down her cheeks with the heel of her hand. "It took two slit wrists for you to care about me again. So please, tell me, why the hell would I want to be married to someone like you?"

Lee set his jaw and cast his eyes to the floor, his blue eyes burning into two dark embers. "It seems after you've had time to think, you know exactly what you want. I won't stand in your way. God knows I've made you miserable enough already."

He got out of the house as fast as he could. It was one thing for him to see her being weak; he was a man, he could take it. But Madeleine could never know just how much damage she had done. With tears streaming down his face, Lee sped off, wanting nothing more than to drink away the pain.

CHAPTER THIRTY-ONE

Doors slammed. First, the front door, shaking the glass in the windowpanes. Then the door to his Range Rover, the roar of the engine following soon after.

Tires squealed, and then there was nothing but pure, deafening silence.

Madeleine had to walk to the foyer just to make sure it was all real. Lee was gone. It was not until that moment, when she was sure he was gone, that Madeleine collapsed to her knees in the marble-tiled foyer, her mind processing what she had just done.

"That was it," she whispered aloud, fighting uncontrollable sobs. "I just ended our marriage. He'll never forgive me."

Every word rushed through her head in a sickening instant replay. *Why would I want to be married to someone like you?*

What had possessed her to say that? Why did she have to say the most hurtful thing she could think of?

A laugh resonated through the foyer, echoing all around her. "The real question is...why would he ever want to be married to someone like you?"

Madeleine cried even harder. Evelyn's stilettos clicked on the marble like a metronome. "Don't be too hard on yourself, Madeleine. You did good for poor white trash. It couldn't have lasted forever. It's going to be hard adjusting back to your old life, though."

Madeleine's sobs ebbed. "It's not about the money."

Evelyn gracefully stooped down to her level. "It's okay to admit you're afraid of losing it. You've never had anything. Your parents were too drunk to care enough to provide for you as long as they got to feed their habit."

"But I loved him. Love him, still. Even now. In a way."

"Ha! So that's why you said all those terrible things to him? That's not love."

"I was just saying what's been on my mind for months now. I was only standing up for myself...wasn't I? It was the right thing to do, wasn't it?"

Evelyn snickered, her pretty features contorting. "If you've got to question it, maybe it wasn't right."

Madeleine saw Evelyn through her tears, and though she hated to admit defeat, she nodded in agreement. Yet again, another failure she could blame on only herself. She had let Lee down, again, and she was about to pay the price for it.

"Don't you get tired of fighting every single

day? Aren't you simply exhausted?"

Evelyn's words were soothing, soft as a mother's kiss, but her eyes narrowed like a beast's that had spotted its prey. Madeleine didn't notice. She couldn't; she was too lost in her mind, drowning in what she perceived as wrongdoing.

The edges of her eyesight faded to velvet black as her heart pounded and her thoughts raced.

What am I doing? What's happening?

Henry Moore's even-toned voice filled her head. *"You're slipping into a dark place."*

He was right, she was. But oh, how good it was, this midnight oblivion of home. She was glad the anti-depressants couldn't find this place, existing despite chemical intervention. The human spirit could not be overcome by knock-off neurotransmitters. This was where she belonged. This was part of her.

"Let's do it right this time, Madeleine," Evelyn whispered. "Lee keeps a gun upstairs, in the safe, in the closet. He said he hoped he never had to use it, but he would, just to keep you safe. He loved you so much."

Madeleine settled into the black. "Yes," she agreed, happy to be home in her darkness once again. "I'll even say my goodbyes this time."

Evelyn rested her head on Madeleine's shoulder. "Stop fighting this worthless fight. The battle's almost over now."

Madeleine lost herself to the dark.

CHAPTER
THIRTY-TWO

"It's super nice of your parents to invite us over like this," Adrian lied as he pulled his SUV into a picturesque upper middle-class neighborhood.

It was one of those subdivisions where the same four house designs repeated over and over on just enough acreage to fool their owners into thinking they had privacy. Kids on their Christmas-gift hoverboards stopped in place when the unknown vehicle approached, staring in wide-eyed suspicion. Adrian could feel Emily glaring at him without even having to take his eyes off the street.

He dreaded being stuck in Statesboro the entire weekend, stuck with Emily's dad and high school-aged brother for company. When Emily, her mom, and her sisters got together, the men were ignored and left to their own devices.

"Please behave," Emily pleaded dully. "I don't want my family to think I'm marrying a complete asshole."

"They act weird around me," he whined. "Like they're scared to death."

"They're intimidated, Adrian. Why wouldn't they be?"

"What? Why? That makes no sense."

"Number one, you're ridiculously loaded. You're the billionaire everyone in this neighborhood pretends they are."

"Like I can help that."

"Number two, you're the vice president of a major corporation."

"Not by choice. At all."

"Number three, you're bourgeois."

"I am not!" Adrian protested. "I dressed normal, and I even drove my cheapest car today."

"You drove your brand new, $230,000 Mercedes G-Class. You're kind of a snob. Especially with cars."

"Still my cheapest car," Adrian quipped. "At least it wasn't the Aston."

Emily rolled her eyes. "And you wonder why they're intimidated."

"I live, breathe, and poop like everyone else! And I have never acted snobby around them," Adrian asserted as they pulled into the driveway of a two-story French-style McMansion.

"Just be nice. And don't talk about work, or trips we take, or major purchases. Better yet, just listen this weekend, okay?" Emily unbuckled her seat belt, and they stepped out of the car.

"Wow, I expected something like, 'Be yourself, Adrian, just show them the man I know and love, Adrian.'"

"I could tell you that, but it wouldn't be helpful," Emily replied. "Come on. Let's say hi first and you can give the excuse you have to bring our stuff in when the conversation gets too awkward for you. Or when you feel the urge to be bourgeoisie."

Adrian stopped on the faux-cobblestone walk, feeling more nervous than ever. "I am not bourgeoisie."

"Oh, come on, Adrian. I'm just playing with you. And they're expecting us."

She knocked on the door a few times, but got no response. Adrian noticed there were no lights on inside. "Where are they?"

"A hundred bucks says the door's unlocked."

"Normal people bet like five," Emily remarked, but she pressed down the door handle and, sure enough, the house was unlocked. "Okay, weird."

"You know what this is, right?"

"Oh my God, do you think they were robbed?" Emily gasped.

"I'd hate to spoil it for you. Go on in."

Emily glanced back at him with a worried expression. With a roll of his eyes, he stepped in front of her and put his hand on the door handle. "Come on, I'll protect you from the big, scary surprise party."

"Mom and Dad don't do surprise part—"

"Surprise!"

Adrian did his best to appear pleasantly surprised while Emily held her hands to her mouth, tears forming. After a pat at each eye, she hugged her mom and sisters and whatever random aunt, uncle, or cousin popped up. Most of the women wanted to see Emily's engagement ring, and as the men walked off in disinterest, they came by and gave Adrian a congratulatory pat on the back or knowing winks.

"How much did that ring set you back, Atwood?" Emily's uncle Craig asked.

"It's a family heirloom."

"You didn't cheap out on our girl, did you?"

"Ask her how much she figured her perfect wedding would cost and I'll let you decide," he laughed, genuinely trying to make a joke.

But Craig's face fell. "Well, it's not like you're hurting for it, eh?" He patted Adrian on the shoulder. "My niece is one of a kind. She deserves it."

"She does."

Craig disappeared in the crowd, chasing down some other relative. Adrian winced. Was this how Madeleine felt at parties? It was no wonder she hated them. He'd play Madeleine's signature move, latching onto Lee for dear life, and went to hunt down Emily, who had been whisked off to the living room along with every female present.

"Y'all remember how we met, right? I was doing a tour in photography, he was there for some class he was taking, and when we stopped to talk about this portrait of Henry Callahan's wife, he said—"

"I said she wasn't half as pretty as you," Adrian cut in with his best charming smile, which actually gleaned a positive response from the gaggle of women gathered around Emily to hear the story of his proposal.

"So here I am, three years later, doing the same

tour, same photograph, and I was just about to speak when he pipes up with the same line. He proposes in front of this whole crowd. I couldn't even finish the tour I was so emotional."

Questions flooded in. Adrian had heard fewer questions at press conferences, but Emily fielded them like a champ.

"So when's the wedding?"

"June sixteenth."

"Emily, that's so close! Can you plan it all in time?"

"It's a lot, because it's going to be huge. The guest list just for Adrian is insane. Apparently, when you own a big company, everyone else who owns a big company has to be invited to your wedding. Otherwise, it's bad for business. Gwynne Shotwell, president of SpaceX, is on the guest list. She probably won't come, but she's got to be invited nonetheless."

"She came to my brother's wedding," Adrian noted with a shrug.

The ladies exchanged expressions, but Adrian had a hard time deciding if they were impressed or annoyed at his apparent snobbery. His phone vibrated in his pocket, giving him the perfect reason to escape. Madeleine's name, and a rather dated picture of her and Lee, flashed on the screen.

"Hey, give me a minute." Adrian nodded toward his phone to Emily, and she gave him a dismissive wave. He said nothing until he was outside. Luckily, no one else wanted to face the January cold.

"Oh, thank God," he breathed, closing the patio

door behind him. "You just saved me from Emily's family."

"Oh, I'm sorry," Madeleine apologized. *"I didn't know you were with Emily."*

"No, no, please. You're a writer. Come up with some long, terrible, business-related issue I've got to put up with. These people hate me."

"They don't hate you."

"Oh, really? Come on up to Statesboro. You're rich. They'll hate you too."

"Are you sure you're not being stuck up?"

"That's what Emily said. I'm not a snob…am I?"

Silence. Then a twinge of worry. He remembered that July day not so long ago. "Madeleine?"

"I just want you to know no one ever showed me the same kindness you did," she sputtered. *"Ever since our first day in chemistry you took the seat next to me, told me that stupid joke."*

"Impossible. My jokes are awesome," Adrian quipped, trying hard to tamp down the concern in his voice. "What do you call cheese that's not yours?"

Madeleine laughed lightly. *"Na-cho cheese."*

There was a long pause.

"Maddie, you know I care about you, right? I always have. I'll never stop."

"I know," she whispered. *"You're the only one. I didn't mean to interrupt your engagement party. Give my apologies to Emily."*

"No, no, you're fine. Talk to me."

"No, Adrian, go enjoy your party. Go be with Emily."

Adrian swallowed, overtaken by a fear he could

not explain, a fear he knew meant something more. "Just tell me the truth. You're not all right, are you?"

"I'm fine," Madeleine argued weakly. *"Don't worry about me."*

"It's too late for that. I'll drive down there right now if I have to."

"Goodbye, Adrian."

"Maddie, don't—"

He could hear the dull roar of the ocean.

"Madeleine Atwood, don't you dare hang up on me!" A cracking sound emanated from the speaker, and the call dropped.

"Adrian, what's going on?" Emily said, placing a hand on the back of his shoulder.

He turned to her, a pain he could not expect welling up inside him. For a moment, he didn't know how to answer because his mind could not come to terms with it. His mind was already calculating the distance divided by the top speed of his car. How fast could he get to Tybee?

"Adrian?"

"I think that was Maddie's rendition of a suicide note," he admitted. "She sounded like she had been crying, and she kept telling me how she'd never forget how kind I'd been."

"Okay, hold on a minute. Just because she was upset and feeling sentimental does not mean she was going to kill herself. You said it yourself— she's not going to commit suicide just because she's upset."

"No, something's definitely up. She was different. She's been better lately and that—it wasn't the same. I need to go."

Emily pursed her lips together. "No," she objected, "you don't."

Adrian looked at her, a fire already blazing inside. He tried to shake it off, unwilling to be angry with her. "I'm not even wasting time discussing this." He stepped away from her.

Emily caught his arm and tugged on it. "Call Lee and let him handle this," she begged. "He's her husband. He should be the one saving her. Besides, it might do them some good."

He paused, studying Emily's face, and saw the concern in her eyes. *Cool it,* Adrian told himself.

He called his brother's cell. Lee should have arrived back in Atlanta a couple of hours ago, but Adrian hadn't heard from him since he'd called that morning to tell him what a disaster the entire trip had been. His phone went to voicemail after a few rings, but he kept calling, pacing around the patio nervously.

All Adrian could think of was ticking seconds, wondering how fast the company jet could be ready for takeoff if he called now, if they could have a car ready for him to take from Savannah to the island. No, it would be faster to drive from Statesboro.

"Damn it," Adrian cursed. "He's probably drunk again."

Emily crossed her arms tightly, her face twisting into one of the sourest expressions she had ever given him. She was seething. "Go. Just…leave before I throw some ugly fit I'll regret later."

"Come with me," he insisted, partially out of fear. He didn't want to do this alone.

"Not a snowball's chance in hell! If she has done something, I certainly don't want to see it. You didn't sleep for weeks the last time. And this party is a big deal for my parents," she declared with the same sour expression.

If the circumstances were any different, he would have apologized for being so crass and insensitive, but his practicality forced him to press a kiss to her lips and promise to be back the next morning. For the first time since he had laid eyes on her, there were things in his life more important than Emily.

CHAPTER THIRTY-THREE

You shouldn't be here, Lee's exhausted conscience chastised.

"Fuck you," Lee grumbled. He knew it wouldn't keep her from divorcing him, but it helped to numb the pain.

"Can I get another glass of Jack?"

"Sure can, sweetheart," the cute bartender replied, bending over the ice chest in her shorter-than-short shorts to refill his glass.

"Just leave the bottle." Lee pushed a hundred-dollar bill toward her.

She looked at the bill in surprise and replied, "No problem, darlin.'"

He poured another glass and drank it in a few greedy gulps, like it was a medicine that might take the pain away, to help him forget her. But he had never been able to forget about her. Why would that change now?

Another glass.

Guzzle it down.

Pour another.

Drink another.

The world around him faded away, molecules at a time, until everything went dark. Another glass and the world started slipping away. Soon, all that would be left was his Darkness, and Madeleine would be lost to him forever.

"I think you've had enough, man."

Glass in hand. Glass against his lips. Swallow and swallow again.

Laughing. It sounded foreign, but the longer he listened to it, the more he remembered.

Sunlight.

He could remember the sunlight burning his skin. The hot sand, the remnants of her kiss on his lips. Her laugh…the way it made him swell with peace, with unadulterated happiness.

"Mom had a dream you lost your wedding ring on the beach. Could be a bad omen."

Her smile was infectious. He always caught it instantly.

"That would be impossible," Madeleine had said. *"It's a perfect fit, and I'm never taking it off my finger."*

A rush of cool night air stole away his reverie, and the awareness he wasn't with Madeleine overcame him. That seconds-long feeling of peace faded into the darkness of night. He heard her laugh again, but this time it was mocking. Lee stumbled to collide with concrete. She laughed again, then it faded into the darkness.

CHAPTER
THIRTY-FOUR

His mind had not ceased racing since Madeleine had uttered the words, "Goodbye, Adrian." He'd kept a close eye on the time, mentally dividing remaining distance by his ever-increasing speed. His thumb drummed on the steering wheel, mirroring his heartbeat. He saw her in his mind, mere minutes from death, her skin so pale, her heartbeat so faint…

He had to push those thoughts out of his mind and replace them with something better.

A glance at the full moon, shining bright in the distance, made him think of "Moonlight Serenade" and the Swan Ball. In its own way, it had been an extraordinary night. The misfit girl he'd always cared for had blossomed again in her emerald gown that fit like a glove, her blonde hair swept up in a wispy coif, framing her ethereal face. How many heads had she turned without even the faintest clue? Even though she'd been knocked down, she'd gotten right back up and danced with him, facing the crowd even though she was nervous and scared. Even now, he could feel her palm in his, his hand wrapped around her silken waist, but most of all he remembered she had smiled again.

It was enough to keep him going full speed the last few miles. If anyone in the entire world deserved to be happy, it was her.

Adrian geared down his Mercedes, desperately wishing for the considerably faster Aston Martin he had left behind in an attempt to appear less intimidating to Emily's family.

He pulled up to the house he'd been to a million times before, his mind already flooded with the possibilities, and he had to admit he was fearful of most of them. Despite it all, Adrian dashed out of the car and ran full out toward the beach, thinking of the crashing waves he heard just as she hung up the phone.

"Madeleine!" he shouted into the darkness, hoping and praying for a reply. He kept running until his shoes hit sand. He reached the water's edge, the darkest parts of his mind searching for her body on the waves, while his ever-present optimism searched for the same flower of a woman clad in an emerald dress. Meanwhile, he pleaded with God for her to be alive, even if the likelihood of that faded with every passing second she didn't respond to his calls.

He had to push through, get the negative out of his mind. He didn't want her to go. He wanted her to be happy.

"Adrian?"

He turned around, and there she was, walking down the shoreline, barefoot. Her face was barely visible in the moonlight, but he could tell she had been crying. Lee's handgun was hanging slack in her right hand. He locked his eyes on it, his jaw dropping as his heart wrenched inside him.

Tears welled in his eyes. He had been right; she was going to do it. This time, she would have succeeded.

"Maddie, please, don't tell me you were—"

She gave him a pitiful stare, then grasped the barrel of the gun and offered it to him. "I was going to. I stopped myself."

Adrian took the gun, deftly released the clip, and emptied the chamber. He shoved the gun in his pocket and pitched the clip out to sea as far as he could throw it. They both watched it arc out over the moonlit bay before it made impact with the water and sank into the dark depths.

Then there was only the roar of the waves, the only sound in the world. Adrian heard a hitch in her breath, followed by a sniff, but he kept his eyes out over the water, trying to sort out what he was feeling before he had to face her.

At first, he was angry. What the ever-loving hell was wrong with her? How could she be so damned selfish?

Then his own breath caught in his throat, a lone tear rolling down his cheek. She wasn't supposed to matter this much. But the possibility of her permanent absence from his life caused a pain that would be impossible to overcome.

She rested her hand on his upper arm. "Adrian,"

she choked. His heart was breaking down to ruins for her. "Don't...I couldn't pull the trigger. I couldn't stop thinking about you and Lee. I promise I'm okay now."

Adrian abruptly turned toward her, angry with her for even thinking about harming herself. "Don't you have any idea how much we love you? Do you have any idea how much it hurt to see you dying once already, with nothing I could do to stop it?"

"You did stop it. You saved me, Adrian. You've been saving me since the first day I met you!" Madeleine cried. "You have no idea what you mean to me because I've never told you. Isn't it funny how we waste so much time not saying the things that matter the most? We never tell people how important they are until it's too late."

His eyes blurred with unshed tears, Adrian said, "I'm sorry if I've never told you. I wish I would have sooner if it could have saved you even the tiniest bit of pain."

Madeleine tried offering him a reassurance that he had done everything in his power, but it was accompanied by more tears. "When I think about it, you're the best thing that ever happened to me. You encouraged me. You were my only friend for the longest time."

He swallowed and did as emotion and instinct dictated. He wrapped her in his arms. He needed so very much to feel her alive and breathing, still here on this Earth. She melded into his embrace. Adrian's heart was pounding but gradually slowed to a steady pace. The peace of the world righted again.

The threat of her death made him express things he should have kept inside.

"Then stop trying so damn hard to leave me," he whispered.

Her breathing slowed, but Adrian could sense her electric pulse; her heart was flying. He slipped his willful hands down her back, while something in the back of his mind kept whispering something unintelligible, urging and begging for something…

The only thought resonating in his mind was the inevitability of what was about to happen, the sneaking suspicion he'd wanted it to happen for far longer than he'd dare admit.

The second their lips met, the memory of her taste was instantly refreshed. It was an unexplainable sensation, different from anyone else he had ever kissed. While there was no bursting of supernovas or fireworks, the entire world ceased to exist for just a few, slow, moments lingering on into the dark night. His entire body felt as if it may combust, every nerve firing as her body weakened in his arms.

The nagging something in the back of his mind came calling, a reminder there was a real world outside this fantasy (madness?) with real consequences. *This is wrong. Pull away from her. Apologize and leave…you have to. God, this can't be real…*

"Maddie," he half protested, half sighed in the relief that could only brought by the release of a darkest desire.

Pushing away, Madeleine began a stumbling apology, already shouldering the blame. "I know. I shouldn't have. I just couldn't—"

Adrian silenced her with another kiss. He could taste the skepticism and fear in her lips, but Madeleine gave up and wrapped her arms over his shoulders, around his neck, as he drank at her lips.

He'd only dared even imagine this a handful of times, though he remembered the way they had kissed at prom so long ago. All he wanted to do now was savor it while he could. It might have been be the last time in life he could be so close to her.

Then she broke their kiss, separating from him. Her absence was like falling through ice. A shocking pang filled his chest as Madeleine withdrew from him. For a moment they just stared at each other, Madeleine's eyes wide in disbelief.

"What are we doing?" she asked, her expression utter panic.

Stunned, Adrian just stood there, eyes fixed on her. For a moment, he could think of nothing to say. What the hell *was* he doing? Where did that come from?

Yet he didn't feel the crushing guilt, the self-loathing he had always expected to feel should he betray Emily. Where was it? Surely he was supposed to feel it.

His characteristic facetiousness came to his defense, trivializing the situation as best he could. "Most people call it kissing," he joked, trying to swallow back his disquiet.

She glared at him, incredulous, then startled, realizing the magnitude of the mistake they had made.

"Oh my God. I-I kissed you," she stammered,

pacing back toward the house.

"Madeleine," Adrian followed her, "it was a kiss. We had one weak moment. We were both very understandably upset."

"I'm married. You're engaged. We're not supposed to have a weak moment. Weak moments get people hurt."

Adrian could not bear to tell her otherwise. After all, she knew better than anyone. He stood frozen in place, knowing she needed space after their unexpected encounter.

For a long time, he stood there on the shore, looking out to the dark Atlantic, watching the waves crash on the shore. In his mind, he was trying to identify the emotion he was experiencing, but it simply wouldn't come to him.

The closest thing he could get to an emotion was the remnants of her kiss on his lips. But why it didn't make him sear with guilt was beyond him.

CHAPTER THIRTY-FIVE

"What have you done?" Evelyn shrieked. "Are you crazy?!"

Madeleine shut the bedroom door, turned around, and glared at Evelyn. Tears distorted her vision, but she didn't let it dampen her fire. "Yes, Evelyn, I *am* crazy. I think we've proven that together time and time again."

"Finally, something we can agree on tonight. How could you?"

"Weren't you just encouraging it a week ago? Telling me how handsome he was, how perfect he was? Damn it, Evelyn, make up your mind! Quit telling me one thing to have me do another!"

Evelyn laughed. "You are insane! I am you! Isn't that what you've been telling me all the time? You made me, you made your darkness. You're the one who wants Adrian. You've always wanted him."

Madeleine's eyes filled with tears as she went on the defensive. "I put that away! Back into my darkness. It wasn't for anyone to see, even me. Yes, I know I've wanted him, but I chose Lee, so I hid all those thoughts away."

"Until now," Evelyn pointed out.

"Until now. And that will be as close as these wicked little thoughts will ever get to reality."

There was a knock at the door. "Maddie?"

Evelyn huffed. "He's nothing if not persistently heroic, with annoyingly good timing."

Madeleine shored herself up and took a quick breath, willing her voice not to tremble when she responded. "Yes?" She almost succeeded.

"I just wanted to make sure you were all right."

She opened the bedroom door. "I'm fine, Adrian. I promise, I'll be…"

And then something in her just…broke. She couldn't lie anymore. Not to him. How could she explain it? She was so confused, and everything, every decision, every wrong turn, hurt. She was so tired of the pain. It was time to heal, but she didn't know how.

"Maddie," he said again, worry dripping. She didn't want him to have to be this concerned over her, to feel he had to fix all her broken.

But she needed him, needed the healing so long overdue. She wrapped her arms around him, and his arms were waiting.

He cradled her face against his chest, his hands on her hair, her back, assuring her he could keep her protected from all the bad in the world. She sobbed, giving up all the pain she'd been harboring inside since the day she'd left Lee.

Madeleine wasn't sure when the decision had

been made, but by the time she'd run out of tears, she was lying on his chest staring into the dark abyss of the bedroom ceiling. Adrian had wrapped his arm around her in a protective hold, and his thumb chased the last few tears from her face.

"You remember what we did after prom?" he asked in a slow, drowsy tone.

"The exact same thing we're doing right now. I told you I didn't want to go home, so we stayed all night at your parents' cabin in Blue Ridge. You were such a perfect gentleman. You just held me. But back then, we were drunk, and I wasn't a squalling ball of mess. I think it was the first time I'd gone to sleep truly happy since I was a kid."

The waves crashed, but Madeleine thought the sound of his heartbeat was infinitely more soothing.

"I should have told you then," he murmured, barely audible, even in the silent room.

Her heart pounded. She didn't understand why it made her so jittery.

"Told me what?"

Adrian didn't answer. He was asleep by the time she had finished the question.

CHAPTER THIRTY-SIX

Lee felt the bile rising. First, it rumbled in his stomach, rising quickly to his mouth. The vile substance spewed from him, affording him just enough clarity to stumble to his car.

As he shakily flopped into his driver's seat, he found the key was already in his hand. Fighting the unsteadiness of his own body, he fumbled to fit the key into the ignition. The engine purred to life, and he turned the air conditioning to maximum. He lay back in his seat, fishing through his pockets for his phone. The comforting weight centered him slightly, the bright familiar screen bringing some focus to his eyes. His fingers, though they were thick and fat, dialed the familiar number.

It rang and rang until he had almost given up. The bright red "end call" button flashed before him, daring him to press it before he could hear her voice again.

"Hi, you've reached Madeleine Atwood. Leave a

message and I'll get back to you."

Madeleine Atwood…He loved the sound of his last name tacked onto hers.

The red button called his name again, and he did not resist. He dialed the same number again when the keypad reappeared. Again and again, until he was sure he'd heard the name Madeleine Atwood a thousand times.

Why keep calling? the Darkness asked. *She doesn't want to speak to you.*

Just to hear her. Just to hear how nice 'Madeleine Atwood' sounds.

Madeleine is never coming back to you.

She will. She must.

But she doesn't need you, the Darkness replied smugly. *Not anymore. You've fucked up for the last time, Lee Atwood.*

But I'll go crazy without her.

Maybe you already are. Just let her go. She's already left you behind. You'd be better off calling up that whore you've been fucking around with.

Brecklyne. It took an enormous amount of effort for his fingers to dial her number, long deleted from his memory, even longer from his phone. Two wrong numbers later, Brecklyne's drowsy tone caused him to cringe with regret.

"Lee?"

He barked a short laugh, harsh and rough as it bubbled from his throat. "I can always rely on you."

"Jesus," she hissed. *"You're drunk, aren't you?"*

Another laugh, this one hurt less. "Maddie left me. She's not…she's never coming back."

A sigh, some muttering. *"Where are you right now? Are you at home or are you out?"*

"I'm always at home in the ATL."

"I'm coming to get you. Do you even know what bar you're at?"

He snorted. "The usual."

"All right, don't you dare even get in the car. I'll be there in twenty, okay?"

"I don't think we should see each other."

"It's all out in the open now, Lee. What's Maddie going to do? She can't leave you twice."

"She doesn't want to be my wife. I love her, though."

Silence. A sharply drawn breath, suspended. *"I know you do. Stay there. Don't go anywhere."*

Although Lee agreed to do as she said, he didn't want to see her. He couldn't look at her without hating himself.

He turned the key in the ignition, engine sputtering in protest since it was already running. With some creative maneuvering and a miracle, he made it out of the parking lot and onto Fifth Street.

Amber streetlamps lined Peachtree Street. They marched past him, one at a time, slow at first. Then faster.

His fingers fumbled for Madeleine's number yet again.

"Hi, you've reached Madeleine Atwood. Leave a message and I'll get back to you."

"I love you, Madeleine Atwood," he said. "I always have."

The Range Rover began to veer, first left, then right, and left again. Headlights blinded him as his head pounded. He could feel her again, the hot sand, a kiss on his lips.

Then the sun exploded. Heat surged over his body, spiraling through the darkness that engulfed him. Her laughter turned to screams, her kiss turned to blinding pain. His body was ripping at the very seams of his being as the world went black.

CHAPTER THIRTY-SEVEN

Madeleine paused before the doors of the ICU. She had practically run there, through the twisting, turning halls of Emory University Hospital, Adrian trailing close behind. Now they were here, and she sensed a sinking sickness in her gut.

Maybe it was the realization she was about to see Lee, battered and bruised to an extent she wasn't sure of, or was is it the idea just six months ago they were in exactly opposite roles? She was the broken one; he was the guilty one. It was almost easier to be the broken one.

Adrian stood at her side, waiting for her to make the first move. "Are you ready?"

Madeleine didn't look back at him to answer. Looking at him was too hard. He grasped her hand, and their eyes met.

Seeing Adrian's face, as guilt-ridden and lined with worry as her own, everything inside her burst. "I can't do this. Not after last night. Not after being so horrible to him," she said, casting her eyes to the floor. She would have cried, but there simply were no more tears left to shed.

Adrian squeezed her hand as if he knew the direction of her thoughts. He understood; having to face Lee, the damage she felt she had inflicted herself, was a load she was not ready to bear.

"We will figure this out. I promise," Adrian said. "You've been through hell and you're still standing. You are so much stronger than you think you are."

Madeleine tightened her grip on his hand, reluctant to let go. She took a deep breath, and they pushed through the double doors together. In a haze of fear and her pounding heart, she told the receptionist their names.

"There's only supposed to be two of you back there, not three. You should mention that before security has to," she noted in a terse tone.

"Three?" Adrian asked, but Madeleine breezed past the desk and wandered down the hall. As she approached his room, the last on the hall, her steps slowed. She could hear Adrian's long strides quickly catching up to her.

"Maddie, wait—"

Her jaw fell as she walked through the glass doors. Between all the bruises and cuts, she was in disbelief that this man lying helpless in a hospital bed was her husband. Everything sank inside her.

"He keeps coming in and out," Maggie Beth said, hugging Madeleine. "I know he's been waiting on you."

She had not even processed who all was in the room. Peering over Maggie Beth's shoulders, she saw Richard, his eyes swollen, trained on Lee's every breath.

And then the entire world went red for a moment.

"She is his wife. Doesn't that mean anything to you?"

Madeleine turned to see Adrian standing before Brecklyne, pleading with her to leave from the second Madeleine had entered the room.

"He called *me*! I came, not her. I have just as much right as anyone!"

"Just leave. Please. You've seen him. You can't keep doing this to her."

Every molecule of hate that had festered inside her since the day she'd first laid eyes on this woman, the one who had made her life a living hell, took up residence in her chest.

"I believe my brother-in-law has asked you to leave as politely as he knows how, given the circumstances." Madeleine kept her voice flat and even, a stark contrast to her inner rage.

"I am not leaving him! And none of you can tell me otherwise!" Brecklyne looked to each of them. "I am the one who has been here since they brought him in off the ambulance. I called his parents. I've been here for him, while you've been off God-knows-where with his brother!"

"You'd best thank God you're a woman," Adrian growled amidst instantaneous protests from Richard and Maggie Beth.

The dull complaints had risen into impassioned yelling within seconds. Madeleine looked toward Lee, who was thankfully sleeping, but beginning to stir.

"Would you all pipe the hell down?!" she yelled above all the commotion.

The room silenced, all of them dumbstruck over her newfound assertiveness, but Madeleine's gaze was zeroed in on Brecklyne. "I want all of you to leave right now, except her. We have a few things to clear up. After that, you'll all follow normal procedures around here until Lee is better, is that clear? And I mean it, Richard, you bribe one single nurse and I will know about it."

Richard huffed, but Maggie Beth walked out, guiding Richard along.

"Come on," Adrian told his parents. "We'll come back later."

Without a word, Maggie Beth and Richard gathered their things and left the room, followed by Adrian. Madeleine went to close the door behind him.

"You don't have to do this by yourself," he whispered before walking out, throwing a glance toward Brecklyne.

"And you can't save me this time."

Adrian nodded and shut the door, leaving her to speak to Brecklyne for the first time since she'd made the announcement that had turned her already shattered world upside down. Turning around to face her, Madeleine filled with almost overwhelming fear and trepidation, but she knew above all, she was going to let this woman know who exactly who she was and what she stood for.

"Whether you like it or not, I am his wife," Madeleine stated confidently, "not you. And you

235

never will be because he doesn't love you. You have no right to be here, and I will not hesitate to file a restraining order against you. He's got plenty of lawyers who would love to make your life a living hell."

"Bitch, I'd like to see you try," Brecklyne spat.

"You're going to leave, and you're not coming back."

"Like hell I will." Brecklyne's jaw clenched in anger. "You can't talk to me like that. I don't care who you think you are. You're no more his wife than I am. He was talking about divorcing you long before you decided to kill yourself."

Inside, Madeleine knew something was rising, something not quite…her. Something more…Evelyn.

A low laugh, one Madeleine could only describe as evil, emanated from her core. "Oh, you poor, poor thing. You knew you'd struck gold with him from the second you met him, didn't you? You're not stupid, I'll give you that. You saw the Armani suit, the Bulgari watch, the two-hundred-dollar haircut, the things on the surface. But you saw even more than that, didn't you? Was it the swagger that all the money in the world couldn't buy? Or was it that fancy Harvard education seeping out of every word he spoke?"

"If you're saying I was only interested in his money—"

"Hardly. It became more than that. You love him in your own way; that much is obvious. But it didn't happen that way for Lee, did it? You've questioned the entire time if he was ever going to fully give himself to you."

Brecklyne looked lost for a moment but recovered quickly, ready to spew more insults.

Madeleine didn't allow her to get the first word out of her mouth.

"I know he talked about divorcing me. But he never said it with quite the determination you wanted. And when he did mention it, it was for my benefit, not his. He loves me. Not even twenty-four hours ago, he was begging me to come home. Has Lee ever begged you for anything?"

"He's never had to!" Brecklyne erupted. "I've bent over backwards since I've met him to make him happy. I did it when you wouldn't. I was there for him when you wouldn't speak to him or even look at him. Do you have any clue how much he's talked about you? How much you've done your equal share of hurt?"

Madeleine swallowed, taking a dose of her own medicine. Every single memory flashed before her eyes. She knew she was guilty of shutting Lee out after they lost Thomas. Nothing could ever justify what her husband did, but there was no ignoring Lee had been hurt too, and he'd been no more able to deal with his pain than she was. They simply chose different outlets—she a knife, and he an affair.

"I know he loves you," Brecklyne choked. "He called me, just before the accident, and you're all he would talk about. What little time he could speak before they operated on him, gasping to even live, all he kept saying was, 'Tell Maddie I loved her.'"

Madeleine felt as if all the oxygen had been

drained from the room. "Past tense."

"He had to think he was dying, but you were the only person he was thinking about. As bad as his body hurt, it can't compare with how my heart hurts."

The room was beginning to rotate side to side. She couldn't appear weak, not yet, so she stood straight up to stare down the expression of sheer defeat reflected from deep within Brecklyne. It was an expression Madeleine had seen on herself a thousand times in the mirror.

"You won't have to worry about me coming back. I'll just be happy to have you people out of my life."

"The feeling is mutual," Madeleine growled. Tears welled in Brecklyne's eyes. The last lingering gaze she gave Lee before stepping out of the room was near-heartbreaking. The second the automatic doors shut behind Brecklyne, Madeleine thought she might collapse.

She turned toward Lee, surprised to see his eyes open.

"There's my beautiful girl," he murmured in what could barely be described as a whisper.

Madeleine went to him, grasping his hand. She finally could allow herself to process everything. The tubes in his nose were a good sign; he could breathe well enough on his own without a ventilator.

Richard had explained what had happened the second she and Adrian had landed. Lee had swerved onto the sidewalk close to St. Mark's Church. The speed and trajectory was just enough to make the

Range Rover roll over to the driver's side. Between the side airbags being deployed and the rollover, a few ribs had cracked and punctured his left lung. His femur was broken in multiple places, but he had made it through with minimal pelvic injury. Lee had had the wherewithal to put on a seatbelt before driving off, but otherwise, the police were convinced the wreck would have killed him. It was a thought Madeleine could not bear to linger on for even a second's time.

"I'm...so...sorry," Lee gasped.

"Shhhh...don't talk," Madeleine breathed. "You need to rest. I'm here now."

"Don't leave," he said fearfully, grasping her hand with as much strength as he could muster.

"I wouldn't leave you for the whole world," Madeleine vowed without a second thought.

She clenched her hand around his, and before she could even tear her eyes away from the bruises and scratches on his arm, Lee had fallen completely asleep.

CHAPTER THIRTY-EIGHT

Adrian breathed a sigh of complete exhaustion and relief and opened the door of his darkened apartment. He could hear the familiar, dull roar of Atlanta traffic and the distant cry of a police siren as he tossed his keys on a table in the entry. His only thought was of slipping into his bed and into a long, all-consuming rest. A guaranteed eight-ten-twelve hour stretch where he didn't have to think about Madeleine, Lee, Emily, or the rest of his family. He meandered like a zombie down the hallway, counting the steps all the way to the bed.

When he swung open the bedroom door, he had to stop himself from letting out a groan.

Emily was furiously shoving clothing into her suitcase and barely acknowledged his presence when he entered the room.

"Emily, what are you doing?" he asked in a tired sigh.

She did not reply.

Adrian stood there, both awaiting her response and being too tired to care what she had to say.

"What does it look like I'm doing?" she responded tersely. "I'm taking my things home."

"And you would be doing this why?"

Emily threw the blouse in her hands into the suitcase and glared at him. "You even have to ask?! First, you just leave our engagement party to go rescue Princess Prozac, then don't even call to let me know what was going on! I had to find out about Lee over Facebook. I've gone from being part of your family to less than an afterthought!"

His guilt had been steadily building from the moment he'd answered his mother's phone call that Lee had been in an accident. Now it crashed over him like a tidal wave.

"Don't you have anything to say for yourself? Aren't you going to argue with me like you always do?"

"No. I'm not. I have no reason to argue with you. You're right. I should have called you the second I knew Madeleine was going to be all right. I should have called you before we got on the plane to come home or when we got to the hospital. But I didn't, and that was wrong. I'm sorry. I've asked you to be my wife, but I'm not treating you like one."

Hadn't he hated how Lee's actions fueled his need to be the one person who saved Madeleine from every heartbreak? Or had it been an innate need to protect her in the first place? Either way, he'd been acting just like Lee and hurting Emily for nothing but his own selfish desires. He couldn't allow that to happen. Emily had done nothing but love him.

"Em, I'm so sorry. You've got every right to leave, but please don't."

Emily's eyes filled with tears, full of an ominous sorrow. Though he felt determined to never make the same mistake again, he somehow knew this wouldn't be the last time she'd cry on his account.

She threw her arms around him and he held her close. Her body was so familiar, yet so different now in a way he could not explain.

I'm going to make this work...I have to make this work, Adrian chanted in his head like a mantra. Yet the same doubts kept creeping about. Every time he promised himself he wouldn't dare stray again, his mind kept churning, *Madeleine, Madeleine, Madeleine...*

"It's not even like I can actually leave," Emily whispered through her tears. "I barely have anything here. Just a few outfits and junk. I'm not even a part of your home."

"See? Wouldn't you rather move all your stuff in, so the next time we have a fight you can drag half the house with you?"

She only cried more. "You don't want me moving in until we get married."

Which was true. There were a few of Maggie Beth's Methodist values he clung to whether or not it was hypocritical, and more for his mother's sake than his own. Since he hadn't even been sure he wanted to propose in the first place, asking Emily to move in with him had been the last thing on his mind. Now was the time to let Emily know he loved her, that he was serious about the commitment he

242

would make to be her husband. "We're almost married. The wedding's only five months from now. Close enough, right?"

Emily backed away as her face twisted into an analytical glare. "You don't want me moving in. You're just thinking I won't be upset with you anymore."

"It's not that. We've made a commitment to each other. What's wrong with moving on to the next step?"

"Because that's not your next step, Adrian. What makes you think I want you to sacrifice everything to just try to appease me? Oh, Emily's always wanted to move in, so I'll ask her to next time she's about to leave me," she mocked.

Adrian started to speak, but his mind went back over the words she had just said. "Wait—the next time? Implying there was a first time you were going to leave?"

Emily was caught off guard for a moment but quickly recovered. "That's not what I meant. Quit trying to change the subject."

"No, that's exactly what you meant. When were you planning on breaking up with me before?"

"I was never planning on breaking up with you."

He looked at her incredulously. "You were going to do it, but I proposed."

Frustrated, Emily pressed her lips together, glaring. Adrian kept his eyes fixed on hers, expectant.

"Fine," she fumed, her fists clenched. "We had been together for three years already. Every time I talked about getting married, it was like you were disgusted. I don't want to be a girlfriend for the rest of my life, Adrian. I want to get married; I want children. What's so wrong with that?"

"That. You said it exactly, just now." A feeling of betrayal rose, although Adrian realized his own hypocrisy.

"What did I say?"

"That you want to get married. That you want to have children. Not that you want to marry me or have kids with me, just that you want those things. Like you're ticking items off a list. It doesn't matter what man, as long as he's willing to put a ring on your finger and give you his last name, is that right?"

Emily pressed the engagement ring into his hand. "There. Now you won't have to worry about me marrying you for anything. Least of all for the sake of just having a husband."

Before he could even protest, she had gathered her things and walked out the door.

"Damn it," he hissed, grasping the ring so tight the setting pierced his skin. "Emily!"

His apartment door slammed shut, silence ringing in his ears.

He wanted to call Lee. Lee would tell him he was better off without her, pour him a drink, and make him feel better, whether he deserved to feel better or not. What the hell happened? Just yesterday, life was all figured out. His parents would simply berate him and blame the entire situation on him. There was no one he could talk to about this.

Only Madeleine.

CHAPTER THIRTY-NINE

Madeleine awoke with a start to the familiar muffled sounds of the hospital room. Bright daylight stung her eyes, sending colorful floaters dancing across her line of sight. Blinking her vision clear, she glanced toward the bed, where Lee was sleeping peacefully. The sight of his bruised and battered body was a shock to her. Every time she looked, she found a new bruise or scratch, some mark she hadn't noticed before.

She stood, ignoring her sore and tense muscles resulting from stress and sleeping in the single chair that fit in the tiny ICU room. The mere rise and fall of his chest was a wonder now, as was the steady tick of his heart rate. How such simple things could be lost in an instant.

She ran her fingers through his hair, trying her best to make it look presentable. Lee would never show how fussy he was about his appearance, but Madeleine knew he was.

Needs a good combing, Madeleine noted. *Maybe Maggie Beth will bring some things later.*

His eyelids scrunched and fluttered. Madeleine backed away, but his hand brushed against hers in a feeble attempt to catch it. Her fingers, moving by instinct, grasped his, and she went back to him, sitting on the side of his bed and holding his hand.

Lee gazed at her with weary eyes. He opened his mouth to speak, but he gave a sputtering cough instead. He winced in pain and held his left side where his ribs had broken. Madeleine didn't know what to do other than stand there feeling useless while he fought the pain.

Finally, he regained some semblance of control over the pain.

"Lee, what do you need? Do you want some water?"

He nodded and began another coughing fit. Madeleine didn't even have to press the nurse call button before one had entered the room.

"Are we having us a good cough? Coughing is good. It lets us know everything is working. We'll get him something for the pain."

"Please," Lee croaked.

"Leia, can you get Mr. Atwood's pain medication?" the nurse called into a small silver intercom Madeleine had not even noticed on the wall behind Lee's bed. "I'm Darla, by the way. Very nice to meet you both."

"Thanks. He said he was thirsty." Madeleine cleared her throat, tight from the threat of tears.

"I'll get him some ice water and send up for some lunch. But I were you, I wouldn't eat from the cafeteria after breakfast. Just a friendly warning," Darla added like she was telling a very grave secret.

She had left and was back within two awkward, silent minutes, much to Madeleine's temporary relief. Darla handed her a nondescript Styrofoam cup with a green bendy-straw and left them to their devices.

The very idea made Madeleine's stomach flutter in anxiety.

She sat on the side of his bed and held the straw to Lee's lips so he could drink.

He drained half the water in one long sip and settled back against his pillow. It brought tears to her eyes.

"Why are you crying?" he asked, his voice hoarse but already sounding better.

"Look at you, Lee. This is all my fault!"

"Don't. It was my stupid decision."

"I was horrible to you."

"I haven't exactly given you a lot of reasons to even speak to me, much less roll over and give me everything I want." Lee took a shaky breath and coughed again. Madeleine offered him the straw, and he took a long drink.

"You were trying, fighting. I wasn't. I gave up the second I went to Tybee."

"Also my stupid idea."

Madeleine put her hand on his arm. "I wish I knew how to fix this."

"Me too." He placed his hand over hers.

CHAPTER FORTY

"I just…I can't believe it," Maggie Beth declared, her hand over her heart. "She was so perfect for you. Why would you just let her walk out, Adrian?"

Adrian wondered the same. Was it because he was just still reeling from everything that had happened? Or could he have just been so completely apathetic at the time that it didn't matter?

There was the matter of Madeleine, but Adrian didn't even dare question if she were the real cause. If she was, even on some subconscious level, he'd rather not know about it.

They were sitting in a waiting room outside the room where Lee was going through his first physical therapy treatment.

"I don't know, Mom." He shrugged. "I was so out of it, I guess."

"Don't you think you should call her and try to work it out?"

"Absolutely not! He's right!" his father cut in. "I

think she wasn't only after a husband, she was after your money too."

"Dad—"

"Richard, really? She was going to, and still could be, our daughter-in-law. Do you have to be so crass?" Maggie Beth chastised.

Madeleine passed yet another tissue and Maggie Beth took it gratefully. Adrian watched his mother dab at her eyes gently, then moved his eyes to Madeleine, sitting next to her. He could tell her thoughts were running rampant as she stared at the floor, biting her lip.

"Adrian, it may not feel like it, but you're better off. If she's so needy you can't even support your own family in an emergency, then she's not the kind of woman who needs to be your wife," Richard explained. "Family comes first, and if she's going to be a part of yours, she needs to realize that."

Maggie Beth gave him a burning glare, and Richard sighed. "You know better than anyone I was not the most involved father. We barely had any kind of relationship until we all worked together."

"Dad, seriously, it's—"

"It's not fine. Who wants to marry someone who isn't going to make their family their number one priority? Ask your mother."

"That's the problem. I didn't involve her. Not once did I call her, send her a text, or even a damn telegram to let her know what was going on. This is my fault." Adrian shot a glance at his mother and gathered his courage to admit how he felt. "But I guess what I'm trying to say is I don't necessarily know it wasn't for the best. Maybe we just need some time apart."

He tacked that last bit on for his mother's sake. While he couldn't quite explain his apathy toward the entire situation, not once in the last twenty-four hours since Emily had left had he experienced any emotion, positive or negative.

"Then you need to tell her that," his mother stated flatly, in a tone that brooked no argument. "Let her know you care, apologize for not calling her, and suggest just taking a break."

"I will."

"I swear, you boys will be the death of me. Madeleine, I'm going to go see Lee one more time before we head home, if that's okay with you," Maggie Beth said.

Adrian threw a peculiar glance toward his mother. "What do you mean?" His over-analyzing skills were in rare form.

"What?" Maggie Beth asked, dabbing at her face, clearing the last vestiges of her dismay.

"By the whole 'before we head home' thing."

"Both of us need to get some rest," said Richard. "We have other responsibilities to attend to."

"You know what I meant," Adrian said, cutting his eyes at his father and then to Madeleine. "Wasn't there something about the way she said that? Something that suggested they were going home *together?*"

"That's ridiculous," Maggie Beth protested too quickly.

Adrian grinned. "You were right, Maddie! They're back together."

"Adrian Flynn Atwood!" his mother exclaimed.

Even Madeleine smiled. "I tried to tell you."

"Tell me I'm wrong," Adrian dared his father with a mischievous grin.

Richard rolled his eyes. "Fine. Jesus, yes, we're dating. What's the big deal?"

"Richard! We weren't going to tell them yet!" Maggie Beth protested, crossing her arms against her chest.

"Aw, Magpie, they're big boys. I think they can handle it." Richard put his hand on her shoulder protectively. "Come on, let's say goodbye to Lee and let these two try to get some rest. And I mean it, you both look exhausted."

"I'll see you tomorrow morning, Dad."

"No, take the day off. You need it."

Maggie Beth hugged her son. "Please don't tell your brother. Not until he's better. I just don't know how he's going to react."

"He would be happy for you, Maggie Beth," Madeleine insisted. "All the same, we'll wait until you're ready."

Maggie Beth hugged Madeleine. "Oh, my girl. I do love you like a daughter. I don't know how we got so lucky."

Madeleine's mouth fell, and she felt lost. Maggie Beth patted her shoulder and then turned to leave with Richard.

For the first time since Tybee, they were alone together. Madeleine cast her eyes to the floor and started after them, but Adrian caught her arm before she could take another step.

"Maddie—"

"If you're wanting to talk about—"

"We never have to talk it about it if you don't want to. But I think it would help."

"Fine. It's not like I'm looking forward to awkward conversations and general avoidance of each other," Madeleine said.

"We were getting close again. I liked that."

"Yeah, too close," Madeleine murmured.

"I care about you. A lot. I always have. I guess that night it just…coded differently?"

"Adrian, I…I am so confused right now. I love Lee."

"I know you do. He's your husband," Adrian said softly, disappointment building although he knew it was wrong. "I just—"

"I told you I didn't want to love him. Then I look at him," she choked on her words. "God, I can't help it."

"No one will think you're weak just because you want to stay with him, if that's what you're worried about."

Madeleine closed her eyes. "I'm not staying with him."

Adrian was shocked. Even though he understood her decision, he hadn't expected those words to come out of her mouth.

"Oh." It was all he could muster.

There was a long pause. Madeleine sniffed, tried her best to stifle a sob, and failed. "I'll get him through this, but when he's back on his feet, I've got to move on."

"I understand."

"Do you?" Madeleine asked. "Sometimes I don't

even understand it, but I'm tired of living this way. I got lonely on Tybee, but I was satisfied with my life for the first time in two years."

"Then that's what you have to do," Adrian said solemnly, unable to look at her.

"Why do you seem so broken up over it?"

"I'm not," Adrian admitted. "There is nothing I want more than for you to be happy. I would think you'd know that by now. And if it means leaving my brother, I get it."

"I think you're the only one who will understand."

CHAPTER
FORTY-ONE

"Sorry, I'm late," Emily said grumpily, making her way through the crowded Midtown cafe. "I decided to drive and traffic was ridiculous."

"I was beginning to think you'd changed your mind." Adrian stood and pulled her chair out for her. She waited patiently for him, following in a routine they'd begun on their first date. Never would he have thought they'd end up here—in love, engaged, then not-engaged. All over a silly argument and unfounded fears.

"I thought about it, honestly. I've been worried about what to say, how to handle it."

"Me too."

They sat across from each other, saying nothing for the longest stretch of time imaginable.

How can it already feel so weird? Adrian mused. *It's only been a couple of days.*

A waiter came to their table and took Emily's order first. Coffee only, nothing else.

Not planning on staying long, he noted, ordering the same.

"So…how have you been?" Emily asked, her voice wavering.

Adrian shrugged. "I don't know. Things are just messed up right now. What about you?"

"About the same. One day you feel like you've got your life on track, and the next, you don't even have a clue what planet you're on."

"Tell me about it."

A server brought two steaming cups of coffee and copious amounts of cream and sugar.

"Lee's doing better, though," said Adrian. "He'll be able to go home after his next surgery, so there's some good news."

Emily blushed, trying to distract herself by fixing her coffee. She looked like she wanted to say something, then pursed her lips.

He opened his mouth to ask a question, more small talk, when she said what was on her mind.

"Adrian, I'm so sorry. I have picked a worse time to unload on you."

"We were both very understandably upset." Hadn't he just said the same thing to Madeleine?

You did, said that dark part of him which was becoming more of a familiar presence. *Just after you kissed her. How many times have you thought about that kiss since?*

Instantly, he was there again, her body molded against his and her lips moving sweet and slow. And her taste—

Focus!

"We were," Emily agreed readily. "And it was

stupid to make a decision before I had time to think about it."

All he could do was nod numbly. Maybe he should just give in, stop being so afraid of commitment. If she wanted to get back together, why not just go with it?

"After we've had a couple of days apart, though, I think it was the best decision for us."

Adrian felt a pang of shock. "What? Seriously?"

"Oh, come on, you never actually wanted to marry me," Emily said.

Adrian took a second to adjust before answering. There was no use in bullshitting her. At this point, what did it matter?

"No, but I love you. I care about you very much."

"I know you do. I've never doubted that. But I'm not the person who sets you on fire. You deserve that, and so do I."

He nodded, completely understanding what she meant, even if he could not quite agree.

"Good luck to both of us finding it," he scoffed.

Until then, Emily had been calm and composed. At his words, her face fell into the most pained expression she had shown so far. "I think you've already found her. Even if you are the last person to know about it."

Adrian narrowed his eyes in confusion. "Do you think I cheated on you?"

Technically you did, the dark side said mischievously.

It was just a kiss…kisses, and sleeping next to her, Adrian protested weakly.

"God, no, Adrian. I trust you. You'd probably die of guilt if you did something like that. I was mad and jealous about it at first. Who wouldn't be? But I know you'll always be fighting it, and I can't help but feel sorry for you."

At that point, Adrian had to stop her. "Wait a second," he said, holding up his hand. "I'm completely lost here. What the hell are you talking about?"

"Are you really lost? Be honest."

Adrian was unsure of what to say or do. "I-I have an idea, but—"

"Then don't insult my intelligence and act like you have no clue, Adrian."

"This is ridiculous. I'm sitting here with my fiancé, ex-fiancé, whatever, discussing...this. I mean, this isn't even a thing."

He knew he sounded ridiculous, but he refused to say her name or to call it anything. It was madness, and he sure as hell wasn't going to speak it into existence.

Emily looked at him as if he were a child attempting to cope with something he simply wasn't mature enough to understand, and he resented her for that. Didn't she know even if he felt something, anything, for Madeleine, he had to live in denial of it? Anything else simply was not an option. He couldn't do that to his brother.

"I didn't say it was the right thing to do or if you actually quit lying to yourself long enough to follow through there wouldn't be consequences. As jealous as I am of Maddie, I don't envy either of you. You've both got some hard decisions to make,"

Emily said with pity. She stood and gathered her purse and jacket. "And I mean it, I think she feels the same way, if that helps."

"It doesn't. It wouldn't make the least bit of difference even if any of this were true."

She gave him another pitying expression, which made his jaws clench. "Call me sometime, when you're ready. You're going to need someone you can talk to."

"You're going to miss me," he said, unsure if it was meant in jest or seriousness.

"Oh, believe me, I already do." Emily pressed a kiss to his cheek and turned, walking out of his life.

CHAPTER
FORTY-TWO

Madeleine, Maggie Beth, and Richard had resumed their positions in the waiting room. Madeleine and Richard were hard at work on their laptops, Maggie Beth wedged between them with her crochet needles.

Richard's mouth formed a hard line as he responded to all of Lee's emails and rescheduled or reassigned his various meetings and duties. It looked overwhelming just handling Lee's responsibilities, much less carrying them all out.

"Please tell me why I didn't get Adrian to do this," he groaned.

"Because Adrian would run Atwood Technologies with Post-It notes and communicate through memes?" Madeleine offered.

Her father-in-law snickered and nodded. "Yep."

"What's a meme?" Maggie Beth asked with a puzzled expression.

"Adrian would make a great CEO if he'd apply

himself," Richard said. "He's got energy, charisma, a passion for what we do, but I agree, Post-Its and memes."

"What is a meme?" Maggie Beth asked a second time.

"Kinda like Lol-cats, Mom," Adrian explained as he walked up to join the rest of the family.

Madeleine did a double take. Her mind sifted through an avalanche of adjectives to describe him. He was dressed up much more than usual in a well-tailored three-piece suit that fit his body perfectly. He'd cut his messy black hair, shorter on the sides and in the back this time. Her mouth went dry and she didn't even dare mutter as much as a "hello" for fear of stammering.

"Oh," Maggie Beth said with a pleased expression. "I like when you send me those."

Richard and Madeleine laughed out loud and Adrian looked at them in confusion. "What's so funny?" he asked.

"Nothing," Richard said, shaking his head. "Grab a seat and help me figure out Lee's convoluted schedule."

"Um, I already took care of that hours ago. It's all been reassigned to me or other execs."

Richard groaned. "You've got to be kidding me."

"I *am* the VP. It's kind of my job to handle these things."

"Grab a seat, baby," Maggie Beth offered. "We're gonna be here a spell."

"About that," Adrian said, taking a seat next to his mother. "I heard about a place I thought you and Madeleine would love, so I got you reservations."

260

"Oh, Adrian, that's sweet, but I can't possibly leave," Maggie Beth said.

"Why not? It's a four-hour surgery, and the reservation is limited for two hours. You'll be back long before Lee's out of surgery."

"I'm not leaving my baby. Lord only knows what could happen in that operating room," Maggie Beth said. "But Maddie, you should go. I know he's your husband, but you've not left this hospital in days."

"I'm not leaving if you're not."

"Madeleine, you've been more than dedicated to him. Please, go and get out of here for a while, get your mind off things. You deserve a couple of hours to yourself."

"I certainly don't want to go alone."

Richard was quick to volunteer. "I'll go. Can this place make a stiff Tom Collins?"

"It's a tearoom, Dad. I'll take you out for drinks later."

"Damn," Richard mumbled.

"A tearoom?" Madeleine asked, her interest piqued.

"See? I knew you'd like it. Wait until you see it. It's got you written all over it." Adrian smiled. "Plus, I hear they make the best Earl Grey in the city."

"You two go," Maggie Beth insisted. "Adrian, you've obviously cleared your schedule to be here, and I'm sure your father could handle any emergencies."

Madeleine looked at Adrian with a panicked expression. They had barely patched over their awkwardness, and Madeleine didn't know how she could even possibly spend a couple of hours with him all alone.

Adrian's eyes met hers, and he seemed to be thinking the same thing. Neither of them thought it was a good idea, but if they shot down Maggie Beth's suggestion, they knew it might appear suspicious.

"Um, yeah, sure. That is, if you're okay with it, Maddie. I'll understand if you'd rather stay here with Lee," Adrian said, giving Madeleine the perfect out.

"I am pretty worried about him," Madeleine played on.

"They're doing surgery on his knee," Richard said. "He'll be fine. Go, Maddie. Maggie Beth's right. You need some time away from this damn hospital."

Her in-laws weren't giving her many options. Adrian threw her an understanding glance, and she reluctantly gathered her things.

CHAPTER FORTY-THREE

"Doctor Bombay's Underwater Tea Party?" Madeleine questioned as they walked up the sidewalk. Until then, conversation had been nonexistent, save for a couple of remarks of small talk and some niceties here and there.

"Yeah," Adrian said nervously. "I mean, if it doesn't appeal to you, we can always just—"

"It's so...whimsical," Madeleine breathed, pausing in front of the shop window. "The name, the design—and all those books!"

Adrian was pleased Madeleine was happy as he eyed the long rows of bookshelves lining the walls.

"Wait until you have some of their pastries," he said, opening the door for her.

She stepped inside, her eyes darting around the rooms and taking them in while he spoke to a hostess who showed them to their table. Case after case of old books with their dull spectrum of buckram and dust-covered spines lined a long length of brick wall in the dining area. Mismatched antiques and décor gave the place the place a quaint ambience.

When they sat down, Madeleine saw the ceiling and gasped. "Oh, I love the parasols!"

Adrian glanced up at the tattered Chinese paper parasols hanging from the ceiling. Emily had been the one to tell him about the place, but she hadn't been terribly impressed with it. Cute, but too dusty for a restaurant, she had said. When he had Googled the place to find something enjoyable for his mother and Madeleine to do for the afternoon, the colorful parasols had reminded him of Madeleine. She loved old things, no matter if it were some old kitchen gadget or a ridiculously expensive, exotic piece of antique furniture. Old things always had a story, she would say.

In fact, as he looked at her, staring up at all the strange and mismatched decor with a patina of story covering every item, Adrian thought he could practically hear the gears grinding in her mind. She was already at work creating something from what others would see as a dusty heap of consignment store finds.

And that, he decided, *is why I'm attracted to her.*

No. No, that was bullshit. He couldn't be attracted to her. He was *not* attracted to her.

Then again, she found beauty in everything. She was beautiful…

Or he just had an obsession with fixing what was broken. He always had. Hell, he'd made a career out of it. But it was Lee's job to fix all her broken parts, wasn't it? He was her husband, after all.

"You must have a lot on your mind," Madeleine said, eyeing him over her menu.

Adrian pinched the bridge of his nose. "Getting a headache," he lied.

"Oh, I'm sorry. Do you want something?" Madeleine picked up her purse.

"A stiff drink and about twelve hours of sleep?"

"We could have gone to a bar. I definitely wouldn't have objected." Madeleine handed him a couple of aspirin. "Although, I've got to tell you, I'm already liking this place."

"Thanks," Adrian said and knocked back the two pills he didn't need.

She was so sweet…Lee didn't know what a good thing he'd messed up.

Then there was silence again that stretched forever. Adrian couldn't stand it, and he had never been more grateful to order a meal.

They ordered the full works for high tea and a pot of Madeleine's beloved Earl Grey. When they brought it in a mismatched set of vintage china, Madeleine was trying hard to suppress a giddy grin. Watching her enjoy such a simple thing made him do the same.

Until she asked something that made his entire mood crumble.

"You said something the other night in Tybee," Madeleine said.

Adrian set his teacup down. "I said a lot of things in Tybee."

"You didn't say it exactly." She leaned forward, speaking just barely above a whisper. "It was pretty vague."

"Like the direction of this conversation? We've kissed, shared a bed, what could we possibly say now to make things more awkward?"

She shifted in her chair, seemingly scared to even mention it. "You asked if I remembered what we did after prom."

"Cabin in Blue Ridge, about the same routine, just fourteen years and a bottle of rum earlier."

"Yeah, and then you said, 'I should have told you then.'"

I should have told you I loved you then. That our lives might have gone completely differently if I'd just been honest with you.

Instead of voicing his wayward thoughts, he shrugged. "I have no idea," he lied, taking a long drink of his tea to avoid looking at her.

When he put the cup back down on the saucer, he noticed Madeleine was dissatisfied with his answer but reserved enough not to pry.

"I was pretty tired that night. Who knows what the hell I was saying?"

"I understand," she stated flatly.

Adrian was nearing exasperation. "Madeleine, why ask a question you know the answer to?"

She stared at him as if he'd started speaking gibberish. "Because I don't know the answer?"

"Jesus. Just stop—"

"What? Adrian, I wouldn't ask if—"

"You know exactly what I was going to say. We both know what I was going to say, and there's no sense in rehashing it."

"I'm not rehashing. How can you re-hash what wasn't hashed in the first place?"

He took a deep breath and suspended it, trying to center his thoughts and decide what would be the right thing to say. "It's not something I should have said or even brought up in the first place, so why ask?"

Madeleine's expression relaxed. "Curiosity?" She shrugged, and Adrian thought she was infuriatingly cute.

"There's an old expression about that, something about dead cats," he said sarcastically.

"Is it the one where the cat's in the box and it's neither dead nor alive until you observe the result?"

"Would you rather discuss quantum mechanics? Because it would be so much easier to talk about."

"They're equally complicated subjects. Pick one." Maddie leaned back in her chair and crossed her arms.

"Okay, multiverse theory—possible or bullshit? Are there really other worlds where our lives took a different course with every decision we made?"

"Totally possible," Madeleine returned. "Like, there might even be one out there, somewhere in the deep, dark recesses of the universe, where you actually tell me what you were going to say."

"Yeah, like deep, deep, dark recesses. Never in a million years would it happen in this version of reality. And to expound on your idea, there's probably a universe where you'll just drop it."

"Hmmm, maybe I don't believe so much in multiverse theory after all."

"And maybe I don't have any clue what you're talking about." He took a long sip of his tea.

Madeleine pouted, leaning forward toward him.

"Adrian…"

"Madeleine…" he mocked her whining tone. "You're not getting it out of me."

With a wistful smile, she lounged back in her chair, teacup and saucer in hand. "It's that bad, huh?"

Adrian cast his glance down to his own saucer, allowing his eyes to get lost in the busy floral pattern. "No, not really. It was a long time ago. Doesn't make much of a difference now."

"So you could just say it, right?" Madeleine teased, her eyes lighting up.

Jesus, Adrian thought, admiring the mischievous expression more than he should have. It was so easy for him to get caught up in her eyes—deep, gorgeous blues that made him feel paralyzed, falling to the bottom of the sea without the least bit of hope. Worst of all, he didn't even care. Sinking deep into the depths felt like a peace he'd never known.

"I was in love with you," he acquiesced, taking a breath and drowning in her eyes. "Back in high school. Hell, I think I spent my whole freshman year in college wishing you'd somehow waltz back into my life. I don't know why I didn't try harder to convince you."

Madeleine was struck speechless.

"See? Weren't you better off not knowing?"

Madeleine swallowed. "So…multiverse theory…"

Everything inside Adrian sank. How could he be so damned stupid?

"If multiverse theory is to be believed, there's a

universe out there where you told me that fourteen years and a bottle of rum ago. Which means a lot of other possibilities may exist out there somewhere."

Adrian relaxed slightly. "Yeah, somewhere out there, I could be making you completely miserable."

"Or we might be happily married, in a charming little house with three beautiful children. We could be the people the Joneses are trying to keep up with."

"I should have told you then."

"Yes, you should have."

Adrian wondered how terribly he'd messed things up now.

CHAPTER
FORTY-FOUR

"Let's get the hell out of here," Adrian said jovially, waltzing into his brother's hospital room with his discharge papers in hand.

"How'd you get those so fast?" Madeleine asked. "We were told it'd probably be another hour."

"Yeah, two hours ago," Lee grumbled from his wheelchair.

"Dated the discharge nurse for a bit junior year. And she wanted me to know she is single." Adrian pointed out a phone number scribbled on the corner of Lee's discharge papers.

"Nice. You gonna call her?" Lee teased while Adrian gathered a couple of bags and started pushing his brother out of the room.

"I just got, what do you call it? De-engaged? Dis-engaged? Un-engaged? Maddie?"

"It's dis- for verbs, un- for adjectives. I'd go with unengaged."

"Unengaged then, and I ain't dating anyone. Not

for a while," Adrian continued. "Hey, how fast you think we can wheel this thing down the hall?"

"You're the engineer. Figure it out."

"How much do you weigh these days?"

"We're supposed to wait on a nurse anyway," Madeleine interrupted. "To help load him in and all."

"But here you are, walking down the hall with us, prepared to leave," Adrian cracked with a mischievous grin.

"Because the phrase *supposed to* isn't in an Atwood's vocabulary." She pushed the down button on the elevator. "Might as well just be an accomplice at this point if I'm going to keep putting up with the two of you."

The elevator chimed its arrival.

"And after how many years of knowing us? Seventeen? Eighteen? She finally gets it," Lee said to Adrian as they boarded the elevator.

Adrian was sure he heard a rather concerned "Mr. Atwood?" as the elevator doors closed, but what difference would it make? If they were concerned, there'd be some orderlies or someone at the main entrance by the time they got to the door. He knew his brother was beyond ready to get home and wasn't going to feel any better until he could repair his broken spirit as well as the doctors had repaired his body.

And then there was Madeleine, who was doing a pathetic job of hiding her anxiety. He'd make sure to ask her if she'd been taking her medication if he could get a second alone with her later. He couldn't be sure if it was a longing to go home or if she was

271

dreading being at home with Lee again, when all she wanted to do was leave. And Jesus, how was Lee going to react?

She was happy when she saw he'd had the forethought to rent a van that would help Lee get around for the next several weeks until his leg had completely healed.

"Stylish," Lee brother joked as a wheelchair lift lowered to the ground with a mechanical grace. "You run out of Lambos?"

Adrian chuckled. "After this incident, you're not even allowed to breathe around my cars, thank you very much."

They'd barely made it out of Atlanta before a dose of pain medicine had kicked in and Lee was sleeping soundly in the back. Madeleine looked particularly contemplative sitting in the passenger seat next to him, and after their conversation at Doctor Bombay's, he didn't know what to say to her for the next awkward hour of his life. He searched through banal topics; it was finally raining again after a dangerously dry winter—he could mention that.

"You tried."

His brow furrowed. "Huh?"

"At prom. All summer before we left for college. I just…I didn't see it until I thought about it."

"Oh," he said, clearing his dry throat in nervousness. "Well, like we said—"

"There was one day. We had lunch together, table close to the dippin' tree."

Adrian smiled. "Ah, the good ole' dippin' tree. I had forgotten about that."

"You normally ate lunch with your so-called friends, but you came out Monday after prom and every day after. You always brought me a Cherry Coke. That's what made me think of all this. Today I pressed the button for Diet Coke and out comes a Cherry Coke instead. Weird, huh?"

"Nothing says 'date me' like free Coke."

"You invited me to your house like a dozen times. Or to the movies, concerts for bands you knew I liked but I knew you didn't care for. And for some stupid reason I could not comprehend, you were trying your best to win me over."

"You know why, right?" Adrian asked as traffic came to a standstill on I-75.

Madeleine thought for a minute. "No, I have no idea."

Madeleine was bathed in the blood red of all the surrounding brake lights. "Because it was beyond your ability to understand someone else could care about you that much. As cheesy as it sounds, you can't love someone else until you love yourself. It made sense to me, even then. That's a big reason why I wished I tried even harder. Maybe you would have realized you were worth it."

"You couldn't have fixed me," she said in a low tone. "As much as I hate to admit it, I've been like this a long time, and I may always be. I need the therapy, the pills. Full-blown depression? That's an awful lot to expect an eighteen-year-old boy to fix."

Traffic started to inch forward, and Adrian turned his attention back to the road.

"Wouldn't it have been easier to go through with someone else?"

273

Madeleine had to look away from him. "Yes, it would have."

CHAPTER
FORTY-FIVE

Adrian had given up the fight to focus. He had been running the company solo now for two weeks, going to meeting after meeting on Lee's behalf, and his brain was fried. Occasionally, he would jot down a few things he thought were pertinent, but more than once he'd found his pen writing a capital *M* before he realized what he was doing.

What the hell are you doing? Are you crazy?

Luckily, taking over for Lee gave him very little time to think about anything else. But with every lull in every day, he was either carefully thinking over what Emily had told him or chiding himself for thinking about Madeleine.

Why was the thought of her so painfully consuming? Every time his mind wasn't dominated by the stress of yet again having to fill his brother's shoes, he couldn't help but replay the way she felt in his arms, the rare-as-rubies smiles he loved coaxing out of her.

He could text her. It wouldn't hurt. He could ask how Lee was doing.

He took out his phone and tapped out a message. He put his phone back down and pretended to be interested in…whatever this was he was supposed to be listening to.

"…and neither private nor public sector businesses are investing to pre-recession levels. To ensure profit margins will continue to grow, we need to make cuts in a few areas. The engineering department obviously deserves the largest portion of the company budget, but there are several places where the department needs to investigate their budgeting to—"

"Wait, what did you just say?" Adrian interrupted.

The young financial analyst nervously cleared her throat. "Um, I said there are significant cuts that could be made in engineering."

"Elaborate on that for me."

It was something Lee would normally say whenever he was about to shoot something down, and Adrian was going to be no different when it came to his precious engineering department.

The young woman stared down at her tablet, shifting pages of her presentation to a slide with her perfectly prepared reports. "There's an above-average amount of spending on the innovative design team, without a lot of return on the investment. For instance, last year, they requested a ten percent hike in budget, but only increased five percent from their marketable—"

"Miss, um…"

"Hartline."

"Miss Hartline, you are aware this is a technology company, correct?"

Her faced screwed into a mix of offense and fear. "Yes, sir, I am."

"You are also aware I oversee engineering's budget and operations, correct?"

"Yes, however, it's—"

"Being an engineer first and foremost, I believe our innovative design team is the heart and soul of this company. Innovative design is what's going to change the world, and if any of you can't appreciate that simple philosophy, then maybe this isn't the company for you."

Miss Hartline's countenance faded from fear to flustered. The change made Adrian's usual sense of compassion return. He didn't think he could handle the guilt of making an employee cry.

"Listen," he said, standing to address his employees. "I realize it's been a few slow years around here and you're all just trying to keep the guys up top's pockets well-padded because, hey, that's your job. But know this—we're not the rich douchebags people think we are."

That statement alone garnered more muffled giggles and surprised expressions than he would have thought possible out of the morose crew in attendance.

"More than anything, my brother and I want this company to be great. We want to lead the industry in technological advances. We want to be such an exciting place to work the nerds at MIT would cream their pants to even get an interview here."

The room broke out in raucous laughter and more shocked expressions. Adrian gave in and laughed too.

"Seriously, though, we need you to stay focused on the big picture here. Think beyond the dollar signs. Sure, innovative design was a little in the hole last year, but they developed a new rover design being tested by NASA to scout the most livable places on Mars. That's something we should get excited about, not money. But I wouldn't say—well, Lee wouldn't *let* me say it—if we both didn't fully believe focusing on our product—life changing, meaningful technology—will make the money come to us.

"Miss Hartline, I'm sorry about your presentation. I'm sure it's been meticulously planned. Find somewhere else to make cuts if we truly need profit margins to increase so badly, but cutting funds from innovative design is never an option."

One of the other financial analysts and the head of engineering began clapping, and the entire room soon followed.

"All right, there's nothing being said in this meeting that can't be put in an email. Send all your presentations to me and we'll be sure to review them. Get out of this office and have lunch somewhere nice. Put it on your company cards; it's on me."

There was a collective cacophony of glee and more scattered applause. Within minutes, the conference room had completely emptied. Adrian gathered his things, his mind already wandering from the meeting to Madeleine. He checked his phone expectantly, but he hadn't gotten a response to his text.

"They all seemed inspired."

Try as he might to hide it, a smile instantly lit his face like a supernova in the darkest reaches of the universe.

"What's a doll like you doing in a place like this?" he asked, positive he sounded like a complete idiot.

Shameless flirt, he criticized. "Did you leave Lee to fend for himself?"

Madeleine huffed. "Hardly. Your mother's with him. After two weeks, I just needed some time out of that house."

"I can imagine."

"I felt guilty asking."

"Don't. Mom'll take good care of him," Adrian insisted. "Anyway, please tell me you're hungry."

"I could eat."

"Good, because I'm starving. Let's get out of here." He placed his hand in the small of her back to lead her out of the conference room. When he realized he was daring to touch her, he fully expected Madeleine to recoil...yet she didn't.

"What about Tin Lizzy's, since Lee's not here to rule against it?" Madeleine suggested, seemingly unconcerned about the placement of his hand.

It wasn't like he was feeling her up.

From there his mind was lost. He pictured his hands moving down her hips, getting a good, firm grasp on her ass and spinning her into him, his mouth crashing down over hers. She'd wrap her gorgeous legs around his waist and—

"Ade?"

"Huh?"

"Tin Lizzy's. Yea or nay?"

Room service sounded better. A half-darkened hotel room, Madeleine beneath him, calling out his name with every thrust and—

He had to get his rampant thoughts under control.

"Absolutely," he said, coming back down to Earth, his heartrate noticeably rising. "We can't pass up that opportunity."

"Are you okay?"

"Couldn't be better. I'm on my way to get a beer and nachos with a hot blonde. Isn't that every man's dream?"

Madeleine's cheeks reddened. "You shouldn't say such things."

"Probably not," he conceded, regretting his tongue's swiftness and reminding himself that he couldn't have her.

They walked through the office together, Adrian doing his best to tear his eyes away from her. He didn't know if the stares they were getting were a result of perception or paranoia; it was as if everyone in the world could see what was on his mind. It was a relief when they stepped into the elevator alone.

Being alone in a small space with her made his mind run even wilder. He didn't snap out of his trance until the elevator chimed and the doors parted to the executive level parking. His car was parked in the CEO spot for once. He had to admit, he liked the parking space much more than the job.

"Ah, I get the pleasure of riding in the Maserati today," Madeleine said. She wasn't quite the car enthusiast he was, but she had always liked his Gran Turismo.

Adrian threw her a devilish glance. "Why don't you drive?"

She looked at him wide-eyed. "No! Besides, you don't even let Lee drive your cars."

"Hmmm…wonder why," he responded sarcastically. "Take the keys, Mads."

It took a moment for her to consider it, but Madeleine nearly squealed in delight and took the keys from his hand.

Adrian felt odd on the passenger side of his own car. He wasn't quite sure what had possessed him to suggest she drive—especially his Maserati—but it was worth the beaming smile he could practically feel from across the armrest. The damned thing was as wide as the Grand Canyon, and all he wanted was to be closer to her.

She crept down Peachtree Road, much to the dismay of the irritable Atlanta drivers behind her.

"Um, you do know it goes from zero to sixty in four seconds, right?"

"Are you kidding me? I'm not risking getting as much as a scratch on this thing," Madeleine said, constantly checking all the mirrors when they stopped at a red light.

"Maddie, doing 20 in a 420 horsepower car is doing it an injustice. You're hurting her feelings. It's a straight shot from here to Tin Lizzy's. Floor the damn thing."

"No, Adrian, I can't."

"Yes, you can."

"No!"

He grinned when an idea struck.

Adrian rested his hand on her thigh, just above her knee. Her lips parted in surprise, but she didn't have time to protest. When the light turned from red to green, Adrian pushed his hand down and the engine roared to life. Madeleine let out a shocked gasp that turned into peals of giggles as the speedometer climbed. The Maserati sped down the street, and Adrian had to force himself to take his hand off her thigh when it was time for her to brake and turn into the parking lot of Tin Lizzy's.

"That was a cheap shot, Adrian Atwood," Madeleine said, shifting the car into park.

"What?" He laughed. "You mean getting you to drive?"

"Or using it as a pathetic excuse to touch me," she countered.

He was beginning to feel lightheaded just looking at her. The light pink flush of her lips was enough to capture the entirety of his attention.

"I, um…I'm gonna need that beer now," he mumbled, unable to take his eyes off her lips.

"Then let's get you a beer." She laughed, the rosiness of her lips spreading to her cheeks.

God, he loved when she was happy.

She's happy when she's with you, a dark part of him whispered as she opened the car door.

His damnable impulses couldn't be helped, and his mind fought against them as hard as he could. All he wanted to do was recreate that kiss in Tybee.

With any hope, one last kiss could tide him over a lifetime and he could move on from this nonsense.

When Madeleine shut the car door, thankfully oblivious to his struggles, Adrian sighed a breath of both frustration and relief.

CHAPTER FORTY-SIX

Lee awoke to an intense itching all over his body. He rubbed his face in his hands, trying to relieve the prickling feeling behind his eyes and forehead. His medication was wearing off, and he could actually feel the pain in his leg and ribs for the first time.

And then he remembered, Madeleine was gone.

Again.

This time it was just for the afternoon, but when she'd left, he greatly feared she might not ever come back.

All he could think about was how much he loved her, and he knew it beyond any shadow of a doubt.

It's not enough. It will never be enough, said a voice buried deep down inside him.

"I've been so fucking stupid," Lee hissed. Months had been wasted, attempting in every way he possibly could to tell her he loved her without showing her, without making even the slightest attempt to change.

He tried to sit up on his own and grunted at the searing pain in his leg. A final push off the headboard helped him to gain some semblance of balance. Then he laid eyes on the wheelchair.

It was only a couple of paces from the bed, but it might as well have been an ocean away. Asking his mother to pick him up out of bed was a humbling blow he was not prepared to deal with. Luckily for his pride, the wheels were locked, and he was determined to get out of the damned bed on his own.

He reached over and pulled the chair closer and then started to push off the bed by pressing his fists into the mattress and lifting with every bit of arm strength he had. With some creative finagling, he was able to turn and lower himself into the chair, dragging his now-throbbing left leg into place on the wheelchair.

He hadn't been so proud since he exceeded his father's percentage growth for the first time.

Feeling determined, he thought that if he could get out of bed, there was more he could do.

Lee peered in the mirror. The bruises on his face had already begun to yellow at the edges, and the cuts had healed into crimson scabs. He looked like hell and needed a shave.

He wheeled into the bathroom and filled the sink with water. He had to make do with a bar of soap instead of shaving cream, but it did the trick. He even styled his hair and threw on a clean t-shirt. Lee he thought it was strange how such small things he'd always taken for granted could make him feel like a new man.

He wheeled into the living room where his mother had been stationed since Madeleine had left.

"Mom?"

Maggie Beth turned in a snap, her eyes wide in disbelief. "Lee! You're supposed to be in bed! How in the world did you make it to the wheelchair?"

"I can't ask for help with everything." He was already feeling the burden of depending on others for so much.

"Do you need anything? Maddie said you could take another pain pill if you needed to when you woke up."

Lee shook his head vehemently. "No. In fact, flush the damned pills. I'm tired of being in a haze all the time. I'd rather deal with the pain from now on. I need your help with a couple of other things too, if it's not too much trouble."

"Whatever you need, baby. Just tell me what to do."

It took hours to collect all of them. Lee knew there were probably a few more stashed here and there across the house, but he'd told her every location he could remember. His mother had even found a few he'd forgotten about.

After a while, they stood staring open-mouthed at 127 bottles of liquor. Some were full, but most were at least half-gone.

"We haven't even touched the kitchen fridge," Lee said, unable to take his eyes off the glistening bottles spread across the butcher table.

Maggie Beth shuffled to the fridge and fetched two six-packs of beer and a half-empty bottle of wine, adding it to the collection of bottles on the island with a clang. For a moment, he watched the heartbreak on his mother's face as she processed the sheer amount of alcohol.

"Think of how many you must have already thrown away," she said hollowly.

He didn't want to think about it or the number he'd have to empty when he got back to his office.

"Let's get them emptied then," his mother decided, taking a bottle of Grey Goose to the sink.

The first one was easy enough, as was the second and third, but as Lee noticed the dwindling number of bottles, he began to feel a sense of panic.

"You don't need them, Lee," his mother stated, looking him straight in the eye.

Lee's throat was closing shut, his chest locking. "What if Maddie doesn't come back? How do I deal with it? I've done nothing but self-medicate for so long."

"Honey, you're just going to have to learn to do what everyone else does. Cry it out, scream it out, throw every breakable thing in the house until you realize how stupid you're acting. Then, let time heal what's broken. Maddie's gonna come back, don't you worry. She'll come back because she loves you. But you know what you and Maddie are both going to realize?"

Lee shook his head, trying to decide whether to focus on the threat of Madeleine being gone versus the bottle of Gentleman Jack in his mother's hands.

"It's not y'all's job to be each other's one-and-only source of happiness, and people these days get divorces all the time because they think that's how a marriage should work. They don't fix what's broken, so they run off and find someone else that's not broken, at least on the surface. Sound familiar?"

"Yeah, it does," he admitted.

"Of course it does! That's where you two got so screwed up. You lost Thomas, and God knows that was heartbreaking. Lee, there's not a day that goes by I don't think about that baby, but you never dealt with it. You just shut off every emotion, and you shut Maddie out too. You shut *her* out. Not the other way around. Maddie dealt with it. She cried and screamed and threw stuff until it didn't hurt as bad, but by the time she got done, she'd lost her husband too."

"No," Lee protested, shaking his head. "I did all that. I did cry, I screamed, I just did it on my own, so I could be strong for her."

"You didn't have to be strong for her. She was strong enough to pick herself up, though in her own time. You needed time together, to mourn together. You tried every which-a-way to stay numb to it. Work, alcohol, Brecklyne…And here you are now, a lot of suffering later, trying to get past all of it."

"I've messed it up too bad to fix it! My marriage is hanging by a thread, I've got the job I've wanted since I was a kid, but my brother has to do it for me. I've got more money than I'll ever spend, and I'm the most miserable man you'll ever meet."

"Not to mention you're an alcoholic, and because of that, you almost lost your life."

"I'm not an alcoholic."

"Lee, you're eyeing that bottle of Gentleman Jack right now, and I'll bet you don't even realize it."

He hadn't, until he had to turn his head to see his mother. "I just want one last drink. Just to get me through this."

Maggie Beth considered it for a moment, then took a highball down from the cabinet and filled it halfway with the very Gentleman Jack he wanted so badly.

"All right, Lee, one last drink." Before she put the glass in his hands, she added, "After you drink this, I want you to ask yourself if it's worth everything that matters to you. Do you want this more than Maddie? Adrian? Is it worth losing your life?"

She placed the drink in his hands, and Lee realized just how much he wanted—no, needed—the glass in his shaking hands.

It all became too clear, and the realization she was right came crashing down on top of him like a wave in a hurricane.

He didn't want to. He wanted to just down the damned thing, then snatch the bottle and take it back to bed with him, but he shoved it into his mother's waiting hands, shaking his head as the tears he'd been holding back for months finally broke free.

Maggie Beth wrapped her arms around her eldest son and let him cry.

CHAPTER FORTY-SEVEN

Adrian was nervous. The plans were simple enough—spend the weekend at Lee and Madeleine's, helping her out with Lee and trying to keep his brother sane while he adjusted to being even a minutia less than fully independent. Although, if he were brave enough to admit it, the only reason Adrian even made the trip was Madeleine. Truth be told, he was still angry with his brother. At some moment in time (he wasn't sure when it was—that first day in chemistry, their first kiss, the moment he'd pulled her out of the water?) she'd become infinitely more significant than his own flesh-and-blood family.

Yet his family had always taken priority over everything else in his life. Disappointing them had always been his greatest fear. That was enough to make his blood run cold.

It happened to Lee and it would happen to him. Someone would find out about this. Or it would come to the point where he wanted her so much, loved her so much, he couldn't stand the idea of her with anyone else. Even if he knew he would never have the right to be jealous over her.

Adrian couldn't convince himself to get out of his car.

This will only end up hurting your entire family. You've already hurt Emily beyond repair. And could Maddie stand another heartbreak if it didn't work out? Since when have any of these situations worked out for the best?

Adrian had certainly heard of scandal after scandal his entire life, whether it was among the Atlanta elite or the blue-collar folks down the street. Some affairs certainly seemed justified, and even resulted in marriage, but those never seemed to last very long.

Sin begets sin. How many times had he heard it growing up? Along with, *Blessed is the man who withstands temptation.*

He had to admit, he was certainly feeling he wouldn't be blessed any time soon.

Adrian was half-convinced to leave when his mother stepped out onto the porch. She waved, and he faked a half-smile, shoring up his nerves, and stepped out of his car. He left his overnight bag in the passenger seat, hoping he could get out of spending the night.

"I didn't know you were coming over," his mother said pleasantly.

"Yep…for a little while," he lied. "There's a few things I may need to do for work."

"Oh, good Lord, Adrian. Don't be like your

brother. You're the acting CEO right now. You can take a weekend to rest."

"Being the CEO means there's a lot of people's jobs riding on my shoulders. That's important, even if it'll only be for a couple of weeks."

Maggie Beth shot a quick glance back to the windows, then faced Adrian, her face very grave. "If your brother doesn't shape up, it may be more permanent. Your father's been hearing rumors from some of the board."

Adrian laughed mockingly. "They can choose me if they want. I'll never accept it."

Maggie Beth narrowed her gaze. "Adrian, seriously, you may have to."

"No. I don't want it. I don't even want to be VP. I was happy in engineering."

"You weren't even making a fourth of what you make now."

"Wow, is my salary public knowledge?"

"Watch the attitude, mister. And no, that information is classified, unless you're a majority shareholder."

Adrian had nearly forgotten—in their divorce, his mother had opted to take shares in the company as opposed to taking any of Richard's personal funds. It was a wise move for both his mother and father. Richard technically didn't lose a dime, and Maggie Beth profited more than she would have if she had taken it from him.

"Either way, the money isn't the point. The point is having a job I enjoy doing, what I went to college for six years to do."

"You're a fantastic engineer, everyone knows

that, but you're good at this too. Your father is impressed with what you've been doing. And like you just said, you've got so many people depending on you. It's important someone with a level head keeps the business running smoothly. Right now, that's not Lee."

"I guess we need to focus on getting Lee put back together then."

He turned his back and walked toward the porch.

"Don't be angry," his mother called after him, following on the graveled path. "You're always underestimating yourself. You could be so much more. You deserve more."

"I'm happy with who and what I am, and there's not very many people like that in the world. I'm a lucky man. It seems everyone else around me are the ones who want more."

"You're being dramatic. I'm proud of you. I just…it's not fair you're the one we can always count on, and you're just as capable as—"

"This would kill him," Adrian stated. "He's going through a rough time with Maddie. Don't take something else he loves away from him."

His mother's eyes widened. "Something else? What about Maddie? Do you know if she plans on leaving again?"

Seeing his mother's face crease with worry, Adrian grimaced. He had not realized the irony of his own words.

"I don't know," Adrian shrugged. "Would you blame her if she did?"

Maggie Beth blinked back a tear. "No, not at all. But…she's been a part of our family so long now.

And who else does she have, other than us? Who's going to watch out for her?"

For Adrian, there was no question who would be there for Madeleine.

"I would," Adrian said solemnly. "She was my friend before she married Lee. I'd take care of her after."

His mother nodded. "You've always been a good friend to her. You're always standing up and doing what's right."

You are a worthless piece of shit, he told himself as he started back up the pebbled path and through the front door.

Inside, he was greeted by warmth and the smell of cinnamon and sugar wafting through the house. It was almost enough to make him forget how much he was beginning to loathe himself. It was time to play the part of devoted brother, and if he didn't do a damned good job, his whole life might unravel at the seams.

"Oh, God bless, she's making cinnamon rolls," Adrian announced with a grin, strolling into the kitchen. As soon as he saw Madeleine, his grin softened and his body unwound. A light blush spread over her cheeks.

Did she have a single clue how gorgeous she was? Adrian was unable to take his eyes off her. The spot of flour just above her cheekbone was driving him wild for some strange reason.

What I would give to come home to her every night...

"You aren't getting a damned one, either. Those are my cinnamon rolls," Lee's voice sounded across the kitchen.

Adrian saw Lee seated at the kitchen table in a wheelchair. He looked like himself for the first time since his wreck. It was a welcome sight, but mixed with his rising sense of guilt, Adrian simply wasn't sure just how to feel.

He cleared his throat. It was time to put on a happy face and pretend there was nothing wrong.

"Wow. You don't look like shit," Adrian teased.

"I feel better. A lot more like myself. Quit checking out my wife and come here. I have something I want to show you."

Adrian's eyes met Madeleine's, and her cheeks reddened. He opened his mouth to protest but soon realized Lee was only joking as he sped by them in his wheelchair and unlocked the door to the back porch.

"Think you can give me a push over this damn threshold?"

Adrian gingerly nudged the chair over the threshold and pushed his brother out into the chilly evening air. He noticed the full, doubled-up trash-bag leaning against the column next to the steps.

"Pick it up," Lee told him, nodding toward the bag.

Adrian's first thought was that Lee had completely lost his marbles. Lifting the bag, he was surprised by its weight and the unmistakable clang of empty bottles. He looked at Lee in amazement. "You didn't—"

"Every one of them. At least I think that's all," Lee said. "Listen, I know there's a ton in my office. Do you think you could get them out of there for me before I get back?"

"Yeah, sure. I don't know what to say. I'm proud of you."

"It's way overdue. I know I'm pretty stubborn, but it's taken way too much for me to realize how stupid I've been. I know you're tired of having to take on all of my responsibilities and I promise, barring unforeseeable catastrophe, you will never have to step in for me again."

"It hasn't been bad. The business end of the company just isn't my favorite, that's all."

"I'm not just talking about the company. You've been there for Maddie when I couldn't or wouldn't, and I feel guilty because you've lost Emily. It's my fault."

"Didn't think you'd care so much Emily was gone," Adrian replied, becoming morose.

As disinclined as he was to admit it, Adrian was lost without her. She'd been an absolute for so long, not having a concrete plan of marriage and children at some point made the future less certain. More interesting, but uncertainty was almost as scary as marrying a woman he could never fully commit to.

Lee pursed his lips. "I didn't think she was perfect for you, no. Right for you, sure, but she just wasn't, to use a phrase Maddie hates—'the one.'"

Adrian's ears perked at mere mention of her name, but seeing his brother sent a guilt searing through him. "I think we've talked about that before. Why doesn't she like it again?"

His brother shrugged. "She's got some philosophy behind it. Makes better sense when she explains it. Any woman married to me for any length of time wouldn't much believe in the concept of there only being one person in the world you could fall in love with."

Adrian grinned. "I agree wholeheartedly."

"This thing's pretty fast and I'm not good at controlling it," Lee replied, jutting his wheelchair toward Adrian. "Sure would suck if I ran you right off this porch."

"And it sure would suck to have to beat your crippled ass," Adrian said, faking a punch to Lee's jaw.

Lee blocked his fist and tried to grab it, but Adrian dodged. As he moved to the side, he accidentally pushed Lee and the wheelchair back into the wall.

"Hey!" Lee laughed, kicking his brother in the shin with his unbroken leg.

"Ouch! Jesus, for a cripple you can pack a—"

The back door flew open and his mother admonished, "Adrian Flynn!" She and Madeleine stood in the doorframe, curious to see what was happening. "Quit roughhousing with your brother! He's in a wheelchair, for crying out loud!"

"What? He started it!"

"You insulted me. I had to defend my honor!"

"Honor? What honor?"

"Mom! Adrian says I have no honor," Lee whined.

"You two haven't matured in twenty years. Get in this house before you kill each other."

For a few hours, Adrian forgot any of the bullshit going on in their lives. If he pretended hard enough, it was almost like Lee was his best friend again, and

Madeleine was genuinely happy.

As the evening waned, Adrian noticed Lee could barely keep his eyes open. It was the most active he'd been since the wreck, and everyone had been proud of him for being so determined.

Adrian helped Madeleine get Lee into the bed, and he was nearly asleep by the time Madeleine leaned over to cover him up and make sure he was comfortable.

"'Night, Maddie," Lee said softly, with a peck to her cheek.

His stomach sank. He couldn't afford to feel even the slightest twinge of jealousy.

She's Lee's wife. Lee gets to kiss her all he wants, Adrian scolded himself. What the hell had ever made him think this would work?

That simple peck made for racing thoughts and the closest thing he'd ever experienced to anxiety in his life. An hour of tossing and turning in their guest bedroom later, Adrian gave up and took his laptop downstairs to the kitchen where he tried to work. He answered a few emails, but mostly his mind was on Madeleine.

What hurt the most was Emily had been so painfully right, and it made him afraid. Even if Madeleine could ever find it in her heart to love him, could either of them bear to hurt Lee so much?

Moving on would be the right thing to do, but if he was in love with Madeleine, how could he dare marry another woman? He'd make his wife's life miserable, just like he would have if he'd married Emily.

The situation was enough to make him Google

houses in Tahiti. When a pajama-clad Madeleine walked into the kitchen, Adrian hated to admit how his heart leapt by just the sight of her.

"Looks like I'm not the only one who couldn't sleep," he said with a crooked grin.

"I've got too much on my mind to sleep. Ice cream should help, right?" She took a carton of Phish Food ice cream out of the freezer.

"Or the sugar will kick-start your nervous system, but hey, ice cream."

"I don't need your science at two in the morning," Madeleine said, brandishing a spoon in his direction.

"Jesus, is it that late?" Adrian asked, taking the spoon.

"It is indeed. Almost the witching hour." She plopped the carton of ice cream on the butcher table. "So…what did you think about Lee's grand alcohol purge?"

"I am proud of him. I hope he can keep it up. Tomorrow will be the real test."

"And all the weeks thereafter."

"You don't think he can quit, do you?"

"It's not that. I know he can do it. As many faults as Lee has, lack of determination is not one of them. I just know what's coming—the withdrawals, the irritability. My daddy tried to quit a few times, and it was never pleasant. Momma told him he was better off being a drunk."

"It's a lot to put up with. We'll get him through it, though. We have to."

For a few minutes, they sat side by side on barstools at the butcher table, digging around in the carton of ice cream for the chocolate fish candies and fighting over them.

"It's my ice cream. Just because you crash here constantly doesn't mean you have rights to it," Madeleine protested, blocking his spoon with hers.

"That means I'm a guest. You should be a gracious hostess and let me eat all the fish."

Adrian scooped a spoonful complete with a fish, then smirked at her in victory. He raised it to his lips, but Madeleine gave a fake pout. Rolling his eyes, he moved the spoon toward her instead. Madeleine grinned and leaned toward him, letting him feed her the ice cream off his spoon.

Adrian wasn't sure if he was more drawn by her mouth or the bit of cleavage he could see when she leaned over. Either way, his thoughts were running rampant and his heart began to pound.

Don't do it, he urged as his eyes met hers. *Shut down those instincts before—*

Cursing his impulsiveness, he leaned over, cupped her face in his hand, and kissed her with the knowledge that each time could be his last. Her cooled lips and tongue set his entire body ablaze, and he drank all of her in, knowing she was a thirst he'd never quench.

Breathless, Madeleine looked up at him, her eyes starry and for once not filled with sadness or regret. They resembled clear skies in the middle of winter.

"I've wanted to do that all day," she confessed, standing to take a timid step toward him.

"Thank God it's not just me." Adrian pulled her close. "Do you have any idea how hard it's been to focus on anything else but you?"

"I think I have a pretty good idea," Madeleine whispered. Her knowing smile set her eyes into a sparkle that Adrian thought rivaled the galaxies themselves.

He wrapped his hand around hers; she laced her fingers through his. "I think this is why I like being around you so much."

"Why is that?"

Could he dare to say it? Everything on his mind?

"Because you're so beautiful when you're happy. And whether we're willing to admit it or not, you're happy when we're together."

Did I really just say that? God, this was a terrible idea...

Madeleine blushed as she averted her eyes from him. "I am happy when I'm with you. It's about the only time I'm truly happy anymore. It's just...very dangerous to admit it."

He understood all too well. "I ain't gonna pretend to know what's come over me. God knows, this is the most reckless thing I've ever done, and I've done a lot. But it makes me feel like I have a pulse, like I'm not some piece of machinery programmed to a basic function."

Madeleine didn't respond immediately. There was a decision to be made. He waited and would have sworn his heart didn't beat once until she spoke.

"Adrian, we can't give in to this." She released her hand from his. "It's so undeniably screwed up."

"I know. I know it is. If you want, we can put this all in the past and pretend it never happened. But if you don't..."

301

She took moment to process. In her silence, Adrian's heartbeat was deafening, but the whole damned world halted when she opened her mouth to speak.

"God, how things can change so quickly. Six months ago I wanted nothing more than to just…stop being."

"And now?"

Her smile flickered like candlelight in the darkness. "And now there's nowhere else that I'd rather be than right here with you, fighting over chocolate fish at two in the morning."

"Me either." Adrian grasped her hands and pulled her toward him.

He wrapped his arms around her waist and breathed her in. Being this close to her cost more control than his mind could afford. She absolutely bankrupted him.

Lust soon took over. She straddled his lap and his mouth was running over hers before either of them could think it through. Blazing heat roared from inside out, and their heartbeats pounded through their kiss. Wanting to explore all of her, he pressed a trail of slow, maddening kisses from her neck to her collarbone, eliciting shivers and an ever-so-slight gasp.

Weak spot, Adrian thought with satisfaction, noting to keep it in mind.

He groaned deep in his throat as she ground her hips against his, and this time, he just couldn't hold back from touching her. Emboldened, he slipped his hands up her shirt, ambling over the gulf between her hips and the blossom of her breasts.

Madeleine shivered beneath his touch, her hands roaming from his face, to his chest, and then stopping torturously at his waist. Adrian wanted nothing more than to take her right then and there. She had every nerve in his body firing, and he needed relief. He cupped the back of her thighs in his hands and placed her on the butcher's block.

"Not here," she said, trying to catch her breath.

He picked her up again, accidentally pushing back the barstool behind him, a great scraping sound resounding through the silent house.

"Ade," she admonished in a whisper as his thoughts turned to his brother.

The mere idea of Lee made his heart sink, but before he could utter a hasty apology, her lips were back on his, ruining every sense of right and wrong. With her legs wrapped tight around his waist, he walked her from the kitchen to the hall, pushing her up against the wall at the foot of the stairs.

"Are we seriously doing this?" he asked between fevered kisses.

She shook her head but breathed, "I don't know."

"I need you to know," he said, purposefully nipping that spot on her neck.

Then a barking cough came from Lee's room that was like a hurtling railroad spike to slice through the rushing of their own blood and fear. It seemed an entire hour had passed before they realized their sin would remain a shared secret for another day.

"Jesus Christ," Adrian whispered, his pounding heart slowing. He held Madeleine just long enough for her to get her feet back on the floor before putting distance between them.

Madeleine held both hands to her forehead, wracking her brain for some kind of understanding. "It's my fault," she tried to explain in an apologetic whisper. "I had no business even being down here."

"No, I'm the one who should be sorry. I kissed you, and I-I wanted more."

"He can be a real asshole, but he doesn't deserve this."

"God, no. No one would deserve this."

"So…we can just put this behind us and move on, right?"

Adrian forced a short laugh. "We don't have much of a choice here do we?"

"No, we don't."

"I'll leave early in the morning. No sense in making this more awkward than it has to be."

"It's going to be awkward no matter what, Adrian. What difference is it going to make now?"

"It's the difference between me keeping some kind of control around you and—"

Madeleine rolled her eyes. "I'll try to be less irresistible."

"Sweet Jesus, Madeleine, you have problems," he huffed in annoyance. "You're the only woman I know who could have a man dying to take you to bed and still wonder if he's attracted to you."

She looked shocked, and when he headed upstairs, she stammered, "I-It's difficult for me to just accept you would genuinely w-want me."

"Then I'll bet it's an even bigger shocker to know I've had the same exact thought about you.

Goodnight, Madeleine."

He left her standing in the foyer, stunned.

CHAPTER
FORTY-EIGHT

The withdrawals were even harder than Madeleine had said they would be, and Adrian got a glimpse into Madeleine's hellish childhood. The delirium tremens set in mere hours after Adrian and Madeleine had forced themselves to go to separate beds, and neither of them had gotten a wink of sleep. Adrian had woken to the sound of his brother's trembling fits of pain. When he rushed into Lee's bedroom, Madeleine was already there, taking off his shirt and pants.

"He's burning up," she explained in a calm flurry of motion as she stripped him down while his body writhed with tremors.

"What should I do?"

"Get him some ice. We need to keep him hydrated, but I'm afraid if we give him water he'll just puke it back up."

"Shouldn't we call a doctor?" Adrian shuddered. "Get him to a hospital?"

"I called Henry to see what we can do. He's on his way. Go get that ice."

For a person who didn't seem to think she was very strong, Adrian was in awe of Madeleine. How was it that she coolly handled things that sent him into a panic? When he returned with the ice, she was sitting in bed with Lee propped up against her chest, fanning him with an old brochure from some place in Brazil they'd travelled to years earlier when they were happy and Lee was just considered a "heavy drinker." If anyone had told them they'd be *here*, fighting through death, infidelity, and withdrawals, Madeleine and Lee would insist it was impossible.

Adrian knelt at the side of the bed. Lee's hands were grasped in white-knuckled fists. His entire arm trembled, but his muscles would flex in a futile attempt to still them. Lee was fighting and trying his damnedest to keep doing it.

"Lee, I'm going to give you some ice, okay?"

Lee attempted a nod and opened his mouth best he could. He breathed out and closed his eyes gratefully, relaxing his head against Madeleine. Adrian saw her lip was trembling, but she kept it together and wrapped her arms around Lee.

Lee swallowed, fighting through the tremors. "Where's Thomas?" he asked. "Is he all right?"

Adrian pursed his lips. "Lee, Thomas isn't—"

"Thomas is perfectly fine," Madeleine interrupted in an even, soothing tone. "Don't worry about him. Try to rest."

"Can't. No time to—"

"You've got all the time in the world."

307

A knock at the door echoed down the empty hall. "That'll be Henry," Madeleine said.

Adrian quickly walked down the hall to let him in.

"I wish you would have told me you were going to do this," Henry said to Madeleine once they reached Lee's room. He readied a syringe full of the valium that would ease the convulsions. "We could have been prepared, gotten him a bed in a good rehab facility."

"He decided this on his own yesterday," Madeleine stated. "What was I going to do? Tell him it's not a convenient time to stop drinking?"

"No, but you should have called me. You pay me too much to not let me take care of you."

"Lee's not your patient. I can't expect you to do that."

Henry averted his eyes from her, overly concentrated on sticking the needle in a vial and filling it with the valium. Adrian narrowed his gaze towards Madeleine; her expression matched his when their eyes met in silent communication.

"I may need both of you help to stabilize his arm," Henry said.

Adrian went to his brother's side to hold his arm as still as he could.

In mere seconds, Henry plunged the vial in and had it back out as another wave of pain set in.

Lee glared at his brother for a moment. "Why'd you hurt me? I didn't do anything to you."

Adrian's nerves were frazzled and his stomach flopped in pure…fear? Terror? Guilt? He wasn't sure, but whatever it was, he felt it to the greatest possible extent. He thought of Madeleine wrapped up in his arms and how much he had, even in that moment of fear-terror-guilt, wanted her.

"That was me, Lee," Henry clarified.

Adrian realized then that Lee thought he had been the one to give him the shot. The guilt was getting to him.

"I gave you a dose of valium to stop the tremors," said Henry. "How are you feeling?"

"Kinda want to die," Lee said with a dry laugh. "This hurts like hell. I just want a drink."

"You don't need it, Lee. It's gonna be a rough go for a while, but we are here to take care of you," Henry tried to assure him.

Lee's body convulsed one more time before giving in to the effects of the valium. He took a deep breath and relaxed his head against Madeleine's chest. "Thank God you're too good for your own good," he murmured. "I do not deserve you."

Adrian swallowed. His heart was thudding hard. "I'm gonna go get some fresh ice," he said as a means of escaping the situation.

"I'll do that," Henry said, grabbing the cup of ice Adrian had brought. "You stay with your brother. You mean a lot more to him than I do."

Adrian gave a nod, and Henry went off to the kitchen to get more ice.

"This is only going to get harder," Madeleine told Lee. "And I'll be honest, I am scared to death of this. Henry suggested a great rehab facility earlier that—"

"Please, don't. This is embarrassing enough. I

want to go through this at home."

Genuine fear radiated through Madeleine's eyes. "Lee, we'll keep it as private as possible," he spoke up. "And we're hardly going to just dump you off and leave you there."

"Bad press," he said, shaking his head and resting against Madeleine.

"Lee, the company is fine."

"Please, no stupid facility."

"Okay. No facility," she agreed. "But if you get too far gone—"

"I'll go," he said, right before falling asleep.

~*~

"Did you catch that earlier?" Madeleine asked that night as she spread the bedsheet over the mattress in her old room.

"I told you not to worry about making the damned bed." Adrian went to the other side of the bed to help her tuck in the bedsheet. "Catch what?"

"Henry. When I told him Lee wasn't his patient."

"Yeah. That was weird, wasn't it? Do you think…?"

"Yes, I do," Madeleine confirmed as they finished tucking. "Why wouldn't Lee tell me?"

Adrian retrieved the comforter from the floor. "That's easy enough. I mean, he's prideful, too worried about appearances. But the next question is when the hell he fits it into his schedule."

Madeleine threw him a questioning look.

"No, seriously. For one, when did he start? And two, I've seen his schedule—he literally has no time to go."

"Maybe he Skypes like I did in Tybee."

"Showing up to a psychiatrist's office isn't Lee's style," Adrian agreed, plopping down on the freshly made bed.

Madeleine frowned playfully. "All my hard work making up that bed and you just jump on it and ruin it."

"I clearly told you not to bother. Twice," Adrian said. "I'm going to ruin the hell out of this very well-made bed doing some hardcore sleeping."

Madeleine laughed. "I'm so tired. And Monday, I'll have it all to myself. I'm exhausted."

Adrian was unable to take his eyes off her. "I'm not going anywhere."

"I can't ask you to do that."

"You don't have to. I'm not leaving you here with him all by yourself. Hell, today was hard with the three of us. I swear, if he'd begged for another drink one more time, I was going to give in and buy him some. I don't know how the man manages to be annoying and pitiful at the same time."

"You've got a company to run on Monday," Madeleine reminded him with a tilt of her head.

He didn't hesitated to respond. "You're more important than the company. Lee's more important."

Her eyes brightened, but after a moment, she bit the inside of her lips and cast her eyes to the floor. "I'll let you get to sleep."

Adrian's smile faded. Madeleine felt as guilty as he did. It was as plain as day. "Was it really that bad?" he asked.

She looked at him peculiarly. "What? You mean—"

"Yeah. I mean, morally, sure, it's not good, but…" He struggled with the right way to phrase what he wanted to say. "Don't we deserve to be happy too?"

For a moment, Madeleine only blinked, staring at him like she was trying to analyze a complex calculus problem. "I…I don't know if I can be truly happy at the expense of others. I think there would always be a nagging feeling in the back of my brain telling me I didn't deserve the happiness I got."

Adrian nodded. He completely understood, and she was right. "I'm sorry. I can't quit thinking about it. One minute it's wrong and I feel guilty and the next—"

"Adrian, I think you're too big-hearted for your own good. You think I need a decent man in my life so you do what you've always done: you put on your armor to ride into battle," she explained as though she were speaking to a child.

"That's not what this is. I know it's ridiculous, and nothing should ever come of it, but when I told you last night it was different, I meant it," he insisted. "Do you think I would say that just to sleep with you?"

"No, but—"

"Then don't trivialize this. If you don't feel the same way, that's fine."

"That's not the case, unfortunately," Madeleine said sadly. "I wish it were. It would be a lot easier."

For a moment, they said nothing, the air buzzing with electric tension. All was quiet in the old house as it added yet another story to its repertoire of tales.

"So…what now?"

"I don't know, Maddie."

Another pause, and then she said, "I'm going to check on Lee."

Adrian didn't even have time to reply before she was out of the room and heading down the stairs.

CHAPTER
FORTY-NINE

Mentally, Madeleine was fuming.

It was 2 a.m., and she couldn't sleep. Partially because she was sleeping in an armchair next to Lee's bed, but mostly because she couldn't stop thinking about Adrian.

Utterly useless conversation, she groused. Nothing but damage would be done talking about their stupid "feelings."

She watched Lee sleeping peacefully, drugged up on another round of valium. He hadn't wanted it, but Madeleine was grateful he'd continued taking it. She knew the dangers of withdrawals, the possibility of heart failure, even tonic-clonic seizures. Although the steady rise and fall of his chest made her grateful, it also brought her to realization.

She wasn't in love with him.

Evelyn stared at her peculiarly through the shadows. "Then why are you sitting here watching him breathe?"

Madeleine considered it for a split-second, then laughed at her answer. "Because I love him."

"Jesus," Evelyn said with a roll of her gorgeous green eyes. "You're all balled up."

"Are the two mutually exclusive? If love is defined as deep affection, that's exactly what I have for Lee, but I don't love him to the depth and breadth and height of my soul anymore."

"Ugh, God, now she's quoting Browning."

Madeleine left the room, sprinting up the stairs to her old bedroom. She swallowed nervously but gathered the courage to open the door and make her way to the bed, her heart pounding in her chest the entire time. She pulled back the covers and settled in next to Adrian.

She reached out tentatively, placing her hand on his bare back. Once she got over the initial shock that she was actually daring to touch him, Madeleine reveled in the feeling of his skin beneath her fingertips. She flattened her palm against his shoulder blade, content in nothing more than such a minuscule contact with him. As her heart was slowing, he turned toward her in a sleepy, cumbersome roll. He put his arm around her and closed the space between them.

He murmured, "Maddie," in his sleep, and she smiled from the inside out.

She couldn't think it—it was too dangerous of a thought, especially now—so instead poetry filled her mind…

To the depth and breadth and height my soul can reach.

315

CHAPTER FIFTY

Time had always had the ability to either cause old wounds to fester or to heal them into scars. As much as Madeleine had resigned herself to the fact she was leaving as soon as Lee was better, they had fallen into a routine of comfortable complacency she found difficult to break. For once, it was nice to just have some peace.

Lee had suffered through the withdrawals, which was a pathetic understatement. The first seventy-two hours had been hell, but she and Adrian had stayed by his side the entire time. On the fourth day, hell started to burn down to embers. By the fifth, he was demanding his laptop, paper, and pen and throwing around new ideas for Atwood Technologies with Adrian.

On his eighth day sober, Lee insisted he was going back to work. Watching him leave that day, Madeleine felt like she was sending her child off to the first day of kindergarten. He must have sensed her worry, because he called and texted multiple times to let her know how he was. Normally, she didn't stand a chance trying to speak to him during his workday, but Madeleine was grateful he'd taken the time to let her know.

For the next three weeks, they fell into a pleasant routine. Lee would leave for work, and she would write, working hard to finish her new book. Lee would be home as soon as he fought through the Atlanta rush-hour traffic. Dinners were spent together, talking about their days, while being careful to avoid the difficult topics they actually needed to discuss. They slept in separate bedrooms and repeated it all the next day. While they were more like roommates than husband and wife, both Lee and Madeleine enjoyed their brief illusion of peace.

On day thirty of being sober, Lee sent a text less than fifteen minutes after leaving the house.

Lee: Let's go out tonight. Celebrate an entire month being sober?

Madeleine thought for quite a while about how to respond. The offer seemed very…date-like. Accepting could give him the impression she still loved him; rejecting would be insensitive.

After an hour of deliberation, she texted him back.

Maddie: Meet you in town later?

She waited a good forty-five minutes for an answer, and when he sent back a simple,

"See you at 6."

The conversation was over. Madeleine thought she was floating on a vast sea of uncertainty, and she was sure Lee felt the same way. They both needed some sort of closure in their lives, no matter how much it hurt. They had to move forward, and they each had to do it alone.

Though she was already regretting saying yes, Madeleine headed into Atlanta early, attempting to miss the after-school traffic. If she was being perfectly honest, it was also for the tiny chance she would get to see Adrian.

Madeleine's stomach fluttered at the mere sight of him. Feeling this way was ridiculous; it needed to stop. And yet, she didn't want it to.

Minutes later, she was lying on the floor in Adrian's office, staring at the ceiling.

"I've been thinking…"

"Thinking's a dangerous way to spend your time," Adrian said.

"You remember at the Swan Ball, how Maisy was telling me about that plastic surgeon who could fix the scars on my wrists?"

"Yeah…"

"I was thinking of making an appointment to see what he could do for mine."

For a moment, Adrian said nothing. Madeleine waited, watching the sunlight wax and wane on the ceiling as clouds passed by. It was a perfectly lovely day, in the very infancy of a new spring. Never had a little extra sunlight made Madeleine happier. Not that all of her markedly improved mood could be completely credited to sunlight.

"I like your scars."

Madeleine sat up and threw him a skeptical glance.

"Nuh-uh-uh," Adrian chided playfully. "You've gotta stay down the whole fifteen minutes."

"Seriously? I don't even work here!" Madeleine laid back down.

"You're the one who dared to walk into Atwood Technologies during 'morning meditation.' Even the UPS guys have to participate. Needless to say, we're now dead last on their route."

"Whose idiotic idea was this?"

Adrian laughed out loud. "Lee's."

"You've got to be kidding me. He's probably off having a good laugh while all of you lay on this scratchy commercial carpet just because he commanded it."

"I would have thought so too, but I swear he's totally into this. It's supposed to give everyone a break to think and refocus, prioritize. A lot of companies do it."

"All the CEOs, they're in on this together?" Madeleine countered. "Next week some study will say clucking like a chicken will increase productivity five hundred percent and you'll have to do that too."

"My, my, Mrs. Atwood, aren't we awfully negative about company policy? I may just have to send you over to HR for retraining."

She laughed. "Yes, please re-train me on how to lie down on the floor properly."

Adrian gave an amused laugh, and then it was

quiet in his office again. A few seconds passed, and then Madeleine felt Adrian's fingers on the inside of her wrist. Shockwaves travelled throughout her entire body as his fingers blindly traced the crooked path of the scar on her left wrist.

"What makes you want to hide your scars?" he asked, clearing his throat.

Madeleine shrugged, which she realized was dumb. He couldn't see her since he was CEO-mandated to stare at the ceiling for fifteen straight minutes.

"I don't know. Shouldn't I be focusing on forgetting my past and moving on? It's hard to forget the past when it's carved into your skin."

Adrian sat up and looked down at her, then gently grasped her forearm and pulled it into his lap. "Do whatever makes life easier." He traced the path of her scar with his fingertips. "If that means you don't want to live with a constant reminder of the past, then have the surgery. But for me, when I see your wrists, I see a story. A story that could have ended but got a sequel instead. Now I know you're focusing on giving it a better ending this time around, but tell me, as a writer of your caliber, what kind of story doesn't have a little conflict?"

Madeleine had to remind herself to breathe.

He is something else.

"You're supposed to stay down the whole fifteen minutes," she reminded him with a contented smile. Without thinking twice, Adrian lay down next to her and laced his fingers through hers.

She was as happy as she could ever remember. A soft, recorded chime rang out three times.

Madeleine guessed, from the crescendo of scurrying and the baritone office phones ringing off the hook, Atwood Technologies was resuming business as usual.

Without a word, Adrian stood and helped her up, locking eyes with her one more time in a last-ditch effort to make that blissful moment last a few more seconds.

"What's going on in Atlanta today that's more important than finishing my book?" Adrian teased.

The blood rushed to Madeleine's head, a blushing smile rising from the inside. She'd rather a man tell her he liked her writing than spewing bullshit her about being beautiful.

"It's almost finished," she said shyly. "Just a few more chapters left and it'll be off for publication. Hopefully."

"Hopefully? From what you've told me, it's off the beaten path for you, but I think it's going to be the best thing you've ever written."

"Really?"

"Absolutely. It's more of a reflection of you. It's like a glimpse into how I imagine your brain works."

"That's scary," Madeleine replied, knowing she couldn't disagree.

Adrian's eyes softened, his gaze lingering on her. "It's amazing," he uttered in the low, honest tone he used when what he said mattered most.

There it was again—awkwardness that settled deep but felt like a tingling, sparking crossroads between madness and happiness all at the same time.

Then Lee walked in.

"This just came up from engineering, and I don't have a clue what it is," he said, busting through the door as he was well-accustomed to doing.

When he saw Madeleine, his face brightened. "I wasn't expecting you for hours."

Madeleine watched Adrian's shoulders fall. It hurt to see him affected.

"Just taking the opportunity to get out of the house and do some shopping," Madeleine squeaked.

"You? Shopping? That's new."

She hadn't the least bit of an inkling to go shopping before the lie had sprung to life and came spewing out of her mouth. Madeleine was taken aback when she realized how easily the lie slipped right out of her mouth. Had it been that easy for him to lie to her?

She'd been skeptical of lies before. If she overthought it, Lee was probably equally skeptical of hers—the first of many, if she didn't get the idea of Adrian out of her head, which was looking less and less likely every day.

"Are you buying something for tonight or just blowing money?" Lee teased.

Adrian's brow wrinkled, and Madeleine's stomach sank. She wished Lee hadn't said anything in front of him.

"Got plans tonight?" Adrian asked casually. His face, however, said all the words he knew he couldn't say.

"Celebrating." Lee grinned and handed his brother the papers and schematics from engineering. "It's been a month sober today."

"Oh," Adrian remarked, thumbing through the stack. "Cool. Good for y'all."

Which was code for *damn it*.

The following ten seconds of awkward silence was stifling.

Just as Madeleine thought she was going to suffocate, Lee asked, "So what are these?"

"Would it hurt you to learn to read one so you know where the money in your company is going?"

"The engineering stuff is your job. I think of how to make money off it."

"It's the obsolescence mitigation for Lockheed's C5-M. It'll take forever to get through this."

"I'll let you get to it then. We needed that, like, yesterday."

"It's a big project. No room for error. I'd rather it be done right the first time."

"Yeah, and Lockheed wants it right and on-time. How soon can you have it approved?"

"By tonight, if I didn't have to go to your stupid board meeting."

"Done. I'll fill you in. I've gotta go. I've got a full day if I'm going to get out of here on time," Lee said, clapping a hand on his brother's shoulder.

Adrian said nothing, but Madeleine thought she caught him rolling his eyes as Lee turned to leave.

"Maddie, I'll see later tonight. Were you planning on staying longer or…?"

It was Lee's way of saying he had too much to do to see her. Which was just fine with Madeleine. It wasn't actually her husband that she had come to see, after all.

"No, I just thought I'd pop in. And I've got a

much better chance of catching you in Adrian's office than yours."

Lee shrugged. "Good point. I really don't know why I even have one."

"Busy man," she chimed in the happiest tone she could conjure. He placed a quick kiss on her cheek before heading out the door. It was the most affection they'd shown one another in weeks.

And, Madeleine knew, it was driving Adrian even crazier. But what else was she supposed to do? Lee was still her husband, no matter how she felt about Adrian. What had started out as a disaster just months earlier had developed into a complacent partnership. As far as marriages went, there were worse fates.

As soon as the door closed, the entire atmosphere changed. That tingling, sparkling feeling had dissipated.

Adrian pursed his lips and would not look at her, staring instead at the Lockheed documents Lee had delivered.

"Adrian—"

"You didn't mention you had plans," he said in a flat tone. Madeleine wasn't sure how to take it.

"Um, yeah." She shrugged. "Nothing big. Just dinner and whatever comes to mind. Like he said, celebrating a month sober."

"Okay. Sounds nice."

Madeleine couldn't for the life of her figure out why she even told him the first place. Adrian didn't need to know everything, especially if it would only hurt him. Yet what else was she supposed to do? She was married, for the time being. To Lee, not him. And leaving wasn't as easy as it sounded.

"Adrian—"

"Madeleine, it's fine. If you want to be with him, that's your business. I'm certainly not going to stand in your way."

"But you know I don't."

"Then you're giving him hope when you have no intention of sticking around." He looked back down at the schematics on his desk. "I'm sorry, I just think it's unfair."

"And who exactly are you more worried about it being fair to?"

Adrian set his jaw, growing more anxious by the second.

"You've got a lot to do," Madeleine said tersely, gathering up her things. "I'll leave you alone."

"Yeah, I'll see you around."

CHAPTER
FIFTY-ONE

Typically, Lee planned out their date nights down to the minutest details. It wasn't a control issue; Madeleine had just trusted his judgment and let him take the reins. He was normally up to date on the newest, trendy thing they needed to try, and Lee knew how to have fun. It was one thing she had always liked about him.

Not that this was an official date night, although Lee wanted to think of it that way. Madeleine had gotten them reservations at his favorite restaurant, and they held pleasant enough conversations, even though it wasn't like it used to be. When she had accepted his offer of an evening out, Lee hoped the wall she'd put between them was finally breaking, that he wasn't going to lose her after all. But judging from her demeanor tonight, like something was weighing heavily on her mind, her will was stronger than ever.

"So where are we going now?" he asked in

anticipation, not that he cared. He'd walk to the ends of the Earth if that was what she wanted.

"I got a reservation at Top Golf to let you get a few hits in since you've probably forgotten how to use a golf club," Madeleine said playfully.

"You didn't. Maddie, you hate golf."

"Bane of my existence," she agreed, shaking her head but smiling anyway.

"You know, typically when we go out, we do stuff that interests both of us."

"I'm sure we'll do something that interests me too."

God, oh God, he hoped she was flirting. It had been too long, and she looked perfect in an unassuming black dress hugging her body in all the right places.

In fact, his wife was such a distraction he didn't think he could have hit a ball straight to save his life. Every drive and putt he took made him look like a pathetic amateur. It was almost embarrassing. The other guys playing didn't exactly have a curvy blonde in a little black dress acting as a caddy, though.

He laughed as he drove one of the last balls. "Jesus Christ. This is the worst I've ever played."

"You're just out of practice. You'll get back into it."

"No, I won't. My golf days are over. My weekends are about to be spent as a husband only."

"You've got one more shot," Madeleine said hoarsely, breaking the tense silence that ached between them.

At first, he didn't think she was talking about

golf. He realized her meaning when she handed him the last golf ball.

"Better make it good then, right?" he said, hoping she'd catch the double meaning behind his words. She would; she was clever enough to catch the subtleties behind words, what they really meant. He just hoped she knew how much he meant it.

He placed the ball on the tee, squaring up his shoulders. He focused on the furthest hole in the course. If he were going to take a last shot, might as well go big.

A breath in, pivot back and…

Release.

Lee watched it soar and, in disbelief, watched it sink straight in the hole.

"Oh my God." Madeleine grinned. "Did you just get a hole in one?"

"Must have been a fluke. I might have to end my streak and drink to that one."

"How about no?" She laughed, and they turned to leave.

He wanted to hold her hand to help guide her out as they weaved through the groups of happy and carefree people on a Friday night, but Lee hardly wanted to push his luck. He wanted this time with her to last a little while longer.

"Want to grab a coffee before we head home?"

"I never say no to coffee."

If she saw through this attempt to lengthen their night together, she said nothing. He'd have done anything to make this night go on forever. Why on Earth had he ever thought life could be better than this? That there could be anyone better than her?

Lee supposed he never thought there could ever be anyone better than Madeleine. Things with Brecklyne had just happened and then imitated life with Madeleine. It was the same illusion he was in now.

Without even discussing it, he drove toward their old favorite coffee shop just south of Midtown. Atlanta parking being what it was, they had to park half a mile away from the shop, but they didn't mind walking up the store-lined streets. Lee jabbered on until he noticed Madeleine was no longer beside him but a few paces back. He froze when he realized what shop had so captured her rapt attention.

Mon Petit Coeur was the high-end baby boutique that charged ungodly amounts of money for all things nursery. It was where he had spent a small fortune when they were buying for Thomas.

Lee stood next to Madeleine before an elegant display of a girl's vintage-style bedroom, with a brass crib and canopy, complete with a gorgeous sage and pink rosette-print bedding set. It was exactly like something Madeleine would choose for a daughter if she'd ever had one.

"Maddie—"

Fighting back tears, Madeleine cut in, "Sometimes I think that if we'd never lost our baby we'd never have a second thought about whether our marriage was worth saving."

"No...I don't think we would."

"I guess we've screwed it up too much for it to be normal again."

"For what it counts, I wish we hadn't. Wish I

329

hadn't."

"I do too."

She would probably push him away, and he couldn't blame her if she did, but he wrapped his arm around her and held her close to his side as they stared at the crib together, wondering how different their life together could have been.

CHAPTER FIFTY-TWO

It was midnight when his phone buzzed on the coffee table. Adrian glanced toward the illuminated screen but ignored it. Whoever it was could wait. Nothing had been right since Madeleine had left his office, and after finishing the Lockheed project for Lee, he'd shut himself in his apartment with a pizza and a six-pack. He had finished both while binge-watching the Travel Channel, wishing he were the one a million miles away from home. Perhaps the change in perspective would remind him there was more to the world than Madeleine or his own selfish desires.

His phone buzzed again. He flopped back on the couch and tried his best to focus on the television again, but curiosity got the best of him. Snatching up his phone, he saw two messages from Lee that warranted a phone call.

"What do you mean she's definitely leaving?"

"I've come home every night since I started back

to work thinking she's gonna be gone. That whole hour drive home, I'm preparing myself for the possibility. But no, it's been thirty days sober, and she's still here, and she's not telling me to leave either. I'll admit, I asked her to go out tonight hoping…hell, I don't know what I was hoping."

Adrian sighed, more out of relief than indignation for his brother. "Did you think one date night would magically fix things?"

"No, I—"

"Or that she'd just climb right back into bed with you?"

"No! Why are you being such an asshole?"

"Because, honestly, I don't know what you expect. Lee, you're lucky she's stuck around this long. How many women would stay with someone who's cheated on them?"

"Not many, I know, but—"

"Jesus, Lee. You're my brother, and I love you. I know you're working hard to fix all the mistakes you've made, but that doesn't free you from the consequences."

Lee was silent on the other end.

Guilt weighed heavy on Adrian's shoulders. "Damn, that was harsh."

"No, you're right. It's the truth, it hurts, but it needed to be said. Guess I just wanted to keep pretending things were going to get better for a while longer."

It took a lot for him to say it, but Adrian did anyway. "Maybe it could—"

"I'm going to file for a divorce. Save her the trouble."

Adrian's heart sank as the feeling of guilt increased. "Are you sure?"

"Yeah...It's not ideal, but what I really want is for Maddie to be happy again, and she's not going to be happy with me."

Adrian winced and took a sharp breath. "How are you going to feel when she eventually moves on?"

His brother laughed. *"Very jealous of a very lucky bastard. She deserves no less than the best."*

CHAPTER FIFTY-THREE

"Maddie, I'm just telling you, you should have heard the conversation last night, that's all."

Madeleine cut her eyes at Adrian. He lounged against the kitchen counter, drying dishes as she cleaned them. In a way of expressing her gratitude to Maggie Beth and Richard for being there for her with Lee, Madeleine had hosted a small dinner party for the whole family. The meal was over, and Lee and Richard had excused themselves to Madeleine's office to discuss business gossip. Maggie Beth, now attached to Richard's hip, had joined them, leaving Madeleine and Adrian on dish duty.

"Let me get this straight—you want me to feel sorry for him? Are we talking about the same Lee?"

"Don't talk so loud," Adrian groaned. "And yes, we're talking about the same Lee."

Madeleine turned with her a soapy hand on her hip and stared hard at him. "You've been agreeing with me all along he's the one in the wrong. He tugs on your heartstrings and I'm the bad guy? *He's* divorcing *me!*"

"I didn't say you were the bad guy. Quit putting words in my mouth. Damn, you fight dirty," Adrian said, keeping his eyes on the dish he was working too hard to dry.

Madeleine's lips tightened into a hard line, and she attacked a casserole dish full force with steel wool.

"You're gonna scratch the hell out of that."

Madeleine rolled her eyes. "It's not like we can't afford more."

"Do you love him?"

Madeleine shook her head. Despite all the things Lee had done, it didn't fill her with any happiness to admit their marriage was over, but she sure as hell didn't want to stay.

"I thought about it all night," he confessed. "I feel guilty."

"Doesn't mean I have to," Madeleine groused.

Adrian slipped his arms around her in a loving embrace.

"Ade," she said dismissively but relaxed her body against his and wrapped her hand around his forearm.

"Would you, just for a minute, consider the possibility I'm not defending Lee, but being selfish in thinking we could finally have our own chance?"

"As much as I want that, you know it can't happen, Adrian."

"It could happen." He kissed the back of her neck.

"Adrian," she tried again, fully meaning to scold him, but it came out as more of a shiver. She could practically feel his self-satisfied smile as he backed away and went back to drying the dishes.

"Is that why you felt guilty?" Madeleine asked. "Because you think you're being selfish?"

He nodded and dried a glass she handed him. "Yeah."

A feeling of dread took over. "Your family would never forgive you."

"I've thought about it. Mom would, eventually. She'd convince Dad to come around. Lee, though...Jesus."

"You could hardly blame him," Madeleine said.

"No, but it doesn't change the way I feel about you either."

Madeleine shot him a sympathetic look, about the time Maggie Beth came into the kitchen. "Maddie, I will never for the life of me understand why you don't use the dishwasher," her mother-in-law said as she flitted into the room.

Madeleine panicked internally, wondering how much Maggie Beth had heard.

"You should take Lee up on getting a housekeeper. You go relax, Maddie. I'll get the rest of these!"

"Oh, I'm fine. I like washing dishes," Madeleine insisted, her cheeks reddening as her heart beat fast in her chest. She was astonished how relaxed Adrian appeared on the outside.

"I insist," Maggie Beth said, masterfully nudging her away from the sink. "You've had your work cut out helping Lee and you need to take a rest."

Madeleine could only throw a silent, pleading expression toward Adrian while her mother-in-law completely took over. Adrian could only shrug helplessly as his mother shoved a plate in his hands to dry.

After a few minutes of gawking at the scene, Madeleine gave up. They would have to finish their conversation later.

"I guess I'll go write...or something," she mumbled, reluctantly leaving the room.

~*~

Glaring red numerals burned into the darkness mere minutes past midnight. Madeleine found it too difficult to sleep. She thought about what Adrian had said. Despite all the destruction and pain they could cause, it didn't change anything—not the way she felt about him, or Lee, the entire screwed up-situation.

She'd already fallen for him. Helplessly, beyond the point of no return, fallen, and she hadn't even gathered up the courage to tell him she loved him yet. Madeleine couldn't bear to tell him now with the possibility he would decide to do the right thing for his family. It wasn't that she would feel angry, but her heart would always ache for him.

There were three options: Stay and make things right with Lee. *Not a chance in hell.* Let him go through with the divorce and start a new life. But that third option—the one where she threw all caution to the wind and made Adrian a major part of a new life—nothing had ever exhilarated her spirit

337

more.

Finally accepting sleep was evading her, she grabbed a notebook and pen from her bedside table and slipped down the hall and stairs, dodging every creaking floorboard she'd memorized since childhood.

Then there he was, on the porch, sitting on the wicker set she'd bought with Lee up in Blue Ridge the weekend he'd decided to renovate McCollum Manor and move his wife back home where she thought she needed to heal.

God, how wrong she had been. The old house had been nothing but a hateful reminder of how her short happiness with Lee was just a glittering speck in the dark, storm-battered waters of her life. In the distance was a lighthouse, the shore and solid ground, and she might be able to make it there. To have a happy ending that certainly would never be perfect, but happy nonetheless.

Adrian motioned for her to sit next to him and she did, and he instantly wrapped his arm around her. She rested her head on his shoulder. The early April air held a chill, but Madeleine was safe and warm there in his arms. For the longest time, they simply sat there, taking in the beauty of the night, the peaceful sounds of newly formed leaves rustling as the breeze toyed with the wispy oak branches towering high over the lawn. When the rain set in on the porch's tin roof, it was sheer perfection.

"I can't think of anything better than this."

"Me either," Madeleine agreed with a soft smile, her eyes trained on the rain dripping from the porch roof.

In the moment, it was all too easy to put fears aside and consider a future together. It was even possible to imagine those semi-perfect ideals she'd forbidden herself from imagining.

"What are you thinking about?"

Madeleine blushed. "Nothing. Just getting lost in the rainfall." It sounded vague and artsy, so she thought it might satiate his curiosity. She might have been dreaming of a life with him, but she lacked the courage to express it. "What are you thinking about?"

He laughed lightly. "Building a house. Maybe on a mountain."

"Oh," Madeleine replied with a nervous laugh, grateful she hadn't poured her heart out to him.

A few moments passed in silence while Madeleine tried to tamp down her nervousness. "Would you even want to live up on a mountain? It gets cold at night, and you could freeze to death in the middle of a heat wave."

"Oh, I get to live there too?"

"Well, yeah," Adrian continued, as if it was as obvious as the color of the sky. "There's no point in going anywhere if I've gotta do it without you."

"What if I don't want to live on a mountain?"

"See, I need to know these things. What do you want out of life? What would make you perfectly, absolutely happy?"

Madeleine took an apprehensive breath, but she knew she could trust him. "I want a new start."

"What would you want?"

Madeleine tried to relax, to be perfectly honest with him, consequences be damned. "A small wedding and a long honeymoon. I want a house in the middle of Savannah, off one of the squares."

"I like Savannah. I could do that."

"I need a place to write. A mountain view wouldn't be so bad, though."

"I just want a huge garage and my own Tony Stark-style room to tinker around in. Oh, and a pool. I've always wanted one but I've never had one. Think we can stuff one into those tiny Savannah courtyards?"

Madeleine gathered up the courage to say what was on her mind. "One day, I want to try having another baby."

"Really?"

She shrugged, nervous again. "I know I've not got the best track record with pregnancies, but if I'm gonna ask for all that…why not?"

A satisfied smile across his lips. "And here I thought I'd have to talk you into it."

Madeleine was trying hard to contain the stupid feeling of giddiness spreading through her entire body. "So you've been putting a lot of thought into all this?"

"You're kind of constantly on my mind now. And yes, before you turn this all sad and pessimistic, I know it'll take a lot of sacrifice. I'm just saying, when you're ready, if ever, I am too. I love you. We can talk about the perfect house and life all day, but if I had to live in a cardboard box with you, I'd still be the happiest man alive."

Madeleine swooned with every word he uttered. She tried to tell herself to stop, to get it together. They were only words, and as much as she believed in the power of words, to others words could be a worthless currency. What if they meant nothing now? What if he just wanted to satiate some old teenaged crush in a rebound to the next possible future Mrs. Atwood, just like Emily? What if—

Stop it.

Madeleine stared deep into Adrian's eyes. "I need to know you mean every word. And if you don't, that's fine, but please just—"

He placed his hand on the side of her face and pressed a long, sweet kiss to her lips. "I mean every. Last. Syllable. Especially that part about loving you."

"I love you too. I've just been too scared to admit it. I should have told you already."

"There are a ton of things we should have told each other years ago. I don't want another ten minutes to go by again before you know how much I want you in my life."

Joy caused the blush in Madeleine's cheeks. "How do you always know the perfect thing to say?"

"I've been listening to my head instead of my heart my whole life. That hasn't gotten me too far, so now I'm going to speak what the heart says before even thinking about it."

"Tell me I can steal that line and put it in a book."

"You can," he laughed, "but it'll cost you."

"Yeah?" Madeleine looked up at him from the crook of his arm. "How much?"

"Oh, it's pricey. It's gonna cost you a house in Savannah, a small wedding, a long honeymoon, and if I'm gonna ask for all that—"

Madeleine punctuated his statement with a kiss, her lips expressing every bit of gratitude and love for him wordlessly while lightning flashed and thunder rattled the tin on the porch roof.

CHAPTER
FIFTY-FOUR

The quiet cacophony of Maggie Beth's house did nothing to calm Adrian's nerves. The tick-tock-swoosh of the grandfather clock in the hall played a hushed waltz, and the shrill scream of his mother's tea kettle did little to muffle his parents' whispered yet heated discussion on how to handle speaking to their son.

Adrian wished they'd just come out and say it. The situation was an elephant in the room, demanding recognition. He imagined his father was telling his mother serving their son Earl Grey in his gram's china was ridiculous, the thing to do was to go straight to him right now and—

He wondered what his father would ask. Of all the scenarios that had played through his head in the past ten minutes he had spent waiting in his mother's living room, none had been pretty. Most ended with an argument with his father and his mother in tears.

Then again, maybe they'd be supportive. Such an idiotic idea was almost enough to make him laugh.

The kettle stopped shrieking. The flurry of harsh whispers ceased. Adrian peered down the hall and into the kitchen. His mother was arranging the silver tea tray, also Gram's.

It was too formal for this to go well, and his nervousness fizzed up again.

Although Richard's mouth was pressed into a hard frown when he entered the room, he patted Adrian's shoulder as he passed by and took a seat in the armchair across from the sofa where Adrian sat. Richard eased back into the chair and perched one leg on top of the other. He was comfortable here, like he'd never left. "You know why we're here, right?"

Adrian nodded silently.

His mother came in the room and set the tea tray on the table. "Want some tea, baby? It's supposed to rain later, and there's nothing better than a hot cup of tea on a rainy day."

His father appeared to be working overtime to keep his eyes from rolling, but Adrian couldn't further upset his mother by refusing her tea.

"Sure, Mom."

Maggie Beth smiled, making her crow's feet crinkle, and sat back with a cup of tea. Adrian fixed a cup of tea for his mother's sake and settled into the sofa, ready as he could be for the impending storm.

"Adrian," his father said, "there's no sense in beating around the bush here, son. We've got a few things concerning us and we're going to find a solution together."

Adrian wanted to tell his father there were no solutions to this so-called problem, but he didn't. He decided to be respectful of his parents and the pain they were already experiencing. And it was all his fault.

Maggie Beth set her tea down on the end table. "We love you and just want the best for you and your brother, right? This isn't meant to hurt you."

Richard scoffed. "Sometimes the truth hurts."

"Richard—"

"No, he's right," Adrian said. "Sometimes it does. Just say what you need to say."

"How long has it been going on?" his mother asked.

Adrian laughed. "You don't miss a beat, do you?"

"No, I assure you, I don't. Maybe with Lee, but not you," Maggie Beth replied in a calm, even tone Adrian certainly never expected. "Are you going to answer my question?"

"Do you mean to ask how long I've been in love with her or how long this...so-called affair has been going on?"

His mother's huff and what she said next was also something he did not expect. "Adrian, you've always been in love with her. I knew it long before *you* figured it out. A mother knows her child's heart."

Adrian's jaw dropped. "I don't understand. Why haven't you ever said anything?"

"The same reason you didn't. You were just kids at first, then Lee loved her. She made him a better man, and she still does." Maggie Beth crossed her arms across her chest. "But it became obvious Friday night after dinner, when I come in to see my son with his brother's wife wrapped up in his arms."

"That's why you're going to put a stop to this," Richard interjected. "Because it's the right thing to do, for everyone involved."

Adrian stared at his parents incredulously. "Absolutely not. You said it yourself—I love her, and Lee doesn't. Not in the way he should."

"Lee is trying to put his life back together. They were happy before," his father said in his patronizing tone.

"He also filed for a divorce yesterday."

Richard and Maggie Beth looked at each other in disbelief. "Lee did? Did Maddie ask him for one?"

"No, she did not, but they both knew their marriage has been over," Adrian stated. "At this point, all Lee wants is for Maddie to be happy."

"But not with you! He is your brother, your blood! Or have you gotten so selfish you've forgotten? Besides, your father and I are the ones who will have to pay the consequences. Do you really want our family ripped apart?"

Maggie Beth was shaking from head to toe, visibly hurt and angry.

Adrian leaned toward her. "Mom, that's not what I want."

"Then why are you doing this to us? You had a good woman in your life, and you gave her up for one you can never have!"

Adrian took a deep breath before continuing the conversation. He wanted to say he already had her, that he and Madeleine were more than just some torrid love affair, that this was real.

"Obviously, Maddie and I having any kind of relationship beyond friendship is wrong. I'm not going to debate you on that."

"Ah, some sign of a conscience," Richard spat. "Have you considered she's going to keep stringing you along? She's gotten used to that Atwood money."

Adrian tightened his jaw and clasped his hands together to keep from wringing his father's neck. He chose to pick his battles today.

"Please tell me you're not sleeping with her."

"We haven't slept—"

Richard snickered. "You expect us to believe that?"

"I understand what it looks like. I also know the truth."

Maggie Beth complained through clenched teeth, "I swear I raised you better than this."

"You raised Lee better too, but here I am, the subject of a family intervention," Adrian jeered.

"Are you serious right now? You're going to sit there like you've done nothing wrong?" Richard spat. "You are about to destroy your own family all for a piece of ass?"

"Don't you dare," Adrian snapped. "You've both admitted it's more than that. The last thing I want is for the people I love the most to suffer because of me, but if all I did was love Maddie when she needed it the most, I can make peace with that."

There was a long, awkward pause, and as far as Adrian was concerned, their conversation was over.

He stood and started to leave when his father fished his checkbook out of his pocket.

"How much, Adrian?"

He looked back at his father in disbelief and laughed. "You're kidding me."

"Certainly not. I've lived long enough to learn two things. One, there's nothing more important than family, and two, everything's for sale for the right price. I've got billions, so name your price."

"Lest you forget, I've got plenty of my own, thanks," Adrian countered, taking another step.

Richard stood. "All right then. You love her that much? If you walk out that door, you're no longer a part of this family."

"Richard!" Maggie Beth chided.

Adrian realized every scenario he'd played out was coming true. "It's not what I want," he said to his father, "but if that's how you feel about it, I have no real choice in the matter."

Richard crossed his arms, checkbook in hand. "Then there's at least some shred of respectability about you left. You're a man who'll do anything to get what he wants. And I thought Lee was the ruthless one."

"Dad—"

"Don't 'Dad' me. I'm not sure who I'm speaking to, but the Adrian Atwood I know doesn't have a selfish bone in his body."

His father opened his checkbook. "Maggie Beth, get me a pen."

"Richard," his mother pleaded, her eyes filling with tears.

"I don't want your damn money," Adrian said.

"And it wouldn't change my mind."

"Oh, I'm convinced there's not a dollar amount in the world that would change your mind. But we have business to attend to."

"What the hell are you talking about?"

"I'm buying you of out Atwood Technologies. I've never wanted this business out of family hands, and I couldn't stand it if Lee were to lose one more thing that's important to him, seeing how he's out a wife *and* a brother now. Maggie Beth, I need a pen."

Shaking her head, his mother went off to her office for a pen, then handed it to him when she returned.

"How much should I make this check out for, Adrian?" Richard asked. "What's it going to cost me?"

"You're being ridiculous. I don't even want the damned company. You can have it."

Richard didn't bother looking up. "How about two billion?"

"You can't afford that."

"I'll tell you what I can and can't afford," Richard grunted. "I'll write you a check for ninety-nine million right now, legally as high as I can go. Consider it earnest money on my part to ensure your cooperation."

"Cooperation for what?"

Richard ripped the check out of his book and held it up for his son to see. "Sale completion depends on three things. Number one, I want a formal resignation on the CEO's desk tomorrow morning by 9:00am. I'll call at 9:30 to ensure it's been done."

"Done," Adrian agreed, not batting an eyelash.

"Richard, this is ridiculous!" Maggie Beth cried.

"Number two, you'll comply with any and all paperwork needed in transferring your half-ownership of the company to me."

"You got it."

"And number three, you have the decency to fulfill this solitary request on behalf of the family."

"Yeah, sure, what is it?"

Richard locked eyes with his son. "I want you to take this money and take a nice, long, extended vacation. Do and see everything you've ever wanted. But you're not to have any contact with Madeleine for the entire length of this trip."

"No."

"Fine, then give the check back. I'll force you out some other way that's much less profitable."

Adrian glanced at the check in his hand for a second, then handed it back to his father, who didn't take it.

"Adrian, if you and Madeleine love each other so much, a month or so away won't hurt a thing, right? And even if it does, you've got two billion dollars you did nothing to earn. You'll have any woman you want."

"I've already got her." Adrian walked to the door and put his hand on the knob.

"Richard, I swear if you let him leave—"

"I'm done with him."

With the slam of the door behind him, one closed and opened so many times throughout his childhood, Adrian walked out of his parents' lives.

CHAPTER
FIFTY-FIVE

"Are you sure this isn't just some rebound?"

Madeleine looked up from her laptop and raised her brow. "Rebound?" she asked, ignoring the question. "That's not a very 1920s word to use."

Evelyn rolled her eyes. "I'm in your head constantly, hearing all this tripe you people dare call English these days."

A Sunday afternoon rainstorm had set in and was pounding on Madeleine's thin-paned office windows. She loved the sound of the drops splattering against the glass on impact. She was alone for the afternoon. Lee was already up to his old routine of disappearing to his office on Sunday afternoons to prepare for the week ahead.

"What do you think of this one?" Madeleine asked, turning her laptop around for Evelyn to see a real-estate listing for a Georgian Revival just off Forsythe Park in Savannah.

Evelyn clicked through the pictures of the grand

house with a skeptical brow. "You can afford this?"

"It's on the extravagant end, I know. But I love it, and I've never had anything that was truly mine."

"It's gonna belong to a bank if you don't have the funds."

"I have the funds. I didn't start making a lot of money writing until Lee and I were married, so I've gotten to save or invest most of it."

"How much?" Evelyn dared to ask.

"More than twice the price of that house. I can pay cash for it right now," Madeleine answered proudly.

"It's got one hell of a wine cellar." Evelyn clicked through the pictures a second time. "The parties you could throw here…Knowing you, though, you'd rather fill up all those bedrooms with babies."

"I'd be lucky to have one baby, let alone enough to fill up the other five bedrooms." Madeleine laughed, but the possibility made her glow with excitement. "Think the downstairs suite's big enough for Adrian to tinker in?"

Evelyn groaned. "Again with this Adrian nonsense. You know this isn't going to work. The poor boy's only being used as revenge bait. You'll end up breaking his heart."

"That's not the least bit true."

"Oh, please. You may have him fooled, but you're not fooling the rest of us. You can marry the man and have a dozen children, but you'll never be happy with him. He'll know he was being used, and he'll resent you for taking him away from his family."

Madeleine cast her eyes down at her shoes, beginning to question everything. Evelyn always had such an effect—creating doubt where there had been none before. "I would never force him to make that decision. Besides, Adrian thinks his parents would come around one day."

"Richard and Maggie Beth? They're two of the most stubborn people on the planet. Where do you think their boys get it? Face it, Madeleine, you're asking Adrian to sacrifice what's most important to him, and you're simply not a worthy investment."

The rain began to fall even harder.

Evelyn smirked. "Do the right thing and let Adrian go, before he ends up as miserable as you are."

A knock at the door resonated through the quiet house.

Madeleine answered it, surprised to see Adrian, half soaked from the short walk to the front door.

"Need a towel?" she asked with a wide grin, her earlier doubts submerged beneath the happiness of seeing him.

His face was shadowed and downtrodden, his typical sly grin nowhere to be found. "We need to talk."

For once, she need to be his saving grace instead of the other way around.

CHAPTER FIFTY-SIX

Lee slammed the single sheet of paper down on Adrian's desk with a hollow thud. Adrian looked up from a set of schematics, a sinking feeling dropping in his gut.

"What the hell is this?"

As much as he knew this confrontation was coming, Adrian had to gather his wits to know how to deal with the very delicate situation he was in. He sat up tall in his desk chair, though somehow felt small compared to his brother. "Lee, I think we both know this had been a long time coming."

Lee scoffed, incredulous. "Are you kidding? I didn't know this was coming! From the second I got back, all everyone's done is sing your praises about how great everything had gone, how efficient you were. And then I get a letter—a letter, Adrian—telling me you're resigning from your position? From a job that's been yours, literally, since the day you were born?"

"Lee, you know I've never wanted this. I'd rather be off creating something."

"I know you would, but—"

"So you should understand, right? And why are you so mad over a letter? Isn't that the formal way to resign from a job?"

Lee acted like he'd just been shot. "Jesus Christ, Adrian. I am your brother, first and foremost. We've held nothing back from each other. Not until now."

"Then you know I don't want to be VP. I've told you since middle school. This isn't what I want to do with my life. It never has been."

"Okay, so is that the only problem? You want to go back to engineering? Fine. It's done. You can be head of engineering or you can go play with circuit boards and lasers down in the labs all day, I don't care, but you are not resigning from your company."

Adrian pinched the bridge of his nose. He was already getting a headache. Dealing with Lee would not be easy, and he hardly had his brother's skills in convincing others he was right.

"Lee, sit down. This will obviously take a while…"

Lee wasn't even full seated in the chair across from his desk before he was already back at it, trying to convince Adrian to stay. "Is it money? Do you need more? Hell, Adrian, all you have to do is ask."

"Of course it's not money! Do you think this is about money? You couldn't possibly—"

"I get it, there's VPs and CEOs out there making

more than us, but we've made a huge comeback since the recession and we can swing a higher salary. Besides, it's *our* company. If I were to put you in charge of engineering, you could take home the same salary as—"

"It's not about the money, Lee. It never has been."

"So it's not money, and obviously, going back to engineering isn't a notion you're willing to entertain. Is it me?"

"No."

"Then what is your problem? I swear, I can fix it if you'll just let me."

Adrian looked Lee straight into his eyes, shades of blue and gray streaking to his focused pupils, and tensed up even more.

What the hell am I doing? This is Lee...my brother. How have I let this thing with Maddie go so far?

Then his thoughts went to her, and his heart ached, torn in two impossible directions. How was he supposed to ration properly, having to face the two of them in the farce everyday life had become from the day he'd realized he loved his brother's wife?

I'm doing the right thing. Just need to press on. But what do I tell him, something powerful enough to convince him I mean this?

"You remember the time you jumped from the top of that waterfall at Cooper's Creek?"

Lee laughed. "Yeah, I do. I was scared to death, but I didn't want you to know that, so I just jumped. Little did I know you'd be right behind me! And then Mom and Dad almost killed me because you got a tiny scratch."

"Like hell! I needed stitches! I was gushing blood from my temple!"

"You survived. What doesn't kill you makes you stronger."

Adrian let the overused sentiment sink in. It certainly seemed appropriate. "Let's hope that's true."

Lee's expression faded, but he was less angry, more willing to listen now. "So what bearing does that story have on what we're talking about today? I know there's a bigger point."

Adrian shrugged. Then he lied. "I guess what I'm saying is...I feel like I'm just following in yours and Dad's footsteps. I know if I keep on this path, I'm going to be the one paying for it later."

Lee took a deep breath and leaned back in his chair. Inwardly, Adrian relaxed. It was a good sign. Lee was silent for a moment, making his final considerations. A deal was on the way, but it would be a compromise.

"All right, Adrian. What I'm going to do is this," his brother said, picking up the resignation letter from the desk. He pinched the top middle and ripped the resignation letter down the middle. "We're going to forget this resignation letter ever existed, and you're going to take a nice, long sabbatical, for a time we can determine at a later date. I've taken off nearly three months over the past year, and you're owed some time to yourself as payback. Now, when you decide coming back to Atwood Technologies is in your best interest, I'm putting you at the head of engineering."

"You can't do that. Bill Hampton's worked his ass off in that position, and he's stellar."

"Bill's retiring next year. Also got that piece of information slapped on my desk this morning. But now it's like a godsend, because once you come back, he can get you prepped to take over the position."

"Lee—"

"Adrian, I've been more patient with you this morning than I have been with hundreds of business associates. Listen to the plan. The VP seat will be taken by Brent McCanless for the time being. When you're done clearing your head, you will act as head of engineering, but your official title will be vice president. Brent will handle the operations side of your position, and all you'll have to worry about is carrying out engineering's operations."

I could just take some time and get myself together. Maybe Maddie and I can—

No. There would be no "Maddie and I" and Atwood Technologies, no Lee, coexisting together in any harmony. It was time to decide what was more important.

"I'll think about it. That's the best I can do. But I can't stay here," Adrian choked, making one of the hardest decisions in his life.

Even Lee knew when he was defeated. He shook his brother's hand but decided to pound-hug him instead. "I wish you would just tell me what is going on with you."

Adrian couldn't stand to look his brother in the eye another second. "I wish I could too."

He leaned down, signed off on the schematics in approval with a couple of added notes, and handed them to Lee. "Give those to Bill, will you?"

"Yeah," Lee said dully. "Adrian?"

"What?"

"Does Maddie know about this? Whatever it is?"

Adrian narrowed his gaze at his brother, panic setting in. "Why would you think she'd know?"

Lee shrugged, and Adrian could swear the man was already putting it all together in his mind. His brother could never claim to be less than intelligent. "You're certainly closer to her these days than you are to me."

Lee turned on his heel and walked out of his office, but he'd lost the distinctive sense of purpose in his step, as if he was carrying the weight of the world.

CHAPTER FIFTY-SEVEN

Madeleine knew, beyond a shadow of a doubt, it must be done.

This time there was no way around it. Too much had happened, and this was undoubtedly the end.

Ironically enough, there was a fly on the faucet. Again.

Madeleine leaned forward through a mass of bubbles and swatted at the fly until it perched elsewhere. She glimpsed herself in the mirror and thought of the great contrast between then and now. When she looked in the mirror, she could recognize herself. She was Madeleine McCollum. She wasn't always the person she wanted to be, but she could always work on that.

She leaned back, cradling her neck in the curve of the antique tub, trying to relax. Her mind was blank. No racing thoughts about the past, only the progression of how things might occur.

Her bags were packed and waiting at the bottom

of the stairs. Lee would know as soon as he walked in. She liked to imagine he would not be surprised. He'd filed for divorce anyway, so maybe it would make telling him easier.

Not bloody likely, but she hoped he wouldn't linger in any pain, that he would see their parting was the beginning of something better for both of them. He deserved a true, second chance to be the man she knew he could be, and she deserved some happiness too.

Madeleine pulled the drain and climbed out of the tub. She brushed her hair back in her typical ponytail and went about preparing for what she imagined would be the last time she left this house. Lee had always said it was hers, and on paper it was, but she neither wanted it nor needed it. Her name was already being printed on the deed of the house she had shown Evelyn the day before. She didn't know what she would do with all the extra bedrooms, but she had always loved Savannah, and there was always a glimmer of hope that one day Adrian would be at her side.

She just had to follow through with the hard part—breaking Lee's heart.

"I always knew you were crazy," Evelyn groused from the bottom of the stairs, her arms crossed tight across her chest, staring down at Madeleine's suitcases like they were some insidious creatures waiting to attack. "How can you do this? He's the best thing that ever happened to you."

"Yes. In many ways, he was."

"Don't put it in past tense," Evelyn pleaded.

If Madeleine was reading Evelyn correctly, she

would have said the formidable woman standing in front of her, the part of her that had made her question her every move for years now, was wavering in her strength.

Madeleine pulled her shoulders back and her chin up. "Past tense. It has to be this way."

"Can't you just threaten him real good? He's trying to fix everything, repent for his sins, all his shortcomings."

"I understand."

"He'll be such a good father. Stay. Try to have another baby. You said it yourself, you thought if you'd never lost Thomas, you'd both be happy right now. He could be a good husband if you would just give him the chance."

"I imagine he could be," Madeleine undoubtedly had to admit.

Tears welled in her eyes, but Evelyn's jaw set and her eyes smoldered in anger. "If you know all this, then take those bags back upstairs now. This is your home. Lee is your home. Give him one last chance."

Madeleine took a deep breath. *One last chance*, she kept chanting in her mind. By all accounts, one last chance was the good Christian thing to do. It was forgiving, selfless. If the tables were turned, she'd certainly want to be granted one last chance.

Do unto others as you would have them do unto you.

That one golden rule was kind of hard to argue with.

Wouldn't it be so much easier? To take everything back upstairs and pretend this whole leaving and imminent divorce thing was all merely a nightmare?

Madeleine rested her hand on the tallest suitcase. She would have enough time before he got home. No need to hurt him at all.

"Why aren't you already up there?" Evelyn raged. "Go! You're making the biggest mistake of your life!"

Madeleine's lip was quivering, her thoughts racing again. The room started spinning and someone sucked all the air right out.

You're panicking. Breathe.

She quickly found she couldn't. Everything was flying through her head so quickly—the consequences, pain, strife, all the tears and yelling and screaming. But most of all, the fact Lee would know irrefutably that she was just as guilty and sinful as he was. She was no better than he was, in any fashion. And that was the scariest thought yet.

Breathe, breathe, breathe!

The afternoon sun disappeared, drowned by the clouds. The room was spinning even faster.

Breathe!

Finally, her lungs filled with air. The spinning room slowed and the sunlight gradually returned with every subsequent breath. Madeleine found herself, yet again, in the old high school courtyard, the closest thing to Elysian bliss in the cold brick-and-mortar teenaged hell.

Adrian was standing at the Coke machine, hands in his pockets, fishing for change.

"Here again, I see," he said. He pulled four

quarters out of his pocket. "Want a drink?"

"Sure," Madeleine said. "Diet Coke?"

He raised a brow. "Diet Coke? Seriously? How old are you?"

"I like Diet Coke."

"Yeah, but there's Cherry Coke in this machine. And I know you love Cherry Coke."

"Cherry Coke isn't always the healthiest decision."

"Sometimes you just gotta live a little. The decision that makes you happiest isn't always the easiest. Franklin Roosevelt said that, you know."

"No, he didn't," Madeleine argued through her laughter.

"I tried. F.D.R. usually makes an argument more credible. But he did say the only thing we should fear is itself. They kind of go hand in hand."

Madeleine considered it for a moment. "I suppose they do."

"So...Cherry or Diet?" he asked, plunking quarters into the machine one by one.

She put her hand on the side of his arm, and once she had his attention, she raised up on tiptoe to kiss him while pressing the button for a Cherry Coke.

She returned to reality, or at least as close to reality as Madeleine ever got. Before her, Evelyn stood with put-on resolution, her bleary, pleading eyes betraying her attempt to appear in charge.

"Go now, Madeleine!" she screamed. "For once in your pathetic life, don't screw up something this good!"

Madeleine could hardly contain the laugh that escaped her. "You must be kidding me. There's nothing left for Lee and me. There hasn't been for years. All he's doing is fighting a losing battle."

"Because he loves you!"

"Because he's Lee! He can't stand to fail! But he did. *We* did."

Madeleine brushed past Evelyn, heading straight for her office, but Evelyn appeared in the doorway, blocking her entry.

"Then all this adds up to is revenge," Evelyn hissed. "You want to hurt him like he hurt you, except you're going hit him where you know it would hurt the most, aren't you? That's why you started whoring around with his brother."

Madeleine clenched her teeth. "You, of all people, know that isn't true."

"Or is it? One of those sneaky thoughts of yours? Do you even love Adrian? Or are you just ruining his life to hurt Lee?"

Her temper igniting, Madeleine pushed forward through the doorway and into her office, her blood rushing hot through her veins. "You'd best leave now, Evelyn. I won't warn you a second time."

"Leave now? When we're just getting down to the truth?" Evelyn smiled cruelly. "I don't think so, Madeleine. Because I'm going to stop you, just like I do every time, taking every doubt and inhibition you have to use against you. I've kept you here this long, kept you from writing what was really on your mind. I've kept you from telling Adrian how much you loved him for years now."

Madeleine's jaw dropped. "You didn't. You

365

weren't there."

"I am always there. With you, it's so easy. There are so many fears to prey on. You've been a veritable fountain of negative energy since the day you were born, and you're never going to be any different."

So many emotions were bubbling up at the same time—anger toward Evelyn, toward herself for being so damned weak, helplessness to an extent she hadn't experienced since she'd realized their baby wasn't going to make it. Every instinct said to break again—flight over fight. Every. Single. Damned. Time. How long was it going to be this way?

"Go ahead," Evelyn laughed. "Cry. Break down, like you always do. Perhaps you should even go for one of the knives Lee's dared to put back in the kitchen. That always makes you feel better."

"Not this time."

Evelyn laughed. "What was that, little mouse? Did you squeak?"

Madeleine felt she were stepping through quicksand to her desk, yet she made it. She placed her hand on the drawer pull and took a clean sheet of paper out of the drawer. "I said, not this time."

Evelyn peered at her peculiarly as she fumbled for a pen. "What are you doing?"

Madeleine looked Evelyn in the eye. "I made you. You were always one of my favorites."

"I am myself. I always existed. You just wrote a setting and plot around me."

"You know," Madeleine put her pen to paper, "that's always the great thing about plots. They're so fluid. They can just change on the author's whim like—"

Evelyn's high-pitched scream ripped the silence of the house to shreds. Madeleine withdrew the knife from her chest, then stepped back to admire her handiwork. Evelyn stood there in the middle of her office, blood dripping down her chest in a quick stream, dotting the cream carpet a garish shade of red.

She was more in shock Madeleine could do such a thing than the fact there was a sizable wound with blood spreading like an ink blot on paper.

Madeleine cocked her head to the side. "Pretty," she whispered, remembering how her rivulets of blood had snaked and expanded into the water on the fateful day that seemed so long ago. "You were there that day too, weren't you? The day I tried to kill myself. You were going to let me die."

She drew back the knife again, high above her head, then sank it down deep into the soft hollow point between her collarbone and shoulder. Evelyn let out another scream, as blood pumped and gushed through each wound, the flow increasing with every heartbeat.

Madeleine grabbed the soaked hilt of the knife and found each stab and retraction grew easier with every wound. She wouldn't have known the difference between her tears and the spatter of Evelyn's blood on her face if it wasn't for the fact her eyes blurred with each thrust of the knife or that every tear signified the passing of her old life.

Finally, Evelyn was no more. Her slim, perfect body sank to the crème-dyed-scarlet rug bearing every drop of her sin, her deep green eyes shocked. Even in death, she couldn't fathom defeat.

Madeleine's blood was pumping full force through her veins, her heart pounding in her chest. It had never felt so incredibly good to just breathe.

Sunlight filled the room again. Nothing could hold her back now. A sense of peace had returned.

Until she heard the front door slam shut.

Two footfalls and a sharp breath.

Then silence.

Thirty seconds, one minute, passing in painfully long seconds.

Madeleine waited. She looked down at the rug, yet again crème and perfect. Her hands were as clean as they had been when she'd stepped out of her bath, save for an ink stain on her ring finger. Blue ink. She took the sloppily scrawled scene of Evelyn's death, folded it up, and placed it safe inside the pocket of her capris.

"Maddie?"

Lee was standing in the doorway of her office. His office now, she supposed. It didn't matter. Especially when he was so downtrodden. His eyes had lost every bit of their light, and for once, his shoulders slumped and his chin wasn't jutted out so much he'd drown in a rainstorm. This was Lee, stripped down to nothing, and as Madeleine had predicted, it wasn't an easy sight to bear.

He swallowed hard. "When are you going?" he asked softly.

"I'll leave when we've talked about it," Madeleine said after a moment of thought. "I can't imagine making you suffer through any more than

368

you have to."

"Terrible time to quit drinking," Lee noted with regret.

A few awkward moments passed during which Madeleine wasn't sure what exactly to say. "I'm— I'm sorry we couldn't ever work it out. I know you tried to make everything right, but—"

"But it wasn't enough," Lee interrupted. "It never could have been enough. I screwed things up beyond repair."

"It wasn't just you," Madeleine replied softly, her heart sinking.

Lee locked his eyes on hers. "I know."

Madeleine stared at him peculiarly. Did he know?

"So...why today? Of all days? Why not months ago, or next week?" he asked, his eyes boring into hers.

"I've had my mind made up for months, Lee. I just never wanted to leave you alone after your wreck or when you got back on your feet. But you're fine now. You've quit drinking. You don't need me. And I need to go."

Lee nodded, mulling something over in his mind. "Sounds reasonable to me. And very selfless."

"It's not one bit selfless."

Lee shrugged. "I wonder about today, though. I mean, it's Monday."

"What difference does that make?"

"Statistically, most people quit their jobs on a Friday."

"You think our marriage is like a job for me? I'm not following."

"I guess I just find it odd," Lee said, thinly veiling the anger rising up red beneath his skin, "the day Adrian slaps a resignation letter on my desk and hops off to Thailand or whatever for some stupid reason, my wife leaves too. I mean, Jesus, Madeleine, I didn't want you to leave, but I knew you were going to. I've been waiting to see suitcases stacked up in the foyer any day now. What I didn't expect was that two people very important to me would just so happen to leave on the exact same day."

"I know."

"Of course you do."

"What is it you're getting at?" she countered, every word dropping like steel on concrete.

"I'm getting at the idea that perhaps you're just as guilty as I am. Maybe even more so," her husband accused.

She walked toward him slowly, ready to end this. Madeleine could not say that even though Evelyn was gone, she wouldn't always haunt a part of her. She looked down on Lee as he slumped in the chair, his eyes full of fire.

"Nothing was done with the intention of hurting you. The relationship I have with your brother was for myself, for him. But if you ever lost sleep wondering if something was going on between us, well, that would just be a nice taste of your own medicine, wouldn't it?"

Lee said nothing as she stood back, her lips hardening into grim visage.

"Have a nice life," Madeleine said, turning toward the door. "And I mean that. I want nothing

370

but the best for you."

"You just don't want to be a part of it anymore, is that right?"

"At least we finally understand one another. Goodbye, Lee."

She didn't shed another tear until she loaded the last bag in her car and the house disappeared in the rearview mirror.

CHAPTER FIFTY-EIGHT

"You know it's not too late to buy another plane ticket," Adrian said, taking a seat next to Madeleine.

Hartsfield-Jackson was overwhelmingly crowded, nothing surprising at the world's busiest airport, but Adrian felt they were the only two people in the room. Everything else was meaningless white noise when she was around.

"Don't tempt me," Madeleine said.

She placed her hand over his and laced their fingers. It sent a pang of fear through his entire body at first.

To hell with it, she's as good as mine, he thought, grasping her hand.

"But us being together would kind of ruin the purpose of this trip, don't you think?" Madeleine questioned.

"I don't think there's a chance in the world I'll get some big revelation that changes my mind."

"I hope you don't change your mind, but I would understand if you did. You know that, right? I know you're already in pain over this."

He interrupted her with a kiss that lasted longer than he intended, but he knew now that any sign of affection was going to have to get him through the next weeks, months, however long it would take to know what he already knew—that he loved her beyond logic. His bond with her was stronger than any connection to anyone else.

"I love you. From the ink that's constantly on your fingers, all the way to that overly caring heart of yours. And I am not going to be changing my mind."

Madeleine smiled, her cheeks blossoming pink. "This may feel like hell right now, but we're gonna get through it, aren't we? Being positive isn't my strong suit, but I know this is right."

"Nothing's ever been more right. Even in the middle of everything else falling apart."

"Adrian! Thank goodness I found you." Maggie Beth's harried voice rose above the din of the crowd around them. They both looked up to see his mother fighting through a line of businessmen with their rolling luggage.

"Mom? What are you doing here?" Adrian asked, standing up.

"I couldn't let you go leaving things the way we did. Your father may be angry now—"

"Angry would be an understatement."

"Royally pissed, then. But no matter what, you are our son and we love you. We just want you to be happy, but this is a hard pill to swallow right now. Hopefully one day, it won't be."

"Dad agrees with you, or are you just speaking on his behalf?"

Madeleine squeezed his hand and gave him a look to remind him to be understanding. His mother's eyes were bloodshot and tired, and he could swear she'd aged years since he last saw her. He knew this could not be easy on his parents, and while his father had been more than cruel, Adrian supposed he could come to understand.

"Your father is at Atwood Technologies right now, giving Lee a hand. Your resignation is causing a bit of stir."

"A stir?"

"I told you, Adrian. You'd make a good CEO. And there's apparently enough board members who wanted to make that happen. Needless to say, they're not happy you're no longer in charge."

"Lee will figure it out. He'll win them over somehow."

Maggie Beth winced, making Adrian think the situation might have been worse than she was letting on. "He always does."

"Now boarding Delta flight DL295 to Tokyo. Please have your boarding pass and identification ready."

"That's my flight," Adrian said.

Madeleine and Maggie Beth helped him gather his things and walked with him toward the gate. Adrian stooped down to hug his mother, whose eyes were filling with tears.

"I love you so much," she whispered. "Please be careful. And think about what you want on this trip."

"I already know what I want," he told her. "But I promise you, I'll do whatever it takes to convince you all that she's all I've ever really wanted."

Madeleine smiled behind his mother, and Adrian took her in his arms one last time.

"You gonna plan a small wedding and a long honeymoon while I'm gone?" he asked.

"I'll wait until you come back, since I already went and bought the house without consulting you." She laughed.

"I love that house. You're proud of it and it makes you happy. There's nothing I love more than a happy Madeleine."

"Don't be too long because I'm just dying to make a Pinterest board," Madeleine joked. "Please, be careful. I don't think I could take it if something happened to you."

"I'm gonna be drunk on a beach most of the time."

"Don't rub it in."

"I'll try not to." He grinned as they made another call for his flight. "I love you, Maddie."

"I love you too, Adrian."

They stepped away from one another, but it wasn't even a second before he caught her hand and pulled her in close for one last kiss. She cupped his face in her hands as he held tight to her waist, unwilling to let her go.

"See you later?" he said, breaking their kiss.

"See you later," Madeleine echoed as he turned to leave.

CHAPTER
FIFTY-NINE

Madeleine trained her eyes on him, standing a good foot over most in the crowd. Regret filled her from toe to the very last stray hair on her head.

"You two are crazy," Maggie Beth sputtered with a lemon-puckered expression as she walked toward Madeleine. "Do you have any idea how many people know who we are? How we're going to be the subject of gossip for months?"

Madeleine kept her eyes on Adrian the entire time. "I couldn't care less who knows us. He's more important than their opinions could ever be."

"What did he say to you?"

"He said he loves me," Madeleine said, keeping up with the back of his head until he completely disappeared into the crowd.

"Do you love him?"

Madeleine couldn't help the smile that played at her lips. He made her happy, and not just in the way Lee had when they had first met a lifetime ago.

376

Madeleine certainly thought of it as a lifetime; it had felt that way. Her first suicide attempt had caused a dichotomy in the timeline of her life.

From the second she'd opened her eyes, rebirthed, disappointingly alive, Adrian had been there. He tended to her wounds in one way or another, trying to fix all the broken things inside of her, and not for his sake, being there for her had only been to his detriment, but because he had wanted nothing more for her to be happy. Madeleine knew what he felt for her was pure, and she loved him for his unwavering, selfless heart.

"There's nothing more absolute in the entire universe, Maggie Beth."

CHAPTER SIXTY

She had waited months for this day. All her waiting had culminated into this one fulfilling moment. Their divorce was final and had gone about as smoothly as one could ever hope. It helped that she'd told Lee she didn't want a damned thing from him, just a quick, peaceful divorce to set them both free to start new lives. Lee had been more than happy to oblige and had even hired teams of movers and decorators so she didn't have to lift a finger to get her new home move-in perfect. Madeleine didn't know whether he did it to get rid of her or as one last gesture of kindness, but she liked to think that one day they could forgive each other for all the hurt they'd inflicted.

But that was the past. Now, she was standing in front of the future.

Madeleine grinned at the glorious place she could now call home. It was a handsome brick Georgian Revival that demanded the attention of all who may pass, but it wasn't imposing. The strong Corinthian columns suggested stability and safety,

378

but the swan-neck pediment and wide front porch were arms wide open after a long journey. Framed up between towering oaks dripping with Spanish moss, it couldn't have been any more perfect.

This was where she would start her family. Where she would get to raise her children.

The thought came to her before she could dare stop it. What-ifs constantly plagued her mind. What if Adrian decided to never come back? What if he decided to stay true to his family after all? She could hardly blame him if he did.

Despite her doubts, she knew Adrian loved her and wanted to share a life with her. The very thought of it made her entire soul bubble with a happiness she'd never known before. She took a steadying breath when she remembered that Adrian had wanted her to FaceTime him as soon as she got there. He was as excited to experience their new home as she was, even if he was taking time away for the sake of his family.

Adrian answered the video call after a couple of rings. Madeleine's screen filled with his image.

"Are we home yet?" he asked with a charming smile, making her heart beat even faster.

"We are," Madeleine announced. "Ready to see your new house?"

"Our new house," Adrian corrected.

Madeleine swelled with happiness, pride, every positive emotion that typically evaded her, but dominated when he was present. "Ours."

"You're so excited."

"Aren't you?"

"Well, yeah," Adrian laughed. *"But you're pure*

giddy over it. It's been a long time since I've seen you this excited over something."

"I was just thinking this is where I get to start my own family. Everything's finally coming together here," Madeleine said before she could even think about it. When he didn't respond, she studied his expression. He was pensive, peaceful.

"Say it again."

Madeleine's heart skipped a beat. "Say what?"

"That whole line about starting a family here, everything coming together."

She turned her phone around and stepped back to give him a good view of the front of the house. "This is where we get to start our family. This is where it all comes together."

"That's better. I like the we."

Madeleine flipped the camera back forward. "Shall we go inside?"

"Yeah, let's go." He stood and began walking. In the background, she spotted a familiar brick wall and moss-draped trees.

"Adrian Atwood, where are you?" Madeleine asked as she tested the front door, which was unlocked as she suspected. She desperately wanted for the theory developing in her mind to be correct.

When she stepped into the foyer, she realized she was.

"I'm home," Adrian said, closing the back door behind him. It took every ounce of self-control not to break out into a full run. He grasped her waist and pulled her into him.

Tears welled in her eyes. "I thought you were waiting, giving your family more time to process everything?"

"I've missed you so much waiting stopped making very much sense." He cupped her face and kissed her for the first time in so many long-suffering days. His tongue danced over hers, and Madeleine needed to assure herself the man she had imagined so many times in the past few months was actually there. Everything was too perfect…it couldn't be real, or it was all about to crumble or…

"Stop worrying," Adrian said, as if he could read her thoughts. He rested his forehead against hers, and Madeleine could feel his heart racing beneath her fingertips.

He was here, he was hers, and he wasn't going anywhere.

"I'm not worried. Not anymore. But when life feels like a dream, a girl's gotta pinch herself every now and then just to know how lucky she is."

Adrian pressed a long, sweet kiss to her forehead. "I understand. But if it isn't real, I'd rather not know. I can't think of anything more perfect than this."

"I don't know. I have a feeling the best is yet to come."

ABOUT THE AUTHOR

"Lorelai Watson has lived in the same small, but ridiculously charming Georgia town her entire life. In fact, this little town became the home of the characters of her debut novel, *Ain't Nothin' but the Devil*. When she's not writing, Lorelai is either teaching, chasing her always-active young children, or ruining the plot of every movie and show for her husband."

Facebook:
https://www.facebook.com/authorlorelai.watson.7

Facebook:
https://www.facebook.com/LorelaiWatsonBooks

Twitter:
https://twitter.com/lorelai_watson

Instagram:
https://www.instagram.com/LorelaiWatsonBooks

Join our Reader Group on Facebook and don't miss out on meeting our authors and entering epic giveaways!

Limitless Reading

Where reading a book is your first step to becoming *limitless...*

LIMITLESS PUBLISHING Reader Group

Join today! *"Where reading a book is your first step to becoming limitless..."*

https://www.facebook.com/groups/Limitless Reading/

Made in the
USA
Columbia, SC